MYSTERY
IN THE
'PORKIES'

Mystery
in the
'Porkies'

D.J. Martin

Library of Congress Control Number: 2017919392
ISBN: Hardcover   978-1-5434-7442-8
               Softcover   978-1-5434-7441-1
               eBook   978-1-5434-7488-6

Print information available on the last page.

Rev. date: 12/26/2017

To order additional copies of this book, contact:
Xlibris
1-888-795-4274
www.Xlibris.com
Orders@Xlibris.com
772327

CONTENTS

PROLOGUE

SEPTEMBER 1964

The Disappearance

THE FIRE WAS down to embers and C.B. was half asleep when the guy grabbed him from behind and pulled him to his feet. As he woke his nose was immediately overwhelmed by the putrid smell of tobacco and old sweat coming from the creature that had seized him. Instinct made him swing with both fists clenched. He fought with all his might and kicked as much as possible, but the big creepy guy had no trouble at all holding him still.

"Let me go asshole", he yelled, kicking as he swing his fists at the huge brute of a man that held him from behind. But it didn't do any good. Charles was almost five-foot-ten and maybe a hundred and eighty pounds but the man that grabbed him was taller and easily twice his size. The other two intruders just laughed at him swinging his arms around.

"What are you doing up here boy?" the man with the rifle asked him.

"I was sleeping you idiot," Charles spit out at his captor. "Now let me go!"

"I see you have friends," the man said, ignoring Charles and looking around at the small quaint little campsite. "Where are they?" the man who seemed to be in charge asked calmly.

There were three ruffians who entered the small clearing and held him captive. The man who appeared to be in charge walked around the small campsite, counting the backpacks belonging to the small group of boys. They were to close and he didn't like it. He had to get rid of them.

"We don't have time for this," he mumbled, mostly to himself.

"Tie his hands. Then destroy the backpacks and everything in this camp," he commanded, giving the orders to the other two men.

"Maybe it'll scare the others boy scouts away," he added.

"We'll bring this one with us," he said, looking into C.B.'s eyes, then grabbing him by the hair. "We'll see what Manny wants to do with him."

"Let me go," Charles yelled, struggling even more. But his efforts were muffled as boss man pushed him to the ground and gagged him with a dirty rag."

Charles was shocked when two of the men took out long machetes and hacked away at his and his friends back packs, tearing them to shreds. One of the men lifted his size thirteen shoe and came down hard on the coffee pot Charles had been keeping warm for his friends. The small aluminum coffee pot crumbled like paper. There was nothing he could do but keep down the fear suddenly rising from his gut.

Once the intruders were done they hauled him to his feet. CB's head was swimming and he thought sure this had to be a terrible nightmare. They forced CB to walk east, away from where the boys had set up camp. Charles could feel his legs shaking as he was forced to walk away from his friends, and safety.

They walked for about fifteen minutes when his captors forced him to stop near a ravine. It was a steep downward slope that led away from the familiar trail he knew.

"OK kid," said the boss man, "I'm going to untie your hands so you can maneuver down this ravine. But I'm tying the rope around your waist. Any unnecessary moves, and I'll pull so hard on this rope you'll be sure to lose your balance, maybe even tumbling a long way before coming to a halt on the bottom. Get the picture?" the man sneered at Charles. Charles was scared and still gagged so he could only nod his head and do what he was told. They headed down the ravine slowly. Charles was breathing hard and none of the men complained when he removed the gag from his mouth half way down the ravine. He didn't talk figuring they would leave him alone if he kept quiet. There was no visible path to follow and the climb down the ravine was steep. The loose scrub brush and jagged rocks made it difficult and dangerous to maneuver. He was scared and had no idea what to expect. He didn't know these men and he certainly didn't know what they wanted or what was happening. He just tried to pay attention to things around him. There was no relief from the uneven and rough terrain as they progressed along the downward slope. All he could do was move as slow and careful as possible.

The bottom of the ravine was thick with white pine and huge hemlock trees. They stopped near one of the giant sprawling hemlock trees and made their way through a small crevice hidden behind it. The fissure in the rock revealed a four-foot opening into a mountain cave. Charles had to duck as he was shoved through. Once inside, he was pushed to the ground near the side wall and told not to move. Across from where he sat he noticed several men packing things into crates. Most of the crates were small but still Charles was surprised at what he was seeing. He couldn't really tell what they were packing, but he knew something wasn't right. He was already scared but now he knew he was in trouble.

Boss man told one of his underlings to guard him and he told the third man to go help the others pack up the crates. Then boss man went over to talk to still another man. Charles noticed this new guy wasn't dressed for hiking or even walking in the mountains. He was in a suit and looked like he belonged in an office. Charles couldn't hear what was being said but noticed the two men arguing. That made the hairs on the back of his neck stand up.

As he sat there he looked around. The cave was enormous. The opening was only about four feet, but once inside the walls reached at least twelve feet, maybe higher. He knew this had to be the other side of the same formation that he and his buddies had camped near. But none of them would have guessed that these caves existed. The walls appeared jagged and toward the back there was a small creek flowing amongst formations of stalagmites. Smaller structures of stalactites were stretching down from the ceiling. The columns were simple and not very high. His captors never retied his hands so Charles played it safe and didn't move. He didn't want to draw their attention. His guard was watching the boss and the guy in the suit argue. He seemed to be getting a kick out of it. Charles knew he had to do something. He slowly untied the rope around his waist as he looked around. He had to find a way to escape. He had to warn his friends. He noticed a couple tunnels not too far away, near the small flow of water that formed the creek. Thing is, the tunnels weren't even close to the entrance he was dragged in through. He just wasn't sure what he should do, but the two arguing men were getting louder. The man in the suit looked his way. Then there was more arguing. The man who looked like he belonged in an office raised his voice enough for Charles to hear, "I don't care how you do it, just get rid of him." That was his que. He knew he had to get away, in any direction. So, he took off running toward the tunnels.

He ran, making a quick getaway into the tunnels.

"Get him!" he heard the boss man yell. In the next second, there was a gunshot. Charles heard a ping off the rocks near his left ear, but he didn't stop and he didn't look back. He heard footsteps too, so he just kept running. The further he went into the tunnels the darker it got. He pulled out his lighter and lit it, but only long enough to see the tunnels in front of him. He could see just enough to notice that the main tunnel divided multiple times into two, or even three branches. Then the one he decided to take branched again, and then again. They'll never follow he thought to himself. Too many tunnels. Charles always took the left tunnel hoping that eventually he could find his way back out again.

After a while the footsteps stopped following him, so he slowed down, then stopped to listen. He was right, they hadn't followed. He was exhausted and needed to catch his breath. Everything was dark, and very quiet.

He had waited what seemed a long time and was about to head back down the tunnels when suddenly, he heard a huge explosion. The ground beneath him started to shake! Small rocks from above started pouring down on him like rain, forcing him to cuddle close to the wall and cover his head with his arms. The noise that brought down the deluge of rocks echoed in the tunnel and made his ears ring. He knew where it had come from and it made his stomach churn until he felt bile in his throat! His gut told him it was man made, but why? Did they seal the tunnel he had run into, or the whole cave? Why? He had no answers.

He snapped his lighter back to life moving down the cave in the direction he had entered from. He hadn't gone more than twenty steps when he found the rock slide that had sealed the tunnel he was in. He tried clearing the way but it was no use. The exit was sealed up tight. Was there another opening? He listened but everything was quiet. He obviously couldn't go back and although the darkness enveloped him, he controlled his fear, and started following the maize of tunnels forward. Maybe, just maybe, there would be another way out.

CURRENT TIME

SEPTEMBER 2016

CHAPTER 1

The Old Man's Memory

THE OLD MAN was pressing his knuckles against his temples, thinking back again!

It seems to him he'd been doing that a lot lately, thinking, trying to remember. Especially since the fifty-year anniversary approached and he still remembered details of that September like it was yesterday. They were always cautious. Always! He and his fellow hikers even wore those stupid matching red bandanas, so they could see each other easily in the woods. No matter who went out, they were careful. They all wore a backpack with a small amount of supplies, like food and a first aid kit. They all took water with them. They watched out for each other. And he still couldn't figure out what happened. None of them could! The only thing they knew was that they left someone behind, for a short time of course, but still, he was left behind, and he was alone. It was something he always told himself he would never do, leave someone behind. They shouldn't have done that. But they weren't hiking. They were at a campsite. And they were all college students for crying out loud, not wandering little children. He picked up the folded red bandanna on his desk fingering it delicately, remembering.

"Dammit", he said out loud, scrunching the bandanna in his fist.

"It shouldn't have been a problem", he said, talking to himself. He did that a lot lately. Talked, and even cussed out loud, to himself.

Dave had been a successful engineer in his prime, but he was a tired old man now. And this was an old ache that wouldn't go away. The frustration was always there, and sometimes mumbling, even cussing out loud, helped. He knew C.B. Denton. He was a careful hiker, always making safety his priority. He could still picture the boy's face. C.B. would not have disappeared on his own. He would not have left his friends like that, on his own, without a trace. One of the new guys maybe, getting bored or whatever, but not C.B. And certainly not without informing his friends. No matter how Dave racked his brain he couldn't figure it out.

Six of them had gone out that weekend. Only five came back. He still can't believe it had been more than fifty years ago now. He was still heartsick about what happened. Mainly because he felt it was his fault. He had been in charge, well sort of in charge. He got the guys together. He started the whole thing, the hiking. It was exciting! And they all loved it!

For a few years after C.B.'s disappearance, they would all gather together again, same place, same time of year, up there, where their friend vanished. Winter had been rough the year he went missing. The snow was heavier than normal, and as spring came, there were a lot of small rock slides due to the melting snow. But the cave opening was lost a long time ago. He and the other boys were lucky they got out. Whatever happened that night, they didn't know, but all the ground trembling they felt must have been caused by something happening inside the cave. They all believed that it probably caused the mouth of the cave to collapse. They had made a pact about that. About the Cave!

The cave was hard to find as it was. They had found it by accident. It was tiny, barely big enough for the boys to fit into, even after digging away some of the dirt. And after C.B. disappeared, and before they reported him missing, they figured since the cave's opening had closed-up and was gone anyway, why bother telling anyone that the cave even existed. Maybe someday they'll find it again, or someone will, so they thought. They were ashamed that they made the pact, but it was the one secret all the guys seemed to have kept. He couldn't even remember anymore why they decided to keep it all a secret. Only when they met again, and nobody else was around would any of them bring it up, or talk about it in any detail. And when alone, they did talk about it, mostly wondering why the hell they couldn't find it again. That was the weird thing, the frustrating thing. They couldn't find it again. There were times when they all felt maybe they just imagined it, maybe the hills were haunted. Dave didn't believe that. Not for a second. A strange twist of nature, maybe! But he simply didn't believe that they had all imagined it.

Over the years several of the guys stopped coming. They had lives to live after all, and C.B. was gone. Dave had gone back multiple times, even visiting C.B.'s mother, but never found any clues. His friend Steve had become a Forest Ranger and lived up there. Steve did some looking on his own. For a couple years, following their friends' disappearance, all of them gathered again, looking. But eventually it was just him and Steve. And he knew Steve searched on his own even more times than Dave had. Neither of them found anything.

His thoughts were interrupted by the doorbell. But he knew who it was. His sister had called earlier. She told him she'd be stopping by to bring him a few groceries. His niece was coming as well, just to say hi. He knew he shouldn't ignore it, but he was feeling crochety. Then he heard the door open.

CHAPTER 2

The Old Man's Story

"WHOSE THERE?" SHOUTED Dave, in his best crochety voice.

"Go check on him," said her mother. "I'll put these groceries away".

"It's me and mom, Uncle Dave," Jane shouted loud enough for her uncle to hear. "We brought you some groceries."

Jane walked to the back of the house. She knew he would be in the library. She saw, and heard him, flipping through pages of a book, or something, as she stood at the library door. He tried to ignore her. She stepped into the simple library, probably too big for the house, but beautiful because of the mahogany walls. She loved it because it had a ten-foot ceiling making it seem more spacious. And she loved books. The book shelves were mahogany too, and the décor was light and simple, with only a couple extra's. A large 'Salvador Dali' melting clock was fixed on the main wall and a large world globe was sitting on a small marble base in the corner. Another map, a flat one, was hanging on the wall. It had small thumb tacks pinned on it in various locations. Her uncle was sitting at his oversized mahogany desk, like always. He was searching through several stacks of books, looking for something. He wrote and journaled a lot, and he always had a stack or two of books on his desk, along with pens and paper, and a dish of candy. He liked chocolate.

"What are you looking for Uncle?" she asked, stepping closer.

"I'm looking for some information I had," he said. "I know it's here somewhere. I wanted to give it to you before you leave on vacation tomorrow.

Here it is!" he said mostly to himself.

He got up slowly using the desk for support as he walked around it. He needed to speak to her, eye to eye and up close. "This is important," he said, staring at her, then handed her an envelope. In his youth, he was a good five-foot ten. Jane was easily five foot-eight, but with his loss of height do to old age, and her wearing shoes that easily added an inch to her height, they were basically at eye level with each other. He held on to the envelope tightly in his old wrinkled hand for just a second before releasing it.

"What is it?" she asked, accepting the envelope and then opening the flap and peering into it.

"Let's go for a walk," he said, waving his hand for her to follow, like she was still a little kid following him to a new adventure, which she wasn't she thought to herself, dropping her hands to her side and rolling her eyes. She loved him dearly, but sometimes she wanted to scream at him, "I'm not ten uncle Dave."

He grabbed his cane as he walked out the library's sliding glass door. Jane followed him, like she always did, but she saw the red bandanna on his desk as she went. She knew he was thinking about it again.

The library's sliding glass door opened to a patio that ran half the length of the house. The patio was long and wide, decorated with wicker style patio furniture. The neatly trimmed garden surrounding the patio showed different varieties of flowers in full bloom. Her uncle always liked flowers in his backyard, and the mixture of assorted pigment intertwined with green foliage made the place look like a bright garden of Eden. He loved the full array of color his garden produced. Ivy grew along the wall of the house. In front of the ivy were the rose bushes. The deep red rose bush alongside pastel colored wildflowers all around relaxed him. The garden always seemed to have a calming effect, even on her.

There were a variety of trees as well. Some were tall arborvitae, set close together to allow him his privacy from neighbors to close for his taste. Others were varied and placed in the yard to allow for sunlight on and off during the entire day. He even had a well-cared for apple tree in one corner. It was almost September so the apples were beginning to ripen. There was a worn path around and through the large flower garden, stretching out to the back of the yard around a large oak tree and back. Jane knew he loved to walk through the garden area just admiring the color. Plus, it was good exercise. The gardener he hired to maintain his flowerbeds was expensive, but it was the one extravagance he allowed himself. It made her smile just looking at it. She followed a few steps behind him waiting for him to talk.

"That envelope has my map," he said quietly. "I know I'll never get up there again. My mind wants to but my knees are getting weak and don't want to cooperate. Besides, I'm just too tired to make the trip," he grumbled.

"I want you to do something for me," he continued, turning to face her and pointing at the envelope.

Jane stopped behind him, pulling out the contents of the standard size white envelope and opening the folded paper. It was an old map, scribbled in pencil. It was worn with age but she could still read it.

"Whatever you need," she said to him, turning the map, studying it. "You know I'll do my best. Maybe I'll draw out a new map for you, you know, in case something's changed."

He turned and looked at her, "you know the story," he said.

"I'm just asking that you look around. I mean, if you have time. If you're in that area. If you can," he trailed off.

He was quiet now and just walked through his garden.

Yes, Jane did know the story. Her godfather had finally opened-up to her. And once he found out she loved hiking, well, it was like he found a kindred spirit he could talk to. They mostly talked about all the places he had hiked. She would tell him of places she had gone, but he did most of the talking, so it was his hiking they talked about. That's when the story came out. It came out slowly, over time, bit by bit. It was hard for him to share. It was heartbreaking for her to hear him tell it. She could see he was in another time, another place, when he talked. She wished she could fix it all, but that was the past, and the past is gone.

"You know I'll do whatever I can," she said to him, when he came back around. She stared right back at him as he walked right up to her, looking into her deep brown eyes. He needed to see it there, in her eyes. See that she meant it. Her eyes were sparkling and she didn't blink and didn't look away. She just waited.

"O.K. then," he said, turning back toward the house.

Just then her mother came out to the patio with lemonade and scones. He smiled at the treats she always brought. The three of them gabbed for about half an hour before Jane and her mom said their goodbyes and left.

CHAPTER 3

Jane's Mom

I T WAS A thirty-minute drive to her uncles so Jane rode with her mom. They planned this visit last week. Jane liked driving herself but she knew it was just easier on her mom if they just drove together.

"Jane, you look tired," her mom said after getting in the car. "Everything O.K.?"

"Everything's fine mom. Things have just been hectic lately."

"You push yourself to much you know," said her mom.

"What do you mean?" said Jane sheepishly.

"You know exactly what I mean," her mom retorted. "It's like you're trying to prove to the world that you can do anything and everything. You're smart and you're capable but you drive yourself to hard. You need to lighten the load a bit."

"What do you mean, lighten the load?" she asked her mom, trying to be casual.

Carol just looked at her daughter before saying anything. But she needed to ask. If anything, it would make her daughter think.

"How many clubs do you belong to Jane? How many things do you volunteer for? How many people do you help?" her mom paused.

"Do you still make lists for everything?" her mom added.

There was a pause before Jane answered. Her and her mom have always been close. They could always talk. Her mom understood her gift and had helped her through a lot. The last thing she wanted to do was hurt her mom's feelings. But she made a life for herself and she had to make her own decisions. She was smart, almost too smart, she thought. She remembered things. They told her it was a gift. Sometimes that so-called gift got her in trouble, especially back in high school. Some of those memories weren't very nice. The problem is, she'll never forget them. That she knew.

But she learned. When she went to college, she hid her abilities. She focused on making herself strong, physically strong. She exercised. She ran marathons. She even took karate classes. She had acquired her purple belt and had gained a lot of confidence in herself. That made her feel pretty good. She still practiced the karate moves at home.

But along with being smart and having a photographic memory, she had this intuitive sense as well, and the two things together sometimes seemed uncanny, even to her. She could sense things. She was careful about telling anyone about it. She was careful about telling people what to do or what not to do in any given situation. She'd been tagged weird and strange when she was younger. She wouldn't let that happen in her adult life. She was more careful.

"Look mom," she said, "I like keeping busy. I know I'm doing a few to many things, but I'm cutting back, some. I just need to do it my way. I hope you understand."

"I do understand Jane. I just worry like any mother would."

"I'm fine mom, honest!"

They both fell quiet, each in their own thoughts. The silence lingered for a couple minutes before her mom spoke again.

"The FBI called again," her mother told her. "Same person."

"You know I'm not interested right now," Jane said quietly. "Maybe someday, but not now."

"That's what I told them," her mom replied. "I just wanted you to know they called."

Jane didn't want her mom to worry, but she didn't want her mom trying to solve all her problems for her.

"You know mom," she said quietly, "I'm having a good time. I'm happy where I'm at in my life. Do I want to do more, yes! But I'm trying to pace myself and not overdo it. Sometimes that's hard for me. You know I like being busy."

Her mom smirked just a little.

Jane continued, "I love helping at the soup kitchen. I enjoy the archeology club. You know I love teaching and tutoring. I like to think I make a difference when I tutor. Todd and I do things together that we both enjoy. We do things separately too. Things are good."

"And yes, I still make lists," she added, after a short pause.

Jane didn't need to make lists. She had a photographic memory. She remembered everything. But she liked making lists. It made her feel normal.

"And Todd," her mom said.

"We've talked," Jane said calmly. "He's good for me mom. He's smart, but more important, he's patient. And he understands my issues. He actually helps keep me grounded, and he's helped me make some important decisions."

Jane's mom smiled.

CHAPTER 4

Thieves

"T HESE ARE WORTH a few dollars", the executive said, sarcastically, perusing through the satchel. "What else do you have?"

Randy was pissed. "There's at least a couple thousand dollars' worth of pieces in there", he gritted his teeth.

Matt was annoyed. "You think I'm stupid", he yelled at his dealer. He picked an item out of the satchel. "I have to sell these. Maybe I could get a thousand, maybe more, but you certainly don't get it all".

Randy was still irritated. He hated dealing with this guy. He didn't trust him. But stolen Indian artefacts are being widely sought after right now. He needed to dump these quickly if he wanted to make any money. He knew the market was good now for this type of stuff but it could change quickly. He took a picture from his pocket and handed it to Matt. There were four items in the picture. They all appeared to be effigies. One was an eagle sculpture and a second appeared to be an Indian Medicine Man sculpture. They were obviously professional grade artefacts and Randy knew Matt had a buyer for such things.

"Why didn't you bring these?", Matt asked annoyed, looking closely at the picture.

"Because I know how much they're worth," Randy said, staring at Matt.

Matt through the picture back at Randy and looked away as he walked around his desk. "How much do you have?" he asked the thief.

"Two small crates of delicate effigies, maybe five or six per crate, and a crate of arrow heads and smaller items. Arrowheads are made of stone, some small, some much bigger. Everything will fit in your van", he said to Matt.

"O.K. I'll give you four grand for the lot", said Matt.

"You know they're worth more than ten", Randy shot back.

"Fine", said Matt, "I'll give you five thousand. That's half. Fifty percent each".

When Randy didn't squawk Matt spit out directions to a meeting place. "Midnight tonight", he told Randy.

"Cash! Matt".

"Yes, Randy, cash. Now get out of here". Matt knew he could sell the items for probably twelve or even fourteen grand. The eagle sculpture alone will bring at least two grand, maybe twenty-five hundred. It appeared a bit bigger than the others, and more intricate. But he wasn't telling this yahoo. Matt didn't like the guy. He was a low life and he didn't like the guy coming to his office. But Randy always came through, managing to get some good merchandise so Matt just dealt with him.

CHAPTER 5

Jane's Love for Archeology

J ANE LOVED ARCHEOLOGY. She had taken some archeology classes in college and she had taken an advanced class even after she graduated. It was more of a hobby to her but she liked it. The advanced archeology professor, Professor Terrance Simmons, encouraged his students to join whatever archeology chapter was available in their area.

Many times, she listened to him brag about being the president of one of the local chapters and how they had lectures and set up digs where everyone shared information. He was always animated and his eyes sparkled when he talked about it. He talked about how exciting it was finding a new piece. He told them it would give them a glimpse of archeology in the real world, a lot of work, but worth the reward. It sounded exciting. So, with several of her college classmates, she joined his local Michigan chapter. That was a few years ago.

She was on her lunch break, checking her email when she read the announcement.

"Another damn meeting," she whispered to herself, just as one of her students walked in.

"Mrs. Bowman," the young boy asked, "could you help me with my project?"

"What exactly do you need help with Brian?" she asked, closing her laptop.

"I don't even know where to start," he said shyly.

"OK," she said, "what's your topic?"

"The Civil War," he said, "specifically Gettysburg."

"I tell you what," she said. "Start by following Robert E. Lee after his victory over Union forces at Chancellorsville. Write about how he got to Gettysburg. You don't have to write about Gettysburg, write about Lee. Sound good?"

The student's eyes brightened. "Yah, I can do that."

"Thanks," he said backing out of the room, waving as he went.

Jane smiled at the boy, opening her laptop as he left. She looked back at her emails.

"Why another meeting," she groaned again, but the email didn't say. She thought about what her mother had said, about cutting back. She loved teaching. And she loved the archeology club. She was beginning to realize that this archeology club was demanding and taking up a lot of her time.

And now, another meeting! Today! And this one being unscheduled is exactly what she didn't like. She just shook her head and sighed to herself.

The hall where they met was clear across town, and she was told that it would be a closed meeting and the doors would be shut and locked at exactly five o'clock. That was all the text said. She thought that was weird but whatever. She was a teacher so she had to wait until school was out. Then she would have to leave right away to get there on time, if she decided to go! She knew she would go.

She thought more about it on her drive there. The amateur archeology society was beginning to disappoint her, at least this chapter was. Oh, she liked it at first, meeting other young people interested in archeology like her. When she first joined there were lectures from people who make archeology their life's career. Their excitement was contagious! Professor Simmons even sponsored a small dig where his students were invited to participate. She found her first Indian arrow head there. It made her smile thinking back.

"Can I keep it, please, please," she had begged him. She remembered how exciting it was. And she remembered seeing the smile of approval creep across his face. She knew he was going to say "yes." And he did.

And there were even several field trips to digs across the country. She loved getting involved. But lately things changed. She expected to continue learning from professionals coming in and giving lectures and demonstrations. She wanted to continue to learn new search techniques and to learn more about professional digs. She was even thinking of getting more involved in something she could do during her summers when school was out. But, her professor was changing. He was becoming almost unapproachable. She tried talking to him a few times but he usually just shrugged her off and changed the subject. She didn't like the feeling she was getting. As the chapter president, he should be setting up things like lectures and events for the members. He wasn't doing any of that. He even stopped sponsoring the small digs students always participated in. She was worried about him.

Lately all he wanted was for everyone to share with him what they were doing, what they found. He was especially interested in students who had found any Indian related artefacts. Thing is, he didn't seem to bring in anything new anymore, and over the last six months or so he stopped bringing in guest speakers that taught members new things. She felt she wasn't learning anything she didn't already know. Usually, if none of the members had anything to share, the meetings were short and sweet.

But the last couple meetings were even stranger. The professor was even more distant. And he looked tired to Jane. He wasn't as friendly and excited about his work. He brought in this new colleague to work beside him, supposedly an archeologist who was a forest ranger somewhere up north. The professor just didn't seem to enjoy himself anymore.

And this new colleague was irritating. He was always talking about finding artefacts in Michigan. He encouraged members to report back anything they felt might be a good place to find Indian artefacts. More and more he would focus on the monetary value of things rather than their historical value.

Recently members have been hearing about problems from friends working on other archeological digs in our area. Some of those digs had been looted, and artefacts had been stolen. It was brought up at the last meeting and everyone wanted to talk about it. But it was weird. This new colleague of the professors talked about thieves and told everyone to watch their backs when they were on a dig but he mostly blew it off. She remembered almost word for word, back to the last meeting, this new colleague's comment.

"Apparently," she mimicked him in her mind.

"The FBI suspects a ring of artefact thieves are working in Michigan." Then he said, "the professor and I have discussed this. We don't believe that the FBI has all the facts. Our sources tell us that these thieves are working in Ohio and Indiana and we shouldn't worry."

"Da da-da da-da! What crap," she thought to herself. She knew what this guy said was absolute nonsense! And she remembered the murmuring amongst the members after that.

"This is bull-shit," one member said.

"Maybe we should report what's going on here," another said.

"Maybe we should just all get up and leave right now," said another.

They were really upset but nobody did anything. Some talked about leaving, maybe joining another chapter. She overheard several conversations.

"Just the idea that someone could be out to steal from an archeological dig scares me, "said one girl.

"I'm kind of waiting for the punch line," said a young man. He perked up waiting for more information. But it never came.

"Why doesn't he talk about the thefts, and what the authorities are doing about them," said a frustrated member.

She felt the anger surge in the normally friendly group. It had bothered her a great deal. Now, another meeting! She didn't like it.

The whole atmosphere of their meetings had changed. It was gradual, but she felt it. It was abnormal for any guest, like this ranger colleague of their chapter president, to just take over. But that's what was happening. He didn't talk about safety precautions or how to be aware of your surroundings while on a dig. He talked about how easy it was to steal from a dig. And Professor Simmons just sat there, not saying anything. Jane watched him. He would just look down at his hands like a scolded little boy.

She didn't like this new guy's approach and she didn't like him. She saw the professor arguing with him once. But the new guy got in the professor's face, so the professor backed down. She didn't know what the conversation consisted of, but it didn't look friendly. If she didn't know any better she'd have thought this ranger guy was a fraud. He talked like he knew more than Professor Simmons, or the police for that matter. She didn't believe he was a true archeologist. He certainly didn't act like one.

Jane really didn't like how the professor and this colleague of his downplayed the problem of artefact theft. The members brought it up at that last meeting and truly wanted to discuss it. After all, the FBI thought it to be a big problem, so who are they to just tell members not to worry about it. But the professor and this new guy, Carl something was his name, just blew it off. They acted like it was no big deal and kept telling everyone not to worry about it. It was very disconcerting. Maybe she should quit this chapter and find another one, like some of the others have been talking about. Maybe she'll talk to her friend Jenny tonight and see what she thinks.

She had known Jenny since college. Jenny was a flirt, easily led and a bit wild for Jane, but since they belonged to the same archeology group, they had kept in touch. They had shared thoughts and ideas about the archeology digs and even roomed together a couple times when they went on an overnight dig. Jenny was in the group of students that joined the archeology chapter when Jane did. They didn't know each other outside of the archeology club and Jane wanted to keep it that way. She had a strange negative vibe about Jenny. Nothing she could put her finger on but it was there. Yet Jane couldn't help but trust her intuition so she decided to keep their association with Jenny purely professional. Jenny seemed like a nice enough person and Jane saw her as harmless but, just the same, Jane was careful around Jenny. She didn't mind if the two of them went on the same digs together, when there were digs that is, but that was the limit of their relationship. Jane never mentioned her gift of intuition to Jenny.

She texted Todd about the meeting. She had to let him know she wouldn't be home right after school. He knew she belonged to this archeological society, but, this was the third time in the last couple months that a special unannounced meeting was called. She had told him some strange things were happening at digs around the state, and that a couple in Ohio had been robbed, so he didn't want to give her a hard time about going. It's just that with them having plans to leave this evening for vacation it was terrible timing. Even so, Todd was a bit leery of this organization she belonged to, so, he decided on his own, before talking to Jane, to make a phone call.

CHAPTER 6

The Professional Downfall

"YOU CAN'T KEEP doing this to my students. They need information. They are members of a professional organization and they need to be treated with more respect. They are professionals in their field and you need to stop playing these cloak and dagger games with them. They need to know if they are in danger!" He was shouting now, so irritated and upset, he could barely hold it together.

Professor Terrance Simmons and this man called Carl Handly were in a side room off the main hall. They had, that is Carl had, called another impromptu meeting of the professors' archeology group. The professor knew Carl was taking over and he didn't like it. The professor took another peek into the main hall. He was upset but didn't know what to do. The members would be arriving soon.

"Your students!" Carl looked at him, laughing.

Carl was a dangerous and ruthless man. He didn't care about Professor Simmons, or the young members of his 'club'. But he was having fun now. He got a kick out of hustling people, especially the part when they finally realize they've been used.

"Of course, they're in danger," Carl sneered. They were in danger from the time you started working for me. They don't mean anything to you!" he hissed back at the professor. "You sold them out months ago."

"I did not sell them out!" yelled the Professor, his face turning fire engine red.

"And I don't work for you!"

"It's all twisted," the professor said, shaking his head and staring at Carl. "You twisted everything around. You hustled me!" he shouted at Carl. "I told you about some important discoveries and then I hear about kids getting injured! You're involved in kids getting hurt!", he repeated vehemently.

Carl stepped up close to the old archeology professor, jabbing his finger into the old man's chest. "Be careful," old man, he said. "Don't forget our deal. You provide me with information, I provide you with money to support your little field trips."

"Kids getting hurt was never part of the deal! And you know it! Besides, you've never lived up to any deal. You have yet to give me a single nickel! You're not even a real archeologist, are you?" the professor hollered.

Carl just smiled back at him. It was an evil smile and it sent chills down the professors back.

They heard noise coming from the hall.

"They're starting to arrive", said Carl. "Don't you dare say a word, or you'll be sorry," he threatened as he walked toward the door pushing the old man against the wall as he left the room.

The professor was despondent. It was all wrong. He felt like he was in a nightmare. He was glad he had finally made some quiet inquiries and was eventually routed to a man named Lacrosse. Lacrosse was a federal marshal who told professor Simmons who Carl Handly really was. It was humiliating, but the professor realized that he had gotten himself into something that was very dangerous and he needed to do something about it. He never thought that his dreams could be smashed so easily. He had made a terrible decision trusting Carl Handly and knew now that he was in trouble. Carl was just a con man, and he was dangerous.

The professor tried to think back on how it all happened. He wasn't even sure how he got tangled up with Carl Handly. Now he just wanted to fix what he broke, if that was even possible.

He was glad he contacted someone. Hooking up with marshal Lacrosse took away some of his despair, but not the guilt he felt for letting his students down. At least the marshal could give advice and possibly help him out of this mess. He met with Lacrosse a couple times and started giving him information about Carl, including names he heard during conversations. But he had more information and with the holiday weekend here he didn't trust Carl. The professor wasn't set to meet with Lacrosse until Tuesday.

"That's too long to wait," he whispered to himself. With the confrontation he just had with Carl tonight, the professor just knew he couldn't wait.

He looked out at his membership gathering in the hall. His anger at Carl was building, but there was nothing he could do about it, or was there. He was a smart man, but not that smart. He felt the life he knew was over. He didn't know what would happen to him, and he didn't care. But he did care about the young people that trusted him. He was afraid for his members. Many of them were former students he had convinced to join his archeology group. He had to do something. But what could he do now. Tonight, Carl had plans on disbanding the very organization the professor worked so hard to build. This would be their last meeting. What could he do? Who could he trust? He walked over to the door leading into the assembly room. His eyes scanned the crowd. Then he spotted his favorite student member and instantly had an idea!

CHAPTER 7

The Meeting of Discontent

S HE ARRIVED EARLY enough to the meeting that she didn't worry about getting closed out, yet sure enough, promptly at five, they closed and locked the doors. She was sitting next to her friend Jenny but before the meeting started, Professor Simmons came up to her.

"Can I please talk to you for a second", he asked, motioning her over to a corner.

"Sure," she said, telling Jenny to save her seat.

"What's he want?" asked Jenny, curiously.

Jane just shrugged her shoulders, grimacing, "who knows." She got up to follow Professor Simmons over to the side of the room, near a corner.

"I know this sounds really cryptic but you cannot ask any questions," he said, his eyes watching Carl at the front of the room, then focusing back at her.

He pressed a small envelope in her hand as he talked, making sure nobody saw.

"Don't look at it," he told her, "and don't let anybody know you have it."

He looked around the room before continuing, then looked back at Jane. "I know you're going away for the weekend," he said, "but when you come back I'll explain in more detail what I'm trying to do. In the mean-time I want you to keep this for safe keeping. Don't open it. Don't tell anyone about it. Just slip it in your pocket for now. I have to go up front," he said as he walked away leaving her in the corner.

She was seriously confused. She didn't know if this was good, or bad. She just knew this professor, whom she had come to like a great deal, had changed a lot over the last few months or so. He had become sad and almost listless at meetings. And now this cryptic message. She didn't know what to make of it. She put the small envelope in her pocket and went back to her seat next to Jenny and sat down.

"What was that all about," asked Jenny, after Jane sat back down.

"I'm not even sure myself," said Jane, "I think the professor is losing his marbles, he just grabbed my hand and told me to be safe on my vacation. Then he just dropped my hand and walked away."

"Well what did he say?" Jenny pushed.

"Nothing," said Jane. "He knows I'm going hiking and wanted to tell me to have a good time." Jane was not a good liar so she didn't look at Jenny. She busied herself looking for a pen in her purse.

Jenny just looked at Jane for a long second, frowning. She was irritated but didn't say anything else. She didn't believe her and thought Jane was holding something back. She tried so hard to be Jane's friend but Jane just didn't seem to notice.

The meeting started and the door was closed and locked. Professor Simmons, the chapter president who presided over the meeting walked up to the podium and brought the meeting to order.

"Thank you all for coming," he said. "I expect this meeting to be short. It's informational only and I'll let Carl explain."

Carl Handly came to the podium. He was a plump scruffy looking man, not to tall, not to short, with a black handlebar mustache and a pock-marked face. He seemed nervous but spoke with authority.

"The professor and I," he began, "are aware that many of you have concerns about the artefact thieves we've mentioned over the last couple meetings. We want to assure you that nothing has changed. We are here to advise you, as professionals, that you are in no danger and that if you are working on a dig here in Michigan, please continue to do so. Our work as archeologists is important and we shouldn't let rumors stop our progress."

The members started grumbling.

"Talk about patronizing!" whispered her friend. "He talks like we're two-year old's. Does he think we're stupid?"

Jane didn't respond.

"That being said," he continued, talking louder," we would like to inform you that this chapter's meetings will be suspended until the first of the year."

"What?" one member shouted.

"Why?" said another.

"What's going on," asked another, "why stop our meetings at the height of these issues? You haven't even told us anything, no details."

The members were not happy at all!

"Next thing you know he's going to want us to steal for him," Jenny whispered boldly.

Jane didn't respond. She was listening to Carl Handly and didn't hear what Jenny had said.

"This is crazy," said Jane. We should be getting more details, not less."

Jenny didn't really care, but Jane didn't notice

Jane sat back in her chair. She was thinking about the last meeting now and how she had caught similar comments whispered between members sitting around her. She didn't like the confusing atmosphere in this meeting or the guidance the professor and his colleague were 'not' providing. She felt compelled to attend this meeting so she could hear anything about artefact thieves working in or around Michigan. But now she wasn't getting any details, and to her, that was just nonsense.

And now, this meeting, felt even more mysterious. The cloak and dagger approach to the unscheduled gathering was bad enough. But this! This basic disregard for the members around her, by a professor she once liked and respected came out totally bizarre. She was tempted to just leave, however, considering that the doors had been locked, she decided to sit it out. Something was going on. Something she didn't like but couldn't explain. She thought the last couple meetings were leading up to something, an explanation maybe, or a leadership change of some kind. But there was nothing. The professor and his new partner didn't seem to care. They gathered their papers and left.

The room was silent.

Everyone, was stunned, including Jane. They didn't know what to do.

"What's going on," one member asked.

"They're just leaving?" said another. "That's it? Just like that?"

"This is bullshit," said a young man Jane knew to be a longtime member.

There was a small uproar, mostly questions being yelled as the two leaders left the room. But then everything went quiet. The members began to file out of the meeting room. Many of them, including Jane, exchanged phone numbers, vowing to keep in touch. She told her friend Jenny that she was going on vacation but maybe when she got back they could gather a few members and talk about going to another chapter. Jenny seemed to like that idea.

CHAPTER 8

The Adventure Begins

"JANE, YOU COMING? I thought you wanted to get going," said Todd.

"I know, I hear you," she said. "I had to go to the bathroom, do you mind."

"I Thought you wanted to be on your way two hours ago."

"It's not my fault they called this crazy meeting, and I had to go."

"I know, I know," he said, calming himself down. "Can we just get going?"

"Look," she said, "we need to talk a bit about what they said at the meeting. Let's get moving and we'll talk in the van before we meet up with Jack and Gail. And, I know we're probably already going to be late."

Jane felt hot and sweaty. She knew it was her nerves. She also knew her blood pressure must be elevated. She took slow breaths in and out, trying to relax. She had planned this trip for several months and was past eager to get going. She thought about her uncle, but she also thought about the things she was seeing at the archeology meetings. She felt things happening at the meeting were turning seriously awkward. The professor and his whole personality had changed, for the worse. Members of her archeology group were getting angry. They weren't getting answers to their concerns. And a stranger had taken over leadership of their chapter. She wasn't sure what to make of it all.

Todd knew something was going on that she needed to think through. He trusted that she would give him the details when she was ready, so he was patient with her. Plus, he had to let her know that he made that phone call.

They jumped in the van. Jane checked to make sure she had her maps and her compass. Todd had packed their camping gear but Jane still made him go over their list, like two more times, before they left the driveway. They planned on picking up their two friends at six, getting a quick bite to eat, and then getting on the road and being on their way by seven.

"How long will it take us to get to Ontonagon," she asked him.

"Maybe twelve to fourteen hours depending on our speed, traffic conditions, and weather at the bridge of course. You know they'll close the bridge if the winds are too high," he said, "but I think you know all that!" She looked at him and smiled.

He pushed her once in a while to trust her instincts, to trust her gift. He had a lot of confidence in her gift but he had to help her learn to feel and trust in it as well.

"And of course, a lot depends on how many times we stop at rest stops along the way, or whatever," he added.

It was meant to be a nice long weekend trip. They all took Friday off, so they could get a jump on holiday traffic. "I hope we're still ahead of traffic," she said out loud.

Jane knew that leaving late Thursday would give them three good days of hiking the trails up in the 'porkies'. By Monday, which was Labor Day, they would have to be on their way back home so they could be back to work on Tuesday. At least that was the plan.

"Look! I knew you'd be late when I got your text earlier in the day," he told her. "I packed everything in the van while you were at your meeting. I knew we'd be delayed a, but I was hoping it wouldn't change our plans by much."

"Thanks," she said. "I appreciate it. I've been organizing things all week so we wouldn't have to rush around when the weekend got her. I just didn't expect this meeting."

But all went well. He was ready when she got home. He knew she would still insist on going through her check list. That's OK, he was ready for it. She also wanted to take a quick shower, change her clothes, and pack a few last-minute things. She still rushed around as she got just a few more things together. He watched her do her thing and smiled. She was intense, that's for sure and he loved that about her.

She saw him smiling. "Stop", she said.

"Stop what", he replied with a grin.

"You know what", she replied back, laughing.

She caught him doing that a lot. Staring at her. Jane and Todd had known each other for well over ten years. They dated for three years before they got married six months ago. They felt lucky to have each other. Many of their college friends were already separated, if not divorced. But, they felt they were a good match for each other. They were both in good physical shape and they both liked the out-of-doors. They liked it differently, he liked learning by doing on-line research, she did on-line research a well but she liked learning by experiencing. They liked the outdoors too, and they loved nature. There was no question. They liked a lot of other similar things too, like cooking and reading a good book, they both liked mystery and fantasy, and of course they liked good movies, but they had individual interests as well. He was a computer nerd and did a lot of research on-line before jumping into anything. She liked hands on field work type research and had traveled a lot. They both knew how to give each other some personal space when it was needed, but they both liked adventurous opportunities offered in the great state of Michigan, especially when it had to do with the outdoors and they could do it together.

They met at Oakland University and were both in their late twenties. She graduated with a Bachelor Degree in History and taught at one of the local high schools. But she really wanted to get her Master degree soon. If anything, it would mean a bump in pay. That would be nice. But she wanted her

Master's degree to be in something special. Thing is, even though she traveled a lot, she was always drawn back and interested in her home state of Michigan. She was especially curious about all the strange phenomenon she had heard about over the years. But she knew full well that there was really no Master's program for that. But, still, she loved solving puzzles, especially historical unknowns, which is why she liked archeology. She thought if she did some research maybe it would help her choose the right program and head her in the direction she wanted her career to take her. She liked teaching but if something more exciting came along she would move on. She liked the strange and unusual. She read up a lot on Michigan phenomena and gave her students assignments related to her Michigan interests. But this would be her first, very own, 'field' trip related partly to archeology and partly to all that phenomena stuff she's been studying and looking into. So, needless to say, she was excited about this trip.

Todd also taught high school history, but at a different high school then Jane. He already started his Master's program and was focusing on Renaissance Studies, with some details of American folklore. He tried hard to focus on 'Michigan' Renaissance and Michigan folklore. He liked what he did, teaching. He enjoyed watching the kids learn. He also valued the unusual and enjoyed discovering different things. But he knew in his heart that he wasn't into, hands on, knees dirty, field work, like Jane. He was more of a nerd than Jane and liked to do his research in front of a computer. He cherished their time camping together and liked when they did zip-lining or indoor wall climbing as partners. And mostly, he loved Jane. So, even though he preferred his camping trips to be during nice warm summer weather, he's doing this fall excursion for Jane, hoping it won't get to cold in the U.P. while they're up there.

Jane was going over her list, asking Todd if packed this or that, even though Todd had finished packing everything already.

"Both the tents are in the car, right", she asked him.

"Yes," he replied.

"The cooler and box of food's packed, right," she said.

"Yes," he replied.

"The fishing gear and bug spray are packed," right", she looked at him.

"Yes," he said rolling his eyes when she wasn't looking.

"What about your metal detector?" she asked

"It's in the van," he said. "I'm not sure if we can use it while we're in the porkies. I asked for a special permit. If I don't get a text by the time we get there I thought we could at least take a little time at a couple of the rest areas on the way back, just to try it out."

"I don't know if we'll get a chance to use it either," she said, "but it's in the van. No big deal, there's plenty of room."

"Your extra ammo is packed, right," she said.

"Yes," he replied. "Everything's packed Jane. You have everything here but the kitchen sink. If we forgot anything, we'll buy it when we get there," he said smiling. "Come on, let's go."

"OK," she said. "I just wanted to be sure," she mumbled to herself.

Todd didn't respond.

He had everything organized nicely in the van and there was even room for Jack and Gail, thankfully. Jane got in the driver's seat. She would drive the first few hours while it was still daylight. Todd preferred driving in the evening. He felt there were fewer idiots on the road at that time.

"What time are we supposed to meet them," Jane asked Todd.

"Six o'clock," he said, "but I changed it to eight."

"Wow! Thanks," she said, but it's already seven-thirty, and it'll take us forty minutes to get to Romeo. Can you call Jack and tell him we're running just a few minutes behind?"

"Sure."

"And make sure they go to Youngers and not Time Square. I like the pizza at Youngers better."

"You sure you want to sit and eat? Maybe we could do carry out," he asked.

"I don't want to eat and drive," she said, "especially on the expressway."

"OK, no problem."

Todd took out his cell phone to dial Jack. The number was in his favorites so he just pushed the appropriate button and was already hearing the ring on the other side.

Jack answered with his normal, "hey, what's up?"

"Hey Jack," he said, "We're running a bit late. Are you at Youngers yet?"

"Heading there now," said Jack, we'll be pulling up there in a few minutes. Where are you?"

"We're about fifteen minutes behind. Can you wait for us at the bar?"

"Sure, no problem. See you when you get here."

"Are they running late again?" asked Gail?

"Yah," said Jack. "Are you surprised?"

"No, Jane's always so involved. She texted me earlier and said that she had to attend some last-minute meeting. She's the one that wanted to get an early start and then she had that meeting. I felt bad for her. She sounded frustrated. I knew that she was all hyped and excited about this trip. I was hoping maybe she would be able to sneak out early, but obviously that didn't happen."

"Are you crazy!" Jack said. "The meeting was about archeology and she's too passionate about archeology to leave a meeting early. Plus, she's a list person, remember? She'll make Todd review the list at least twice to be sure they don't forget anything. And Todd will do it because he's a very patient man and he knows that will help calm her down. Can you imagine the preparation she put into this trip? Todd said she's been planning it for quite a while. And the camping equipment and supplies she probably packed? We'll be lucky if they have room for us in the van."

Oh, no!" he said, creeping up close to Gail, "we'll be squished between all the gear!"

Jack had cornered Gail, pushing her into a corner just outside the restaurant, like they had to share a tiny space together in between all the packed gear stuffed into the van.

"Stop that," she said, laughing. "And try to behave".

"Maybe we should think twice before we drop our car off at Aunt Dianna's," said Jack. "Maybe we should drive separately."

Gail just laughed. "Yah, right, I don't think so. We'll be fine, and there'll be plenty of room, I'm sure," she said with a smile.

CHAPTER 9

Vacation – Plans don't always work out as you Expect

JACK WASN'T REALLY in a hurry. He was used to them being late and always had patience for it, mostly because he knows Todd would do the same for him. They'd been best friends for a long time. Todd had been there for Jack, many times, pulling him out of jams when Jack had pulled some stupid stunt as a kid. Todd always stuck with him, no matter what. Todd was one of the good guys. He was Jack's best friend and they always had each other's back. Jack was best man at Todd and Jane's wedding. Someday Todd would be his best man. They would do anything for each other.

The two of them grew up on nearby farms north of Romeo and hung out as youngsters. If they got in trouble it was usually Jack's fault. And although they both lived in Romeo, they went to different schools. Until high school that is. In high school, they both ended up at Lutheran High North. Jack's family was Lutheran and Jack went to Lutheran schools all his life. Todd's parents were Catholic and didn't always attend church services, but their faith was strong and even though Todd didn't go to a parochial grade school, they wanted him to have some kind of religious influence. So, they found Lutheran High North had the faith background they wanted for their son. Funny thing was, as time went on and the boys went to college Todd always seemed to take his faith more to heart than Jack. It seemed to have a calming influence on him.

Gail went to Lutheran High North as well and dated Jack off and on since high school. He always seemed to be a goof off so she was concerned about taking their relationship very seriously. Until this past year that is, when he seemed to start settling down a bit. That's when they moved in together. She figured he was just growing up, maybe, so far so good. Maybe teaching did that to him. They both graduated from Oakland and were also teachers like their friends Jane and Todd. Gail taught elementary Art and loved her first graders. Jack taught high school drafting, math, and mechanics. He was good with high school kids, and he had a big reputation for influencing some of his high school graduates to go into engineering. Gail loved him and was beginning to have dreams of spending the rest of her life with him.

"Come on, we'll just wait for them at the bar," said Jack. "They'll be here before you know it." Jack held the door open for Gail as they both looked around the restaurant. The tables were almost full, but the bar had plenty of space so they headed over there. The bar tender took their order and delivered their drinks within a minute.

"Are you ready for this?" asked Jack.

"Yah! Said Gail. "I'm actually looking forward to camping in the U.P. I hear the Porcupine Mountain area is beautiful and I've never seen Lake of the Clouds. I'm actually very excited. I told my first graders where I was going so I have to remember to take pictures."

"What about you," she asked.

"I've been up to the U.P. quite a bit," he said. "I almost went to school at Northern Michigan University, in Marquette. But I've never seen Lake of the Clouds either. I hear they call it Lake of the Clouds because it's actually situated between two ridges in the Porcupine Mountains, and that it's above sea level. That sounds pretty cool to me."

"I didn't know you almost went to Northern," said Gail. "So, did I!"

They looked at each other and just grinned.

"Cheers," said Jack.

"Cheers to you," said Gail, as they bumped glasses.

On their ride up to Romeo, Jane filled Todd in on some of the details of her archeological meeting.

"This discovery of the theft of archeological artefacts, Indian artefacts to be exact, freaks me out, "said Jane. "And the meetings have just been weird, chaotic to say the least, "she said. "The chapter president brings in this ranger colleague guy nobodies met before. We asked all kinds of questions but he literally side stepped every one of them."

"He just gave me the creeps," said Jane. "I know he's a forest ranger and all, but why have him come to a meeting? Why not one of the more well-known archeologists, maybe from Michigan State or Michigan Tech? It just doesn't make sense. He's just way to knowledgeable and way to comfortable with information related to the artefact thieves. And he tells us not to worry."

"And then," she said with such enunciation, that Todd could almost feel her blood boil. "Then," she said, her voice calming down, "they cancelled all chapter meetings until the first of the year."

"What!" Todd responded. "Why would they do that if there's possible danger out there for anyone working on a dig?"

"Good question," said Jane. "I wish I knew. I just have a bad feeling about this guy."

"Well," said Todd. "Tell me more."

"Over the last few weeks," she said, "until today that is, they seemed genuinely concerned. That's what I thought at first. This ranger dude said that the organizers of all the archeology groups seemed more and more concerned about the thefts. And he told us that they've been keeping in touch with each other more than usual lately, and sharing information. I guess there was a problem in Ohio where some workers were injured, nothing serious but these thieves are taking more and more chances. We fully expected to start hearing about how they operated and what to look for, you know," she continued, "advice".

"When the thefts were first discovered," she said, "we were told that the thieves were very crafty and in and out before anyone knew anything was missing. Now they're getting more brazen. They almost got caught in Ohio and purposely caused a rock slide as they made their get-away. A few people were injured, none seriously."

"Are you thinking they'll be anywhere near us," Todd asked.

"Naaa," she said, "I really don't think we have any worries. There's no real dig going on in the Porcupine Mountains. I checked with the Michigan Tech archeology group. It's just that I really liked my professor, Mr. Simmons. He was always enthusiastic about his job and he shared a lot with his students as well as with the members of our archeology chapter. His whole personality seemed to really change lately, and it just bothers me. I don't know, maybe I'll just find a different chapter to belong to after we get back from vacation."

She was silent for a moment and Todd let her think.

"I just wanted you to know what was going on," she finally said.

"And about that ranger guy," she said. "Who the hell is he anyway? And why did he come and talk to us? Why didn't our Professor Simmons, our chapter president, bring in an actual working archeologist. I mean he's got all the connections. I don't know," she said, "it just all seems weird to me. And I get a strong 'something's not right' feeling about this new guy."

"I appreciate you letting me know," said Todd. "And I think you should absolutely trust your feelings. You need to develop that gift of yours, and the only way you'll get to understand it better, is if you trust it and use it."

She smiled at him and was quiet for a while. She knew he was right. She has this gift and she should trust herself and her feelings.

"It's just that artefacts were disappearing from both new and old digs throughout the country," she said, "and for some reason, lately, Michigan Indian artefacts were being targeted. The meeting I went to was secretive and required ID to attend because, we're told, thy are close to identifying one of the thieves and they didn't want that knowledge to be made public quite yet. That's what we heard last month."

"Then this so-called colleague of our professor shows up, this Carl guy, and the whole focus of our meetings seemed to change. And now they cancel our meetings until next year. So strange," she said.

"Oh, and one more thing," she said. "A very strange thing happened just before the meeting started. The professor asks to talk to me, no big deal, right? So, I follow him off to the side, and he gives me this tiny envelope. He says he knows I'm going on vacation and we'll discuss it when I get back. He tells me not to open it right now or tell anyone about it. What do you make of that?"

"I truly don't know hun," Todd said. "What was in the envelope?" he asked.

Jane looked at him. She had a strange look on her face.

"What!" he said.

"I was so wrapped up in getting ready and getting in the van, I forgot it."

"Well, where is it?" asked Todd.

She looked at him sheepishly.

"What!" he said again.

"It's still in my pants pocket, in the laundry basket", she said softly.

Todd started laughing. Then Jane started laughing.

After they stopped laughing Jane grew quiet for a second before speaking again, as if collecting her thoughts. "Nobody even knows what they're doing with the artefacts," she says, thinking of the artefact thieves. "Somebody has a nice little collection because they're not showing up anywhere. Not publicly anyway," she mumbled, mostly to herself.

"OK," he said, changing the subject. "My turn. I need to let you know that I made a phone call."

"What kind of phone call?" she asked, turning to him with a puzzled look on her face.

"I have a buddy that lives up north and he has some contacts to 'real' law enforcement," he said. "He's really good at what he does, and I just thought he could look into things for us. You know, anything related to archeology and artefact theft, and such, especially anything up in the U.P."

Jane was quiet for a moment. "Well, I guess it can't hurt," she said. "Will he contact you later?"

"Yes, I gave him both our cell's."

Jane thought for a minute. "That's good," she said. "Yah! I think that's good. Thanks".

CHAPTER 10

Getting it Together

I T WAS GETTING late when the two of them walked into Youngers about twenty minutes later. Jack and Gail saw them as soon as they walked in, picked up their drinks from the bar and headed over to meet them. The restaurant had started thinning out and they were only chatting at the door for a couple minutes when a table became available and a waitress led them to their seats. The waitress asked if a booth was acceptable, which of course it was, and seated them at a window booth. She was both observant and efficient and noticed immediately that Jack and Gail already had drinks.

"Would you two like to start with a drink?" she asked.

"Absolutely", said Jane.

"I'll have iced tea."

"I'll have a beer", said Todd. "Whatever you have on tap. Thanks."

"I don't even want to eat," said Jane, out loud, all excited with adrenaline dripping from every word she spoke. "I just want to get on the road and get going."

"Well it really doesn't matter if we get there at six in the morning or eight in the morning, now does it?" said Gail, giving Jane that calm your butt down evil eye.

"I guess not," said Jane, smiling. "We don't want to get to the Park before the Ranger Station is open. We would just end up sitting in the van waiting."

"OK you guys," said Todd, "what do you want on your pizza."

"No anchovies," said Gail.

"Yuk! No way, me either!" said Jane.

The guys just laughed.

"Yah, yah", said Jack, "we know, no anchovies."

The very efficient waitress came over with drinks for Jane and Todd, then she took their pizza order. One large pepperoni pizza with mushrooms, onions, green peppers, and olives. Once the waitress delivered their drinks and took their pizza order the conversation got very energetic. Mostly because Jane was as excited as a monkey in a room full of bananas.

"I love hiking," she said, "and I'm really glad you guys decided to come with us. I want to know everything I can about Michigan, especially the upper peninsula. I could hike all around the U.P. for a month and still not see even half of it. It's a beautiful place and I can't wait to get started. Can you imagine what it was like hiking a hundred years ago?" she asked them, but didn't give them time to respond before she started talking again.

"I've been reading up on Michigan history, especially Upper Peninsula stuff," she said.

"What kind of things?" asked Gail, picking up on Jane's excitement.

Jane's enthusiasm was starting to get them all in the mood for their big adventure. Even Todd and Jack were excited to be on their way. They've all been camping before, but this will be different. Rustic camping is different.

The pizza came to their table and they all dug in. It was hot and it was good. The waitress brought them drink refills as they ate and gabbed about their trip.

"I've been doing a lot of research," said Jane. "There's a lot of things about Michigan most people are very unaware of," she said.

"You know I'm interested in archeology so I'm always looking for something new in Michigan," she continued.

"For instance, did you know that Michigan may have held a very important place in the ancient world? And that it was thought at one-time Michigan may have been about ten degrees north of the equator? Historians and archeologists alike believed that at one time all the land masses of the earth were all squished together as one continent? There are always discussions about it at the archeology meetings I go to. That continent was called 'Pangaea'. And many geographers agree that before the continents split, Spain and New York, yeah, our New York, were on the equator and actually touching, kind of like Michigan and Ohio touch now? And that it's possible Vikings wandered these lands. You could be a descendant from a Viking," she said to Jack. "What do you think about them apples?" she added sarcastically.

At first the others just stared at her. Then Jack said, "my ancestors come from Jersey."

That made everyone laugh. And it took the edge off Jane's nervousness. She took a huge bite out of the slice of pizza she held in her hand. "This is really good!" she said, smiling.

"Of course, that was about 300 million years ago," she continued, as she swallowed a mouth full of pizza. "And," she said, "because the area we now call Michigan was kind of in the center of the continent, they say that the belief that it was a population center would have been quite reasonable. Archeologists love Michigan. We know that at one time there was a great Indian presence here in Michigan. We all know that there are Indian artefacts all around Michigan. Many of our towns and cities are named after Indians or Indian Tribes. But Vikings, and Viking artefacts! Who'd have thought! I've heard that archeologists love to talk to the historians about the possibility of Viking artefacts in Michigan! It was the bases for many very interesting discussions at new archeological digs, should historians be in charge or should archeologists be in charge?"

The others were speechless. They had no idea where she was going with this, but they all knew she was serious, especially Todd. He knew she had been to the library a million times over the last couple months, and that she spent lots of extra time on her computer. And, with this meeting she just attended, and the news she just acquired, it was becoming obvious now, to him at least, what she was doing. She was preparing. But for what! Even he wasn't sure. He had questions. They all had questions. They just weren't sure quite how to ask them. But it was Todd who first spoke up.

"Jane", he said, as mildly as possible. "Just what are your plans for the Porcupine Mountains? What do you expect to find near the Lake of the Clouds? And, most important," he said, "are any of us going to be in danger?" He had to put that question out there. He prepared for fun. He didn't prepare for danger.

"I mean, we all know that the archeologist in you comes out every once in a while, but are you into some kind of hocus pocus, mystical Viking mumbo jumbo stuff?"

He said the word 'stuff' slowly and deliberately, trying not to antagonize her, but at the same time be serious.

Jane saw all their faces sort of freeze in place when Todd asked his short, but serious, questions.

"No, no, no," she said. "There's no danger. At least I don't think so, she mumbled."

"Jane!" said Todd.

"OK, OK, look," she started, "I really didn't think this was any big deal. I truly believed we would do some hiking, maybe use Todd's metal detector that he brought to look for old metal from those times or any metal for that matter. If something Viking shows up, well, all the more interesting. But," she hesitated, "well, the meeting I went to, the one that made me late", she indicated. "It concerned me at first, but, the more I think about it, I really don't think it's any big deal."

"Tell them," said Todd.

"OK," she said, "relax, I'm getting to it, quit pushing."

She continued, "the meeting I went to was basically about the discovery that there are some archeological thieves working in Michigan. The society is warning everyone to be on the lookout. You all know that the reason I chose the Porcupine Mountains as our destination was because of my uncle, and some of the things he's told me over the years. I really don't think we'll find anything, but, I want to look around, as an archeologist, you know.

I thought maybe we could try out the metal detector Todd brought. We're not even sure how well they'll work or how easy it'll be to carry them on a hike. We just got them so we've only had time to try them out twice. Both Todd and I did a little research on metal detectors but we've talked about it and are still not sure if we'll even have time to use them or what exactly they might detect. But we brought them just in case. I'm an archeologist, remember, not an engineer. The area is well known for its copper deposits. You can detect copper with a metal detector. That much I know."

She was changing the subject, but only Todd caught on. He decided not to say anything.

"I can tell you about metal detectors," said Jack. My dad used one on the farm to locate old farm machinery before putting his plow in. It prevented him from breaking expensive equipment while putting in the crops. Besides," he said, "I may not have a science degree but I am mechanical and can figure out how things work!"

"I can vouch for that." said Gail. "He likes to take everything apart. I just don't know if he can put things back together again!" she said with a smile.

Jane just let Jack take over the conversation.

They all laughed at Jack's animated description of metal detectors, and their chattering went on for another 45 minutes before Jane realized what time it was.

"Oh my gosh," said Jane. "Do you guys know what time it is?"

Jack and Gail whipped out their cell phones at the same time.

"We still need to get our car over to my Aunt's house," said Jack. "She lives on Campground Road, only about a mile or two from here." "It's going on nine o'clock already so we should get moving. Dropping our car off should only take a few minutes. We can do that and be on the expressway headed toward Flint in no time at all."

They paid their bill, leaving a pretty nice tip for the waitress, and headed out the door. They were parked close enough to each other that Jane and Todd just followed them to Jack's Aunt's house. They were on I-69 headed toward Flint by nine-forty-five.

CHAPTER 11

Finally on the Way

IT WAS A little past ten-thirty by the time they actually reached I-75 and were headed north. After leaving the restaurant they had to drop Jack's car off at his Aunt's house. His Aunt Dianna knew they were coming and waited up for them and directed them where to park their car. She didn't delay them at all, just took the car keys (in case the car had to be moved) and handed them a small bag.

"Just a small something for the road," she said. "Have a fun time, and be safe."

"Thanks, "said Jack, hugging her goodbye.

"Todd, can you open the backend of the van, "said Jack. "I think these backpacks will fit back there.

"I'll get the other stuff, "said Gail.

They only took a few minutes to move Jack and Gail's backpacks and any supplies they had into Jane and Todd's Ford Expedition. They didn't have a lot to move over because they dropped off tents and some other camping equipment at Todd and Jane's earlier in the week.

Jack's Aunt Dianna waved as they pulled out of her country driveway.

"Oh, you have plenty of room in here, "said Gail.

"Sure, I told you we would, "said Jane.

Gail looked at Jack ready to slap him for his earlier comments. He just laughed knowing full well they wouldn't be squeezed into a small area between all the supplies.

"What kind of van is this?" asked Gail.

"It's an old 2010 Ford 4x4 Expedition," said Todd. It's not exactly a van but it's big, with lots of room and lots of power to get us where we wanted to go. We like it, "he continued. "It fits all our camping equipment, plus yours, and the other supplies we need, nicely in the back. And it still leaves room for passengers."

The only thing Gail insisted on keeping close to her was her pillow and her quilt.

"What are you keeping that up here for, "asked Jack, pointing at her pillow and comfy quilt.

"I always take them on these kind of camping trips. "she told him. I call this my comfy quilt because it's not too heavy and it's easy to clean once I get home. Besides I plan on getting a little sleep in the next ten hours. It's a long trip to the U.P. After all, I did work today."

They all laughed. They had all worked today. It was just before the Labor Day weekend and school for all of them had started in late August for the new school year. This was a three-day weekend vacation that they stretched in four days mainly because Ontonagon was quite a drive. They took an extra day mainly because they all knew a large part of their time would be driving there and back.

They were still excited when they took off, but as the driving melted into a quiet routine they all drifted into their own thoughts. Jane's mind drifted to her research, and some of the things she learned at the archeology meeting. She told Todd about the archeology thieves, and how her professor had changed after bringing in this new guy, and how she didn't trust this new guy and the way he took over. She told Todd about how the group members were frustrated at the lack of communication in their meetings since this guy took over and then how irritated as hell they were when this new guy basically cancelled the next few meetings for no apparent reason, just as information about these archeology thieves was needed. Her head was swirling at the thought of how much their wonderfully progressive archeology seminars had gone downhill in such a short time.

She looked at Jack and Gail and felt guilty that she hadn't told them much of anything, especially about her uncle. She wanted to let them know. They were all friends and she felt it was important to open up and tell them a little about what happened to her uncle fifty years ago. She should at least let them know why they were going hiking in the 'Porkies' instead of somewhere else in Michigan, somewhere a little closer to home.

And she hadn't told anyone about some of the things she read about lately in the archeology journals, especially about the extent of theft involved and how dangerous it was getting for archeologists doing field work. She wasn't sure how they would take some of the unknowns. She wasn't sure if it was even important. They weren't going on an archeological dig, or anything like that. They were just going hiking.

Her intent was to try to find Michigan artefacts, and more specifically she wanted to determine if Indian and Viking artifacts crossed paths. The Porcupine Mountains would be a good place to start. She wanted to watch for anything related to historical Michigan, even if it included just Indian artefacts. It could be a hieroglyphic tablet or Indian cave art, or maybe she would be able to uncover signs of a hidden Indian village. Indians lived in this country for generations and different tribal artefacts are found all over the country. When you really spend time searching, it's surprising what you can find. She thought she could do that while hiking.

She thought about the journal article she read about a Norse altar discovered on top of the Huron Mountain in the U.P (in the late eighteen hundred's). She certainly didn't expect to find an altar, but it was an interesting article none-the less. Finding a Viking altar would be too obvious. But, finding an ancient Indian highway like many found throughout Michigan, or any Indian artefact for that matter, would be amazing. She could dream all day long but she also wanted to be realistic. Even a couple old

Indian arrow heads would be nice to find. She needed to give Todd and their friends more information related to the hiking adventure she planned around her uncle's map. She also needed to figure out if the archeology thieves were really an issue to be concerned about. She just didn't know enough about the artefact thieves being in Michigan to tell anybody anything worthwhile, even if the thieves were here at all. She really didn't even know herself if there was a problem, but what if! She had a lot to think about.

Right now, she couldn't stop thinking about the fact that they only had the weekend, so time was precious. She was just glad that her Uncle had given her a few ideas from his experiences. And she wanted to do something for him too. She didn't say too much to anybody, accept the little she told Todd, because right now, they were just ideas about where to hike and what to search for. However, with the information she received earlier today about the danger these artefact thieves may pose on them, she knew she had to tell her friends something.

Although Todd, like Jane, was in his own little world, Jack and Gail were having a lively discussion about metal detectors and what they 'might' find.

"You don't understand," he said to Gail. "Metal detectors find all kinds of metals, but metal detectors have different properties and it depends on what you're looking for which property is most important. And there are all kinds and qualities of metal detectors out there. They all work off the concept of electricity and magnetism. Those two qualities have simply been refined over the years, but a person should still understand how the thing works."

Jack was on a roll now. And even Jane and Todd started listening to him.

"You could probably go buy a basic metal detector, push the button on the top, and do your thing. Today, that's what a lot of people do. The new detectors out there are pretty good. But, in the past, if you were serious about finding something special than you needed to understand the tool you were going to use, and the item, or items, you want to find."

Jack went on and on about metal detectors and what types (there were three types) he told Gail.

"The first type is called 'Ferrous'," he said. Ferrous type metals are basically metals that can be attracted to a magnet. It's the easiest metal to detect, and the biggest contaminant in our environment. You know, it includes paperclips, thumbtacks, and nuts and bolts left behind by different types of small industry."

"The second type is considered non-ferrous," he continued. "That includes copper, aluminum, brass, lead, and even manganese. Even gold falls into this category. These are harder to detect and these metals are especially harder to detect using the basic metal detector that most people buy."

Then he told them about the third type of metal, stainless steel. It has very poor electrical conductivity which makes it even harder to detect than the other two.

I don't want to bore you with all the details of how the different types are used," he said.

"No, keep going," said Todd. "This is kind of interesting."

Jack didn't need much coaxing to continue. He talked about the type used most often, the 'beat frequency oscillation'. And he talked about the 'very-low frequency detectors' used by experienced treasure hunters, looking for maybe silver or gold. Then he mentioned the third type, 'Pulse induction', used by different security Guards to search for concealed weapons at all types of security stations.

"Wow!" said Todd. "Where did you learn all that crap from?"

"You want to hear about my introduction to metal detectors?" asked Jack.

"Well we're all driving in the same car and none of us are going anywhere for a few hours at least," said Jane, "so tell us your story."

"O.K.," said Jack.

"Basically, when I was younger I remember my dad running over some crazy old piece of combine with his new tractor when he plowed this new field he had just purchased. The piece of metal from the combine was mostly buried so he didn't see it until it was too late. It cost him a lot of money to get his plow fixed. And he was not happy!"

When nobody said any more Jack continued.

"After that, he got an idea. He figured it would be cheaper for him to buy a metal detector and pay me a little cash to sweep the field before he plowed, than to run into something like that again. It was kind of fun. I found all sorts of things, most of it junk, but I found some very interesting coins as well. Then after I got older, I started looking into metal detecting, and I got to know a little more about metal detectors. I also found some fascinating old farm machinery, which is one of the reasons I took math and mechanics in school."

"That's why I had him help me choose the metal detector we brought along with us," said Todd. "I've heard him go through all this information before. One day I asked about metal detectors. You should have seen him go into teacher mode," he chuckled. "You just got the same lecture from teacher Jack that I got about three or four months ago."

"Anyway," Todd said, "since we're on the subject, I might as well let all of you know. I brought two metal detectors with us. Jack recommended the two I bought."

He looked at Jane. "We bought!"

"Yeah, right," said Jane as she rolled his eyes and shook her head.

"You and I are going to have to get together on this finance and spending money thing," she said.

"Yeah, yeah, I know," said Todd, as he continued. "But this would be the perfect trip to use them, "he said. "I just hope we get to use them."

Todd didn't say any more. He just listened as Jane started talking.

"We all know there's probably lots of copper where we're going," she said. "But there may be other metals as well," she continued. Maybe we'll touch on an area where Vikings lived a million years ago."

Jane knew that was a stretch but, whatever.

"And with two detectors we can search more ground."

Todd chuckled to himself. He knew he could get her interested in the metal detectors. She's beginning to talk like it was her idea. That made him laugh more.

"Vikings!" yelled Gail, in a voice louder then she had planned. "Are you crazy?"

"I mean … well not crazy!" She stammered.

"I'm sorry," she said. "That didn't come out right."

Jane laughed! Then Todd laughed! Jack just gave Gail a big hug, and then they laughed as well.

"I really didn't mean it that way," she told Jane.

"I know," said Jane.

"You are sort of right though Gail," she said.

"I did so much research, and have all this stuff in my head. Wouldn't it be cool if we found something really historical?"

"Really valuable would be cool too," said Todd.

They were all quiet for a couple minutes.

"How about a quick stop to stretch our legs?" asked Jane.

"Absolutely," the rest of them said all at once.

Jane had been driving now for three hours. She was making good time. They weren't yet to the bridge, but they were getting close. They were about fifty miles from the Mackinaw Bridge when she finally pulled over for a quick rest stop. It was late, almost one in the morning, and she knew she was getting a little tired so it was time to change drivers as well. When she pulled into the rest area they all moaned as they started moving their bones a little to wake them up.

CHAPTER 12

Into the U.P.

"I NEEDED TO STRETCH my legs, "said Gail. "It was a good idea to stop. Thanks."

"No problem, "said Jane, "I needed to stretch my legs too. I just don't like sitting for long periods of time. "

"Check this out, "said Jack, pointing to the Michigan map on the rest area wall. "We're not far from the bridge."

"Yup. Not far," said Jane. "It's getting chilly out though, don't you think."

"Yah! A little. "said Todd. Want me to drive a while? You can cuddle up with your blanket and take a nap."

"That actually sounds good, "said Jane.

They were back in the car now and on their way again. This time Todd was driving and Jack sat in the front with him. The girls sat in the back with their pillows and blankets. The heat in the car was on, helping them shake off the chill from being outside the car for the few minutes it took to run to the restroom and back without a jacket. The temperature wasn't that bad but it had gotten colder after the sun went down and you could tell it was September. It wasn't quite cold enough for coats, maybe in the low 60's, but chilly none the less. Maybe jacket weather. But jackets weren't necessary when you've been in a warm car for the last three or four hours.

They were about to cross the Mackinaw Bridge but decided to stop for gas first. They had already devoured the snacks Jack's Aunt Dianna gave them (cheese and crackers, beef jerky, and homemade chocolate chip cookies), so they also picked up a few snacks. It was almost two in the morning when they crossed the bridge. Todd asked Jack to help him watch for M-28, the East/West Highway they would be turning onto next. They'll be on M-28 for at least a few hours.

They were well on their way now. Jane and Gail were both ready to fall asleep in the back seat. Jack and Todd had gotten into an interesting discussion on Michigan's Upper Peninsula. It seems Todd knew more about the U.P. than Jack realized.

"My mom always liked the U.P.," said Todd. She went to school in Marquette, at Northern Michigan University, which is why I almost went there. And her brother, my uncle, went to Michigan Tech in Houghton. They used to do some camping at Tahquamenon Falls, and someplace up in Baraga county. They were never specific about where in Baraga County. They just said those were the good old days."

"Anyway," he continued, "when mom and dad got married and had Ginny and me, they would take us camping. We've been to 'Tahquamenon Falls' of course, more times than I can count. And I've been to 'Pictured Rocks', the Porcupine Mountain and 'Lake of the Clouds', where we're headed now, and a lot of different light houses throughout the U.P."

"You should check out 'Whitefish Bay', continued Todd. "We ran into a writer there. He wrote a book about how he was the lone survivor of one of the shipwrecks that occurred in Lake Superior. His name was Hale I believe, yeah, Dennis Hale. We talked to him for a few minutes. I think his ship sank sometime in the sixties. He was cool. He signed the book for us too."

"Wow!", said Jack. "I knew you'd been in the U.P. but I didn't know you'd been up here that many times."

"Yup!" said Todd. "I've even gone swimming several times in Lake Superior too. And all that stuff about it being 'cold' – it's very true, it's shivering your ass off in a freezer kind of cold. But my dad said he wanted all of us to do it at least once so we could say we swam in all the great lakes."

He talked about family camping with pleasure. His parents always made it fun.

"Hey, have you ever been to 'Christmas'?

Jack looked at him, then remembered. "Oh, yah, 'Christmas'! My mom mentioned it. But I've never been there."

"Well you're in for a treat!" said Todd. "We'll be passing right through it! It's just the other side of Munising. And it's the middle of the night so you'll see it all lit up. It's very impressive!"

"It's not even December," said Jack.

"Doesn't matter, "said Todd. "They have Christmas lights up all year. It's tradition because of the town name. I think it's kind of cool. But then I'm a nerd anyway."

Jack just laughed. After that they just fell quiet as Todd drove the miles away.

It was almost four in the morning when he noticed the sign leading into Christmas, but Jack had dozed off.

"Hey Jack!" he said. "Wake up!"

"What?" Jack was still groggy but he woke up when Todd called his name.

"Check this out," said Todd.

Jack stared out the front window of the van in awe. Then his whole face lit up and a huge smile broke out from ear to ear. He looked like he just saw Santa coming down the chimney. There was the city of 'Christmas' lit up in hundreds of sparkling red and green lights. Yes! Christmas lights. And there were other decorations too.

"Should we wake the girls", he said quietly.

"Sure," but you better do it quick. The town isn't that big," said Todd.

Todd slowed the van down as Jack ruffles the blankets the girls were buried under.

"Gail! Jane!" wake up. "Check this out".

"Come on. Come on. Wake up!"

"What are you doing, give me my blanket ba........." Gail's voice trailed off as her sleepy eyes focused on the green house with the fifty-foot Santa figure waving down at her.

"Holy shit!" she blurted out.

"Yah, it does kind of hit you out of nowhere doesn't it," said Todd.

Jane looked up too.

"I've been here before," she said. "But not at night time. This is awesome."

"Who doesn't like Christmas?" Todd said sarcastically, with a big grin on his face.

"Yeah, we're all nerds," said Jack. "But I love it, "said Gail. It makes me feel like a kid again."

The city of Christmas isn't very big so, even going slow, they passed through quickly. But that didn't stop their eyes from feasting on the displays of bright color and the menagerie of lights. Their smiles were like kids on Christmas morning for at least a few more miles.

CHAPTER 13

Passing Christmas

THEY WERE ALL awake now. It seemed like the lights of Christmas snapped them all alert and the excitement of the trip was starting to re-ignite.

"Where are we?" asked Gail. "I mean I know we just passed Christmas. Very cool by the way. But how much longer to Ontonagon?"

"Maybe three more hours, or so, maybe a little less," said Todd.

"Do you want me to take over driving," said Jane. She had her nap and was wide awake now.

"No, I'm good," replied Todd. "But we should hit Marquette in another hour or so, and that would be a good place to stop for gas. Plus, it'll be close to six by then so maybe we should think about stopping for breakfast. Or is it still too early for everyone?"

"I'd rather wait until we get to Ontonagon," said Jane.

"Fine with me," said Todd. "You guys want anything when we get to Marquette?" he said in general, but aimed more at Gail and Jack.

"I'm good until we get to Ontonagon," said Jack. "How about you Gail?"

"I'm fine until then," she said.

M-28 ended at US-41 and Todd turned north toward Marquette. They arrived in Marquette just after six.

"You really made good time," said Jack. "I think you were going a little faster than the speed limit."

"I don't know what you're talking about," said Todd, as he got out to pump the gas with a sly smirk on his face.

He filled up the big tank, got back in the van, and pulled out onto US-41 heading out of Marquette.

"So, what's the plan anyway," asked Gail.

"We'll stop for breakfast of course," said Jane. "Then we'll head into the Porcupine Mountains Wilderness State Park. It's like fifteen miles from Ontonagon," she said.

"I could give you a whole history lesson about the 'Porkies', that's what they call the Porcupine Mountains. Todd knows, don't you Todd?"

"Yeah, I know some. But not as much as you."

"Anyway," Jane continued, "I've reserved us a 'Yurt', but I'm not sure if we'll need it or not. It didn't cost much so I thought it would be worth it."

"What's a 'Yurt'?" asked Gail.

"So, we're getting close, right?" asked Gail. "I'm getting a little nervous," she said. "I don't have half the camping experience as you guys."

"Don't worry," said Jane. "There's a first time for everyone. But this isn't your first time, is it," she asked Gail.

"No," said Gail. "But it's my first time doing this rustic camping thing. My camping experience includes showers just down the road and a grocery store in walking distance. Jane smiled. "Don't worry, Todd and I have both done rustic camping."

"More times than I can count," said Todd.

"Yeah, I've lost count myself. I've gone camping all over the country with friends and family members. Most of it was like you mentioned, hot showers down the road and a place to buy whatever you forgot to pack. But I've done a lot of rustic camping too. Lately I've focused most of my camping experiences in Michigan's Upper

Peninsula. The difference between rustic camping and the camping you've done," she said to Gail, "is simply taking care of yourself."

Jane explained the whole rustic camping adventure to both Gail and Jack. She explained the going to the bathroom outside, and carrying your trash out with you, the 'leave no trace' concept.

"I know neither of you have had much experience camping quite that extreme, but we're actually going to do a combination of the two camping styles," explained Jane. "We're going to rent a Yurt as a kind of home base. A yurt is kind of a hotel room in a tent," said Jane, as she ruffled through one of her packs and handed a brochure about yurts to Gail. "We'll be hiking mostly, and camping on the trail. But if the weather gets bad we'll head to the yurt and spend the night there. This IS the wilderness you know, and we could encounter harsh weather or even wildlife that might not like what we smell like. The 'porkies' do have wild animals like the wolf and black bear yah know. They always post any black bear siting's so hikers and campers can be aware. And there's some of the friendlier types that are just plain exciting to watch in the wild, like all the deer and porcupine, and birds like the bald eagle and the peregrine falcon. I heard someone even spotted an albino deer not too long ago," she said.

"So," Jane continued. "Like I said, we'll be out on the trails most of the time but the Yurt gives us kind of a home base sort of thing, should we encounter any problems."

"Are you expecting problems?" Gail asked, just a little astonished.

"I'm not 'expecting' problems," said Jane. "But I like to be prepared. I mean the weather report calls for nice weather the whole weekend, but you know how weather reports are. Not always accurate Although I want this one to be perfect."

Jane had been talking with such excitement and Jack and Gail were asking so many questions that the time melted away. Todd had already driven past the L'Anse/Baraga area and past the Keweenaw Bay, leaving M-41 and turning west onto M-38 toward Ontonagon. Before they knew it, Todd interrupted them because he spotted a rest area and decided it was time for another stop.

"There's a rest area just ahead so I'm making a pit stop."

"Good, I have to go to," said Gail.

Todd barely pulled up to the rest area when everyone piled out of the van.

"Good decision," Jane said, with a grin, as she gave him a small peck on the cheek. This time they all threw on light jackets.

Rays of light were starting to come up over the horizon making for a perfectly beautiful sun rise. They all took two minutes to watch it come up, making it look like the coming day would be perfect.

They drove into Ontonagon just after ten o'clock, stayed on the main road, which changed from M-38 to M-64 and headed west They were all hungry so they picked out a local restaurant for breakfast. Each of them ended up ordering a really big full breakfast. They didn't say it but they were all thinking it. Even though they're on vacation, good or bad, this might be the last good and hot sit-down restaurant style meal they'll have for the next couple days. Jack and Todd both had the big country style breakfast, complete with bacon, eggs, hash browns and pancakes. The girls were a little more conservative. They left out the pancakes. They also had both coffee and orange juice.

C H A P T E R   1 4

Todd's friend Arnie

THEY WERE HALFWAY through their breakfast, gabbing about their plans for hiking.

"I want to get an early start, "said Jane. "That means getting to the yurt, unpacking our gear, getting our backpacks ready for an overnight hike and maybe even getting ourselves ready for some hiking even today. Maybe we'll even stay out on the trail tonight, "she said. She was in her element and ready to go.

He came up abruptly and they all looked up as the tall man's shadow crossed their table. Todd got a big grin on his face and jumped up from his seat. He immediately gave the big burly guy a hand shake and a hug which was returned in earnest. He then turned to introduce him to his friends.

"You guys," he said, "this is a really good friend of mine, Arnie Sorenson. Arnie, this is my wife Jane, my best friend Jack, and his friend Gail."

They all said their hello's and since he was such a good friend of Todd's, welcomed him to their table. Arnie grabbed a nearby chair and sat down. Arnie was barely sitting when Todd spoke up.

"Jane," said Todd, "Arnie is the phone call I told you I made earlier today."

"Oh, wow," said Jane, putting her fork down. "Can you tell us anything?"

Arnie's smile faded as he began to talk.

"Well," he said, "I need to be careful," he noted as he looked around. Besides the waitress and the cook in the back there was only three other customers. A truck driver sitting on a stool at the counter, drinking coffee and minding his own business. And a mother and her young daughter, maybe ten, out for an early breakfast. The girl should have been in school but there could be lots of reasons why she wasn't. Arnie didn't see any trouble in either of them.

"I've been watching for you to come into town," he said. "When Todd called I put out a quick inquiry as to your approximate arrival. I've also talked to a few of my friends about more specific details on the issue."

"I'm sorry," said Jack, a bit perplexed, "who are you exactly."

"Oh man, I'm sorry Jack," said Todd. "Arnie is a Federal Marshall," he whispered.

"What? Really!" said Gail.

Arnie put a hand out and quietly hushed them before anything else was said. Things were at a point where he really had to be careful. In his business, he's learned that there are ears everywhere.

"Didn't you tell them anything?" he asked Todd.

"I haven't had time," said Todd.

"OK," said Arnie, "let me help." So, he did. He reiterated the fact that he was a federal marshal and he told all four of them that there were indeed some artefact thieves in Michigan and that the federal marshals have a tail on them. He looked at Jane and told her to be careful who she talks to about archeology. He told her that yes indeed there was something going on in the UP (upper peninsula) concerning artefact thieves. And he told all of them that no matter what, if anyone were to ask, they are up in the Porcupine Mountains hiking and camping, nothing more.

"Jane," he said directly at her, "Todd tells me you're an amateur archeologist. Is that right?"

"Yes, that's right," said Jane quietly.

"Not this weekend!" he said. "Be a historian this weekend, or a geologist. Don't be an archeologist, OK? And you don't know anything about digs, or any such thing. You and your friends are up here strictly for the hiking, nothing more."

"I can do that," said Jane. "Are we in any danger," she asked? Our archeology chapter has been hearing things but couldn't seem to get any details. Our chapter president hasn't exactly been full of knowledge that he would share. It's been bugging the heck out of me." She looked around the room to make sure nobody was paying any attention to their conversation.

Arnie took a minute before answering. "There should be no danger," he said.

"Unless you find something really strange," he told her. "I think you'll be fine. Plus, this is supposed to be a great weekend," he told them all, "so enjoy it."

"OK then," said Arnie. "I really need to go. And Todd, keep in touch, will ya."

"Sure thing," said Todd, "see you next time."

With that Arnie got up, excused himself, and left the restaurant.

"He seemed nice," said Gail.

"He seemed concerned to me," said Jack. "Should we be worried?"

"Naa", said Todd. If anything, I know he'll be keeping an eye open for us. We'll probably be the safest group in the porkies if anything were to happen.

Jane laughed. A bit nervously, but she laughed. She got the distinct impression that Arnie had something more to say but just held back.

"Shall we go?" she said.

"I am stuffed," said Gail.

"Yeah, but it was de-licious!" said Jack, opening the van door for her. They both climbed into the back seat. Jane and Todd were in front now with Todd still driving.

They stopped at a local store to pick up the last of the supplies they needed including some ice for their cooler. They planned on providing at least a couple meals with fish caught from local lakes or rivers but they still needed a few things. Highway M-64 turned south just before Big Iron River, but Todd followed M-107 west toward Porcupine Mountain National Park. They stayed on M-107 and were entering the Park by about eleven-thirty and were at the visitor's center shortly after that. The visitor center hours were10am until 6pm so their timing was just fine.

They parked the van near the ranger station and they all followed Jane inside. She registered all their names with the park ranger, received their camping permit and the directions to the 'yurt' she had reserved, and a packet that included trail conditions, maps of the rugged terrain, information about campsite set-up and cleanup, and the location of latest siting's of any local black bear. It also included information on scenic vista's, places of interest like the Lake of the Clouds scenic overview, and some geological history of the area. That's what Jane wanted, geological information.

CHAPTER 15

Into the 'Porkies' – First Day

WHILE THE OTHERS were looking around the visitors' center Jane verified the GPS coordinates with the ranger for specific spots within the Park. She also asked him about local issues related to the parks geology. She avoided asking anything about archeology, even though she was curious about any digs that may have been done by the students at Michigan Tech. She knew they had an archeology program there. The ranger was an older gentleman, at least twenty years older than Jane, maybe more, and very knowledgeable about the parks geology and Porcupine volcanics, as he called them.

"You're pretty knowledgeable about geology, "he said to Jane.

"It's a hobby, "Jane said to him, smiling, and remembering what Arnie had said. "I'm just a normal high school history teacher who likes to throw a little of this and a little of that into her lectures," she told him.

"Well I don't run into too many people who have any knowledge of the subject, "he said, smiling at her. "Most folks aren't even interested in that type of information," he continued. "They're just here to hike."

"Well, like I mentioned, I teach history to teenagers," she told him, "so, sometimes it comes in handy when explaining things in class. It's a hobby, but one I've incorporated into my teaching," she told him.

"Well, wait right here a minute," he said.

He came back quickly with a couple brochures, handing them to Jane.

"I'm kind of an amateur myself, "he commented. "And I've been hiking all over the porkies, more in my youth of course, "he said as he smiled. "I still hike a little but no longer on rugged trails. My knees don't like it much anymore."

Jane liked him. He reminded her of her uncle. And, he was obviously interested in this topic and glad to be having this conversation about geology with her.

"I'm sorry," the old man said. "I'm Ranger Steve. I'm here most every day. If you need anything, just let me know."

"Thanks," Jane said

They talked for about ten more minutes, mostly about how interesting volcanics of the area are layered and what type of rock you can find in what area of the park. The ranger told her all he knew about the area rock formations and was quite intrigued by what she had told him about historical geology of the area.

Jane was hoping to hike south of Lake of the Clouds, near where the rock formations, indicated by her uncle, are shown on his map, and where they would likely locate the peak he talked about so much. She was being careful though and didn't mention anything about having an uncle.

She took a quick glance at her friends and then looked back at the ranger.

"I'm really sorry," she told him. "I need to get moving. We want to get some hiking in before the sun goes down and I'm not sure how much ground we have to cover."

"No problem," said the ranger. "I totally understand. Enjoy the hiking."

"Thanks again," she told him, as she walked away, waving the brochures to acknowledge her gratitude.

When Jane walked away, she took a quick look at the brochures he had given her. She smiled as she noticed that the volcanic rock called rhyolite and andesite were both mentioned. Those were exactly the two rock types she wanted to check out. These are the oldest rocks in the Porcupine Mountains he had told her. He noted that most people don't know that these two volcanic rocks are sometimes grouped together and called felsite. But Jane knew. She also knew that this grouping is especially prevalent near the Upper Carp River. She was thrilled to say the least. But she thought they could be found somewhere not noted on the map.

The ranger watched her leave. He liked her. She reminded him of his younger days and how he was anxious like that to get out on the trail. He had lots of memories of the area, but not all his memories were pleasant.

Jane gathered everyone together outside the ranger station.

"I paid the camping fees," she said. "Backcountry camping was $15 each per night. The Yurt was $65 a night. I paid to have the Yurt for three days, today, Saturday, and Sunday. We need to be out of the yurt by ten Monday morning. That's not too bad."

She was getting excited now.

"We can square all the money's up later, if that's OK." she added.

"Sounds good," said Jack.

"Right now, let's head to the yurt so we can get out on the trail. Most of our supplies can stay at the Yurt. Once we're there we'll pack our backpacks for a two-day hike. We may not be hiking for two days but you never know, and that way we'll be prepared."

They all jumped back in the van. They knew she was eager to get out on the trail. Todd was still in the driver seat so Jane just gave him directions to the yurt.

"The yurt we reserved is on the south side of the park near Lost Creek, "she told him. "It's a good days' hike from Lake of the Clouds, but no big deal."

"Go out the parking lot and turn south," she told him.

They turned south and followed 'South Boundary Road'. They followed 'South Boundary Road' for a few miles before it turned west.

"The turnoff to the yurt should be just a couple miles from here," she told Todd.

"OK," she said, pointing to the parking area near the yurt. "We park there."

Todd pulled into the small parking area, stopped the van and turned off the engine.

"We're here!" she said all excited, opening the van door and jumping out.

"We need to get all of our supplies to the yurt. From there we'll review our plans for today and tomorrow, and pack our gear for the first leg of our hike".

She sounded like she was in teacher mode, but only Todd noticed, and he just smiled. Everyone got out of the van and started grabbing equipment. It took them a couple of trips. The yurt wasn't exactly next to the van. It was about a hundred yards in from where they parked. It took about half an hour to get everything from the van and into the yurt. Then another half hour to organize their gear in the yurt and to take a quick inventory of supplies. Jane was the experienced one so the others just followed her lead as to where to put everything. They each had their own personal bunk where they stowed their individual belongings, but besides that they had camping equipment, fishing equipment, backpacks, a first aid kit, and food supplies. Todd even brought his climbing equipment. They had a cooler for perishable food and lots of easy to carry packaged food. They had a fry pan and a small sauce pan as well. Plus, an axe and Todd's rifle.

"OK," Jane said. "Let's review what we need to pack for this first trip out."

"For individual use, we need one change of clothes. If you want an extra pair of sox that's fine, but remember, we're not going to be gone for a week. It's day trip, maybe two days at the most before we come back here and re-group for supplies etc. And everyone should be wearing their hiking boots. Bring a sweater and a jacket for evening. Make sure you have a rain jacket just in case. I don't think it'll rain but you never know. Remember, this is September in Upper Michigan. I checked the weather several times and I think we'll probably have clear weather during the day, and maybe as high as sixty-five or seventy, but it'll be chilly at night. Hopefully not less than forty-five or fifty, or so. Once the sun goes down we'll make camp and build a fire so we should be fine. The sun this time of year will be going down somewhere around eight-thirty and twilight will be around nine. Plus, we'll have our sleeping bags to stay warm. We have two tents but I also suggest you each sleep in your own sleeping bag, but, and she looked at Jack and Gail, that's your decision. Besides our own personal supplies, we'll split up common supplies so we're all carrying about the same load. Jane paused so everyone could start their packing.

"She always this regimented?" Jack asked Todd.

"Only on trips like this, "Todd said. "If she were like this at home, our house would be much neater."

Jack just chuckled.

Jane finished packing her backpack.

"The guys can carry the fishing equipment, "she said. "Jack can carry the axe and Todd will carry his rifle. Is that good with you guys?" she asked.

"Good with me," said Todd.

"Me too," said Jack.

"Good," she continued.

"The guys will also carry the cooking supplies and one of the metal detectors Todd brought. We don't need both metal detectors right now. The girls can carry the tents and anything related to setting up the tents, and the food. The girls will also carry the first aid equipment and emergency flairs, and toilet paper. And everyone will carry their own sleeping bag, their own water bottle, at least one refill, and their own pocket knife.

"Everyone has a pocket knife, right?" she asked.

Everyone responded yes so Jane continued her instructions.

"I have a compass and a GPS. Plus, I have these." She handed out trail maps to everyone. "You should be able to find your position in the park using these maps," she said. "The parks big, but not that big."

"Does anyone else have a compass?" she asked.

"Yes," said Jack, "I have one too."

"That's good," said Jane. "We'll all be staying together but just in case we get lost, if we are separated for more than three hours, unless otherwise planned, head back here to the yurt. And, you two, pointing at Todd and Gail, stay with either Jack or I, since we have the compasses. Jack, you and I will review coordinates before we leave."

Jack nodded in agreement.

"OK," she said. "It's almost two. Let's have some lunch then pack up and head out."

"Are ham sandwiches O.K.?" asked Gail. It's the only lunch meat we brought. And we have some chips to go with it," she said.

Nobody complained so they ate ham sandwiches and potato chips.

They each drank a bottle of water with their small lunch and once they were done eating they cleaned up, filled their canteens with water from one of the five-gallon water containers they brought and headed out.

On their way out, they each grabbed a couple spare water bottles from the twenty-four pack they had brought with them.

"OK," said Jane," I need to explain the direction we're hiking, what we're doing and why. I know this sounds weird," she continued, "but I have these two things I'm interested in. One, and I'll probably never find it, but I want to look for it, is the rift in one of the rock faces here in the porkies I've read about in some of my journals. It's a geology thing that has to do with copper content and the supercontinent I mentioned earlier. And the second thing, I'm looking for a specific rock face my uncle told me about. My uncle's rock face formation I hope to find. But I'm just saying, you know, if I see something related to the rift I mentioned, I'd like to follow it and check it out."

"What does that mean?" asked Gail and Jack together.

"And what's a 'rift'?" asked Gail.

"Well, it's really not a big deal," Jane continued. If not tonight then tomorrow, depending on what I see, we'll probably leave the trail system."

"Why would we do that?" asked Gail.

"Do what?" asked Jane.

"Leave the trail system. Why would we leave the trail system?", Gail asked.

"Because," explained Jane, "the peak we are looking for, where we're liable to find the rift, as well as my uncles rock face, takes us off the trails. And a 'rift' is a crack, or break, or crevice in the rock."

"Oh," said Gail. "OK."

"And we all have maps so we really can't get lost," said Jane. "And," she hesitated, "what I really want to do is look for that rift I mentioned, near the specific rock face my uncle told me about, a two for one sort of thing. You never know, maybe they're related somehow. He asked me to look at some of the rock formations near this cliff for him. He gave me that map I mentioned. The cliff my uncle talked about is near Cuyahogo Peak here in the porkies, and like I mentioned," she said, "it's just a short walk off the trails."

"It shouldn't matter," said Jane. "I mean we registered for hiking and the rangers know we're here, and there are trails in every direction that would be easy to find if we got lost."

Jack and Gail looked at each other.

"Whatever," Jack finally said. "It might be fun, plus we're all together, so whatever, "he said, arching his eyebrows.

Gail laughed. "Sure, let's go. Whatever you want," she said. "I'm just here to enjoy the wild life and get some pictures to show my first graders. And, I would really like to see a bald eagle's nest."

"Thanks, you guys."

She looked at Todd but he was just smiling at her.

"Go for it," he said.

It was a bit after three o'clock when they finally put their backpacks on. Jane lead the way heading north toward 'Lost Lake Trail' not too far north of the yurt. She had showed them all on their maps where they were headed. They would follow Lost Lake Trail up past Government Peak Trail toward Union Spring. There's a backcountry campsite just north of Union Spring. Depending on how fast or slow they walk, Jane was thinking spending the night there. It's only a six to eight-mile hike, and they're all in good shape, but they've also had a long day and she didn't want to push them too much.

CHAPTER 16

Beauty of the Porkies

IT DIDN'T TAKE long to get to their first stop at Lost Lake. It was only a couple of miles from the Yurt.

"Look!" Gail exclaimed. "A beaver dam! Wow!"

She couldn't see enough. After spying the beaver dam in the river, she took out her camera and started taking pictures. Then she spotted a mother deer and two small baby deer in the brush. They ran away when the four friends came down the path, but Gail saw them run off and got a couple pictures before they disappeared.

"Oh my gosh!" chirped Gail. "Check that out, "she said, pointing at a bald eagle, soaring up above the lake. It looks like it owns the sky," she murmured. The smile on her face said it all. She loved it.

Jack saw the same things, but was more excited that Gail saw them. He was simply enjoying her excitement.

Todd walked up next to Jane. "What are you thinking," he said.

"They're beautiful," she said, as she watched the deer run off.

"That's not what I mean," he said.

She turned to him, sort of surprised, but not really.

"Tell me what you're really looking for," he said.

"That obvious," she said.

"Yup." He replied. "We're married remember, and I'm getting to know you quite well."

They walked a little off to the side before she started talking.

"You know Todd," she began. "I know that sometimes I can get a little tenacious about things." She took a quick glance over where Jack and Gail were checking out the fish in the lake.

"This is probably one of those things. You know I've been trying to decide on my Masters studies. I was thinking of archeology. I know that's not exactly a high school curriculum, but it really intrigues me. I'm not even sure if I have the pre-requisites to get into the program. If not, I'd like to at least take a couple classes. I've been reading up on so much Michigan mystery, trying to separate the real folklore from the folklore we use to tell strange stories, that I need to step back a minute and think through it all. I'm really interested in Michigan's prehistoric copper. Prehistoric minors dug pits all over Michigan you know. They're discovering huge chunks of almost pure copper at the bottom of some of these pits. Some of these boulders weigh as much as 6,000 tons. They found human remains there as well. But," she continued, "that information given out at the archeology meeting is just bugging me. I was really hoping to find some Indian artefacts as well. But, that falls right into what those thieves are after. And I have no idea where they are or what they're looking for. And I've been thinking about what Arnie said too. He didn't mention where any of these thieves might be. All that put together with the fact that we only have a weekend to play with, just means I need to narrow my focus."

"You know, I was thinking of that myself," said Todd. "Why don't we just play it by ear and see what shows up in front of us."

"I do want to find something," she said, "but maybe I'm hoping for too much. You're right of course. Enjoy the hike, right?" she said, looking up at him. "Even if we find anything, it'll be cool and I would be happy, even it isn't anything big. Besides it's not like we're at a registered dig. If we find anything nobody will know until we tell them."

Jane looked up at Todd. He was just maybe a half inch taller than her.

"Do you think I'm crazy?"

Todd chuckled a little.

"Taking more classes is fine with me. And no, you're not crazy," he said.

"Your just passionate about things and I think it can make people who don't know you, just a little crazy trying to keep up. If you realize the rest of us are hear for a good time, to enjoy nature and have fun hiking the 'porkies', then we're all good. I may not be as enthralled with some of the archeology stuff or supercontinent stuff that fires you up, but I do like being with you. I like listening to you talk about some of the strange things you find. I don't do the research you do so it is kind of interesting just listening to you explain it all. Besides, it helps me keep up, and, put simply, like I just said, I like being with you."

He put his hands on her shoulders and pulled her in for a kiss, light and tender but meant to zap her energy, which it did.

"But," he continued, "please realize that I don't have the answers about these thieves any more then you do, but either way, even though Arnie said a little, we still need to discuss this with Jack and Gail. I know you're concerned," he said, "I can see it in your eyes."

"Figure it out in your head how we're going to tell them."

"I will," she said, "I promise." She kissed him back.

"I love you," she said.

"I love you too," he whispered in her ear, sending goosebumps down her arm.

"Hey, you guys, check this out," Gail yelled over.

They walked over to where Gail and Jack were peering into the lake. The shore was rocky and small ripples created by the wind blowing on the water lapped up against the few small rocks buried near the edge. Just off shore, a small school of minnows were swimming against the light current. They were so thick that when they moved with the ripples of the lake, it resembled a dance routine. Gail was enjoying every moment this little piece of nature was showing her. She took a video of the minnows with her phone.

She wasn't sure if it would turn out, with the reflection of the sun on the water and all, but she had to try.

They all enjoyed the moment, and shortly all four of them were off again hiking up the trail and enjoying all that nature was showing them. It was a beautiful day.

From Lost Lake, they headed up the trail toward their destination, Union Spring. With all the stopping and sightseeing they did along the way, it took about three hours to get to the campsite just north of Union Spring. But that was O.K. because Gail must have taken a hundred pictures to show her first graders.

Union Spring is a rustic campsite area and there were not many overnight visitors. One couple had just left and another was setting up their tent on the other side of the clearing. So, with so few campers, they had no trouble finding a place to set up their campsite. It was almost six so Jane suggested they start setting up their tents, and maybe someone could go fish for dinner.

"Cool, can I go," asked Gail.

"Sure," said Jack. "How about you and I go fishing and let Jane and Todd set up camp."

"Leave your gear," said Todd.

"I'll set up your tent, and you can organize the rest when you get back. As you can see," Todd continued, "the campsite is close to the river so you can't get lost. Try to gut and clean the fish at the river, please. We don't want wandering bears smelling fish guts at our campsite."

"Bears!" yipped Gail.

"He's kidding," said Jane. "There's no siting's of bears in this area right now. Let's just be safe and not draw them over in our direction."

Gail still had a nervous look on her face when she and Jack headed to the river to do some fishing. Jane just looked at Todd.

"What," he said, with a terribly hidden smirk on his face.

"She's not as experienced as the rest of us," said Jane. "Just try not to scare her to death," she said, chuckling under her breath.

Jane and Todd worked together setting up the two tents. They organized their sleeping bags inside their tents but left Jack and Gail's gear near the other tent for them to set up as they liked. They also gathered wood to cook dinner and Todd started a fire in the circular fire pit provided at the campsite. Jane took out four of the potatoes they had pre-wrapped in aluminum foil, and placed them on the edge of the fire. Todd also located the bear pole where they would hang any food they had carried in with them. It was a short distance from their campsite but within sight.

They had a few minutes, at least before Jack and Gail would be back, hopefully with dinner, so Todd took out the metal detector while Jane warmed herself by the fire. Todd just did a ten-minute sweep around the camping area. It was fun. When he sat down at the campfire next to Jane he proudly displayed a handful of coins to Jane.

"Wow!" she said. You found these in that short of time.

"Yup," he said. It's really not much, but this is a camping area, right? People drop things."

Jane fingered through Todd's find. Two old quarters, three nickels, four pennies, and an old coin she couldn't identify. It had markings on it but it would need to be properly cleaned before you could read them.

They sat by the fire looking over the coins Todd had found. It was only around six-thirty or so, still a couple hours before dark, but they could already feel a chill in the air so they put on sweatshirts and cozied up together.

"Todd," said Jane, looking up at him. "I'd like to go off trail tomorrow. It's not about waiting to see a sign of some kind. You know I'm not that good, or cocky enough to think I'd find something nobody else could. I'm not even sure how much worthwhile hiking we'll be able to do. You just never know how much time we'll have to do things, like using those metal detectors. What's important to me is making an effort to follow this map my uncle Dave gave me. You know he went to Michigan Tech," she said, waiting for a reply.

"Yeah, I remember you mentioning that", he replied, poking a stick at the embers in the fire pit. "My dad went there like ten years after your uncle, or something like that. And I did meet your uncle you know".

"That's right, you did," she said. "I forgot."

"Well, he and his buddies were always hiking in the porkies. They always hiked all through the U.P., but mostly the porkies. Well, they found something.

"They found something!" he repeated, looking over at her.

"Well Yeah, but there was an issue," she continued.

"What kind of issue?"

"Well," she hesitated, "a kid was lost."

"Lost!", Todd said, "surprised, how did that happen?"

"Good question," she said. "I'm not sure."

"The story goes something like this, and mind you I put this together from multiple telling's of the story, both by him and explanations from my mom added in here and there. Remember, the guy's like twelve years older than my mom, and she's already going on sixty years old now. He seems pretty sharp at times, but sometimes I'm not so sure. He probably has a few marbles mixed up in that old noggin of his and I just don't notice. I just really, really like him, and when I was younger he told us some cool stuff. I just didn't listen very intently back then. I was just a kid."

"Anyway," she continued, "when he went to Michigan Tech, and him and his buddies were always taking off hiking and camping here and there, all over the U.P., they started focusing their camping here in the porkies. Well, in their last couple years especially, they stayed up at school during summers, took a couple classes, and spent most of those summers hiking and camping. They were four of them that were always hiking, and three others that would sometimes go with them and sometimes not. One weekend, Labor Day weekend, just like it is now, they packed their gear and headed out like normal. On this trip, there were six guys. Only this time, one of them didn't come back."

"What?" Todd said, staring at her unbelievably.

"That's right," she continued. "One of the regulars. His name was Charles Barrow something or other. I can't remember the guys last name. Anyway, they called him C.B. for short. It reminds me kind of like that guy D.B. Cooper. You know, the one who jumped out of an airplane with lots of money".

"Yeah, I remember the tale."

"Only they called him CB instead of DB," she said. "They all thought calling someone by initials was funny, and cool at the same time, and it clicked. Anyway, they camped at Mirror Lake, and the next morning they walked around to the east side of the lake and went off trail there. They hiked the park so often they felt they knew every inch of it. But something happened when they left the trail. At first everything seemed fine. They followed the river so the terrain wasn't bad. A couple miles in, they ran into a marshy area, so they left the river and headed over a ridge, so they say. And at the top of the ridge they thought they saw one of those altars. Like the Norse Altar that was discovered on top of Huron Mountain, not too far from here. They never actually found it according to my uncle. The Altar I mean. Nobody seemed to be able to pin down the exact location of where they thought they saw this thing. And, nobody could find it later either."

"I'm thirsty," she said. "I need to get my water."

She got up and walked over to her backpack and grabbed her water.

"Do you want anything?"

"No, I'm good."

"Think Jack and Gail are catching anything?"

"I sure hope so. I'm getting hungry."

"Anyway, come finish your story before they get back."

Jane came back and sat down again.

"Did you know," said Jane, "that it's only, maybe five miles, tops, between Mirror Lake and Lost Lake, just down the path there." She pointed to the path they came up from earlier in the day. "Probably more like four miles," she continued. "That's like nothing. That's barely room to hike without running into someone else on the trail. That is, for all the people out here hiking, and nobody saw anything, or heard anything. It's just weird. And the thing is, they scoured the area, looking for the lost kid, as well as the so-called altar the others swore they saw. But nothing. They had the rangers, the local police, the state police, and they even eventually called in the FBI. Nothing. Nobody found anything. They closed off the park to hikers for a month, mostly because they didn't know if there was a danger issue. They didn't want any more hikers disappearing. By then of course winter had set in. They figured nobody could survive Michigan winter in the porkies, so they called off the search. And according to authorities that was that. They listed the boy as missing, presumed dead. Maybe eaten by a bear. Nobody really knew. Of course, all the boys were questioned, and questioned again, and then questioned again. And all their parents were called up to the school. Mom said it was a terrible time for my uncle, not to mention my grandparents."

"O.K.," said Todd. "You've told me this really intriguing story. I must admit, it sounds pretty damn strange. But, what exactly are you thinking? You obviously have a theory. You said yourself that there was this huge uncanny search. For both the lost boy as well as the strange altar they say they saw, but, what are you not telling me? What map did your uncle give you and what did he tell you that he didn't tell the police?"

Just then Jack and Gail came back to camp all excited. Gail was giggling like a little girl. "Look, look, look," she said, holding on tightly to a string of six fish. And they weren't little. They were small mouth bass and each was about fourteen inches long. They had already been gutted but the heads and tails were still attached.

"Wow!" exclaimed Todd. "Those are some awesome looking fish! Did you catch those?" he asked Gail.

"I caught two!" she said proudly. "It was so much fun. And they really wiggle a lot. But they didn't get away."

"You goofball!" Jane blurted out, smiling. "You've been fishing before," she said to Gail.

"Yeah, but this is different," said Gail. "All the other fish I caught were tiny compared to these. And I hardly had to do anything to bring them in. But these guys fought. I had to really hang onto my pole. It was fun."

"Oh, and one got away. Ask me how. Come on, ask me how!"

"OK," said Todd. "I'll go for that one." "How?" he asked smiling.

"An Eagle came down and swooped it away! Grabbed it with its two huge claws, and flew away with it," she said, with pride that she was privileged enough to witness the event.

"Wow!" said Jane. "That had to have been exciting to watch."

"Oh, it was!" said Gail enthusiastically. "Just like this". And she swooped her hands down from above her head down to her knees, like an eagle diving into the water.

"And it grabbed the fish. And it was close too! Probably twenty feet away from us! So cool! So cool!"

Both Jane and Todd couldn't help but grin, Gail's excitement was so catchy.

Jack just sat back and watched her animation. He was an avid fisherman and a bit calmer when telling the details of their obviously successful little fishing trip. But he was certainly having an enjoyable time watching Gail get all excited.

"We did pretty good, he said. We used a couple lures I have. I wasn't sure if they would work. Usually I use worms. But hey, whose complaining."

"Not me," said Todd. "They look delicious. Bring them over here and I'll get them ready to cook." "Unless you want to cook them," he held them up, looking up at Gail.

"Mmmmm," Gail was tempted.

"Nah," I'll let you cook, as long as you don't mind."

"Not at all," said Todd.

"How about Jane and I get dinner ready while you two organize your tent the way you want it. And don't forget, we need to put any food we have up the bear pole."

He pointed across the way to where the bear pole was located.

CHAPTER 17

The 50 year Old Mystery

"I'LL TAKE CARE of cooking the fish," Todd said to Jane, "if you set table."

Jane laughed. "You have a deal handsome," she teased. "The potatoes are almost done anyway."

Jane had been turning the potatoes while Jack and Gail had been fishing. The last time she checked they felt soft enough to be ready. She got out the paper plates and plastic silverware they brought for eating, and she found a nearby log to use for a table.

"I'm glad he just gutted these," said Jack. "It makes them easier to cook."

He laid them over an open fire on the small cooking grate Jane brought with them. "It beats trying to cook them on a stick!" he mumbled.

All he had to do was flip the fish over a couple times and they were ready to eat.

They were all hungry so once the food was ready and dished out, they all dug in.

The fish were amazing. And for dessert they had, what else, smores.

"That was the best campfire dinner I've ever had," said Gail.

"It might have something to do with the fact that you may have caught dinner, but someone else cooked it," said Jack.

"Not really," said Gail. "Well, maybe a little of that, but I think it was also because I was hungry," she said. "But fresh caught fish is always good," she continued.

"That's very true," said Jack.

"And the potatoes were good too. That was a great idea," she told Jane.

"Thanks," said Jane.

"I'm also glad we have this fire," said Gail. I think it's getting a little chilly and the fire's keeping me warm."

"I think it's also because it's been a long day," said Todd. "It's only eight o'clock but I feel like it should be ten, or even later."

"You have to be tired," Jane said to Todd. "You drove here all the way from the bridge. At least I got a nap."

The fire temporarily mesmerized all of them. And as they settled down allowing the heat from the fire to envelope them, sleep started to draw them in. They were perfectly content sitting by the warm fire, but it was soon getting dark and the fire was dying down. Jack put a couple more logs on it to keep it going. It felt good to be at their destination and they were all finally able to just sit back and enjoy the evening.

The time drifted by when Jane asked everyone.

"Does everyone want to go over plans for tomorrow," she said, mostly to Jack and Gail, but holding Todd's hand as she cuddled up next to him. The evening was moving on and the temperature was dropping. Jack held a blanket around them both, keeping their body heat together and keeping them both warm. Gail and Jack were cuddled in a similar fashion, only Gail was sitting in front of Jack and Jack had his arms wrapped around her, cocooning them both in the heat of their bodies.

"I have this map," Jane finally began.

"You have a map," Gail said, suddenly sitting up, full of excitement that still warmed her blood from her and Jack's fishing expedition. "Is it a treasure map? Wouldn't that be cool!"

"No," she said quietly," watching Gail's excitement simmer down a bit. "It's a map my uncle gave me. It's sort of a hand written scratchy incomplete map to a hidden cave."

"So, it could be a treasure map," Gail said quietly, leaning back against Jack, but still a bit excited.

They all smiled knowing the map was probably nothing at all. At least that's what the guys were thinking. Jane was more optimistic. Jane had her hopes up that it would lead them to something, anything really. But, mostly she was hoping for some kind of archeological find, no matter how small. Even something little. Her uncle was very emphatic that that a cave existed. She wasn't really sure there was a cave, at least nothing obvious. If it was, someone would have found it by now.

"Well, you never know," said Jane, more to appease Gail, then believing that a treasure could be out there.

Gail just smiled.

"Anyway," she continued, "this map from my uncle is supposed to lead us to this hidden cave. And the cave had some remains of old carvings of some kind, Indian hieroglyphs maybe. He really wasn't specific about the carvings."

They were all listening intently now as Jane told the story. She mentioned a little about her uncle and his friends hiking in the porkies when they were in college, but she didn't go into any of the detail she did with Todd.

"The porkies became a park in 1945," Jane said.

"It was just maybe fifteen years after that, or there about, when my uncle was a student at Michigan Tech. The park was pristine, which is why they declared it a park. There was a lot of lumbering going on in Michigan back then and the idea was to preserve the virgin wood and the natural splendor of the area. My uncle loved the woods. And, once at Michigan Tech, he ran into others who loved hiking in the woods as much as he did. So, that's what they did whenever they had extra time on their hands. Sometimes they'd be so enthralled by the beauty of everything here, they'd spend the night. More and more they'd plan on it, spending the night that is."

She stopped talking to take a drink of water, and as it got darker, they all noticed the stars as they started to pop out. Millions of them just started appearing as if they were watching and listening. Somehow, they looked bigger up here than they did downstate. And with the sun ducking down below the horizon, the stars just got brighter and brighter.

Jane continued. "It was one of these nights when they came across the cave. They were looking for a place to camp for the night. They really couldn't find a flat spot so they were looking for a place protected from the wind, where building a fire wouldn't cause any problems. They didn't want a small campfire to get away from them and cause a forest fire. The trees were dense back then and they didn't want to be the ones to ruin the beauty of this place. My uncle kept saying, 'You can imagine what a fire would do to the forest'. I think he should have been a forest ranger, she said. "Anyway, they found an area close to a rocky cliff. The cliff went almost straight up, except for a slight overhang with a shelf wide enough to sit on, about fifty feet up. My uncle said the shelf was kind of strange looking so they planned on checking it out in the morning. But the area they selected seemed perfect because they felt any fire they built would be protected from the wind. My uncle was very adamant about that. They didn't want to start a forest fire. He said that over and over, she reiterated. "So, they built their fire and they all laid out their sleeping bags for the evening. Then one of the guys wandered off to go to the bathroom. That's when he came across a weird crevice in the side of the cliff. It was kind of small but these were guys looking for adventure. So, the kid who found it told the others about it and of course they all had to check it out. Thing is, somebody had to stay back and mind the fire."

"CB," said Todd.

"Who? What?" said Gail.

Jane ignored the question and just kept on with her story.

"So, all but one of them went to check out this crevice. At first it looked hidden. It was low to the ground and barely visible. But pushing some sand away from the opening and pulling some brush away, they found that it was more than just a crevice. The first kid had a small lantern and reached his hand in and around the crevice. It wasn't just a crack in the rock wall. He found that if he sucked in his gut, he could squeeze himself through the crevice, and beyond. The others moved away more of the sand and brush around the opening and they followed him in. It was exciting my uncle said! He told me that when that first kid went into the cave, it was like he just disappeared from view. When all of them squeezed through the crevice and finally look around, they were dazed. It was a cave of course," she said, "but, according to my uncle, it was about as big as a small house inside, and as tall as one too. They couldn't believe all that space was inside this mountain. But what was inside the cave mesmerized them. They found writing on the walls. They didn't know what they were looking at. They thought maybe it was an old Indian cave or something. I mean, they found lots of things. Bones too I guess."

"Bones," said Jack. "Like human bones."

"I think so, but he wasn't real clear on that," Jane said.

"You'd think that would be something a young kid would be very clear about," said Jack. "I mean, I would sure remember that piece of information."

"Yah, I know," said Jane. "But, he just didn't elaborate."

"He kept telling me that all of them were just exploring and looking around. He said he remembered telling all the guys to be respectful and not to destroy anything. Him and his friends seemed to think that they were in there for an hour or two. Then he said, the ground shook beneath them.

"What does that mean?" asked Jack.

"I'm not sure," said Jane. "I'm only telling you what he said. He told me some small rocks started falling from the ceiling. That's when one of them decided it was time to get out of there. They certainly didn't want to get trapped, and they needed to get back to their camp. After all they left one of their friends to tend the fire. They wanted to tell their friend about the cave, even though they weren't sure if it was safe to back in it anymore. Anyway, they hightailed it out of there. After all, if the opening collapsed they'd never get out. If it was just a minor tremor and the opening was intact they could explore more in the morning. But when they got outside the cave, more than a couple hours had passed. When they decided to leave the cave, and all of them squeezed out through the crevice, the sun was coming up and it was almost daylight."

"That's a pretty tall tale," said Jack. "How can they not know how much time they spent inside the cave?"

"Just repeating what I was told," said Jane, remember?

"It gets kind of creepy after that," she said.

"What do you mean," asked Gail, cuddling closer to Jack, "like bad creepy?"

"Well, yes," said Jane.

"Do you want to hear more?" she asked.

"Well, dah, yeah!" said Gail.

"It's kind of like a campfire ghost story," laughed Jack.

"More than you realize," said Todd.

"What?" said Jack, not really expecting a reply.

Jane continued. "They couldn't believe that they had spent most of the night in that cave. They were all talking at the same time about all the different pictures on the walls, as they walked back to their campsite. To them that's all they were, just pictures. It was a few years later that my uncle understood what they had found. He only started sharing it about ten years ago. I think as he got older, it haunted him. So, he did some research and found a couple interesting things. He started sharing them with my mom, and then when he found out I was a history major, and maybe even interested a little in both geology and archeology, he started sharing with me as well. He was getting older then and truthfully I wasn't sure how much was based on reality and how much was just his nightmares coming to life."

"What does that mean," asked Jack. "Did he have nightmares about the cave."

"Not about the cave really. More about what happened when they got out of the cave. The cave was pretty much forgotten. But you see, the problem was that when they got back to their campsite, their friend was nowhere to be found. They looked all over. And the weird thing, that no one has ever explained, is that their campsite was torn apart."

"What," said Todd. "You didn't tell me that part," he whispered, a bit annoyed.

"I didn't get to it, remember, the fish arrived."

"Oh yah," he said. "I forgot."

Jane explained to Jack and Gail that her and Todd were talking about their hiking plans for tomorrow while they were fishing. She also told them that she had started to tell Todd her uncles' story while they were setting up camp, but dinner arrived so she couldn't finish. And that's why she was talking about it now.

"No big deal," said Jack. "So, what happened."

Jane continued explaining as best she could. She wasn't trying to keep any secrets. She wanted not just Todd, but both Jack and Gail to totally understand what she wanted to do and where they were going. She never dreamed there would be any kind of danger for any of them, but, this is the wilderness, sort of, so they all needed to be on alert, always. Not to mention the stupid artefact thieves.

"Well, like I said, their campsite had been torn apart. I mean really torn apart, like shredded sleeping bags and camping gear scattered in ten different directions. They had brought along a small coffee pot. They found their coffee pot smashed in like a paper cup. That's when panic struck the boys. What happened? Was it a bear? Was it some mad killer hiding hear in the woods and they stumbled into his living area? They didn't know. They just knew their friend was missing and their gear was destroyed. That's when they noticed that there was no blood anywhere.

"Oh wow!" said Gail, "That's a nasty thought."

"Yah!" Jane continued, "But, it made things a little hopeful. So they thought. Maybe their friend saw something coming and hid. Or, maybe he's already back at the car, waiting. They double checked, looked all over for blood, and found nothing. They yelled his name. Nothing. They split up in two groups. There were five of them now. They set out in two different directions around the rock wall they had camped at, or planned to camp at, planning to meet back at the at the campsite. But it didn't take long. Both groups were back at the campsite in no time. They were young, but not unfeeling, and they were afraid for their friend. For some reason, they decided to cover the entrance to the cave so it wouldn't be easy for anyone to find, which they did. To this day, my uncle doesn't know why they did that. Anyway, they all decided they'd better go straight to the ranger station. They needed to get help finding their friend."

"The way my uncle explained it, when they couldn't find their friend, they headed directly to the ranger station. He told me they were all so frazzled they just all started talking at the ranger at one time. When ranger on duty finally realized something serious was wrong he calmed them all down and told 'one' of them to tell the story. He told the others to keep quiet. So, my uncle told the ranger what happened. They never told the ranger about the crevice, or the cave, or any of that. They just said they were exploring and he was left back to watch the fire. It was sort of true. That's what my uncle said anyway. The ranger followed protocol, thinking of course they would be looking for a lost hiker."

Jane stopped talking.

"So, what happened," asked Gail.

Jack was listening for that answer as well. Todd already knew the answer.

"Nothing," said Jane.

"Their friend was never found. No trace. His backpack was left back at their campsite and was ripped apart like all the others. The rangers called in the police, both local and state. But they didn't find anything either. They even called in one of those cadaver dogs. Nothing was found. To this day he's still listed by the state police as missing, presumed dead."

"What!" exclaimed Gail. "How can that be?"

"That is so weird," said Jack. "I mean, I would have a zillion questions! What was the tremor? Was it felt anywhere else in the porkies? Were there crooks, or thieves up there at the time? Or kidnappers? How could this mountain have caves in it nobody knew about?" said Jack. "Lots of questions!"

"Hey guys look," said Todd. He pointed to the night sky. It was not only lit up with a million twinkling stars, but the lights of the aurora borealis were visible as well. They were just above the horizon to the north, where Todd was pointing.

"Wow! They're so beautiful," said Gail, "look at the colors!"

"Yes, I forgot just how beautiful they really are," Jane agreed, "and they say that on a clear dark night, Michigan's upper peninsula is one of the best places to view the show."

"They're the 'Northern Lights'," said Jane. "And they are indeed mesmerizing."

They watched just above the trees, in respectful silence, as the spectacle of lights seemed to wiggle their way across the star packed night sky, giving them a show they couldn't possibly capture anywhere down state. It wasn't a full view because there were trees all around, but what they saw was magnificent and they all knew they would remember this moment for a long time.

It looked like the lights could go on forever, but Jane spoke up. "OK, you guys, I'll be the first to admit it. I'm getting tired and am about ready for bed. How about we all hit the sack so we can get an early start. The sun's going to wake us up anyway, and we can talk about tomorrows destination over breakfast."

"I'm all for that," said Todd.

"Me too," said Jack and Gail together.

"But what about this hiker friend of your uncle's?" asked Gail.

"He was never found," said Jane. "My uncle and some of his friends came back, year after year. They found nothing. It was heartbreaking really!"

"Wow," said Gail, as she got up. They all headed to bed.

Todd made sure the area was clean before heading to the tent himself. He hung what food they had left on the bear pole. There was no bear siting's in the area but he didn't want to attract them either.

CHAPTER 18

The First Full Days Hike

JANE OPENED HER eyes to a smiling Todd staring at her.

"You are so weird," she said, half yawning. "I love you, but you're still weird," she added.

"I love you too," he said. "Do you know your left eyebrow twitches when you sleep?"

"OMG! You know some day you'll wake up with me staring at you."

"I look forward to the day," he said, laughing. "But we all know I always wake up first!"

Even after her advice to Jack and Gail, Jane and Todd zipped their sleeping bags together so they could share their body heat. Well Jane could share Todd's. She was always a tad chilly and he always had enough body heat for the both of them. She just cuddled in close and stayed warm. And he loved every minute of it.

They could tell the sun was starting to rise, but they could also tell that the temperature was a bit chillier then they would have liked.

"You know we have to get up," he said.

"How about you go start the fire, and let me know when it's ready."

Todd laughed so hard the whole tent shook.

"Not on your life miss hiker woman," he said, whipping off the sleeping bag, and letting in a chill that forced Jane to get her butt moving for the day.

"Oh man, now I have to go to the bathroom."

"It's that way," said Todd, pointing outside the tent. He had to go too, but he wasn't going to let her know. They heard rustling from the other tent and decided it was time to get moving anyway. By the time Jane got her boots on and left the tent, Gail was coming back from the lady's room and handed her the toilet paper.

"I love hiking, but this is the part where I'd like to turn the corner and find a flush toilet."

"Let me know when you get the magic to produce that product," said Gail. "I'll invest in your company."

Jane just rolled her eyes and went off to the lady's room.

Todd had done his business, came back, and was starting a fire to cook breakfast by the time Jane came back. They were only having oatmeal but it still required a fire. He had left the necessary wood out last night before they all went to bed, but he needed a little kindling because everything was a bit damp from the morning dew. Todd was good at making campfires so even with the wood being a little damp he had a small fire going in no time.

Jane started rustling through her pack for the things she needed. She would heat the water in their coffeepot. They were having oatmeal for breakfast and the girls had packed individual packages. They only needed to pour the oatmeal into hot water and stir. They were hoping to have toast as well but Jane knew that without proper embers the toast would come out anywhere between still being bread to being a square piece of charcoal. She was going to try anyway so once Todd's fire was burning good she placed their cooking grate across the fire. Before he went to bed, Todd had taken the grate to the river and cleaned it. Good thing otherwise their toast would be tasting like fish this morning. Todd was good like that, clean and orderly.

They were all standing around the campfire trying to warm up. Gail was deciding whether she should wear a sweatshirt for the day, or her coat.

"It's cold," she said out loud, "maybe I should wear my coat today."

"It'll warm up," said Jack, hugging her to help her keep warm.

"Yeah, it is nippy this morning, but the temperature will start rising with the sun," said Jane. "I'm going to start with my sweatshirt. I think with us moving and the temperature starting to rise as the sun comes up, a sweatshirt will be fine. I am definitely wearing my jeans though. We had a nice breeze yesterday so we didn't have to many bug problems. I know it's already September but they're still around. If we're going off trail later today I don't want to run into any deer flies. I hate it when they bite."

"That's because they don't just bite," said Jack, "they take a chunk of skin from you back to their den."

They all laughed.

"I'm also wearing my bandanna around my neck today," said Jane, "for the same reason."

"So, we're still going off trail today," asked Gail, just a little timid. She wasn't as experienced a hiker as the others and was always worrying about getting in over her head. Jack had assured her that hiking in the porkies was quite safe. Besides, Jane was really being nice and always giving advice. She didn't know Jane long but she liked her adventurous spirit.

"Yeah, we're headed for a place on my uncle's map that I was telling everyone about last night. Here's my uncles map and here's the Porcupine Mountain Trail map."

She spread both maps out side by side as she explained. She pointing to the location they were heading, as she explained.

"The starting point is up ahead not really far off the trail. We'll just go off trail there and then follow the Upper Carp River a bit."

"Following the river takes us off the trail, but it should make the going pretty easy, although you might get your feet a little wet as we near the swampy area. My uncles map has a few distinguishing landmarks, so, if we find those landmarks without too much trouble, we should find the wall with the crevice he described, just as easily."

"Can we get lost?" asked Gail.

"Not really," said Jane. "We're really not that far from the trails. We could head in any direction and find a trail in a very short time. But what we're looking for is on the south side of Cuyahoga Peak. That's the other thing. Once we are just below Cuyahoga Peak we'll run into some marshy area. As soon as we feel the marsh under our feet we'll head north. From there we keep heading north and there's no question that we'll be doing some uphill hiking."

"Uphill!" said Gail. "Like in mountain climbing uphill?" she asked. She was getting excited now. "That'll be cool."

"Well it's not really mountain climbing. It's just that the land starts rising from there. Cuyahoga Peak is about 1550 feet or so. Not terribly high by any means, but like climbing up a big hill that's rocky. We might run into some cliffs so, we will certainly need to be careful."

"Let's have some breakfast, then we can be on our way," said Jane.

"The water's already boiling so all you have to do is grab a bowl. Here's your oatmeal."

She pointed to where she had placed the bowls, and she handed out the packets of oatmeal. She gave two packets each to the guys and her and Gail each took one. She worked on the toast as she was talking about the days hike and she was pleased at how the bread turned into a fairly decent piece of toast. She had jelly if anyone wanted it but she just dipped her toast in her oatmeal. And they all drank water with their breakfast. It was easier to keep it simple. They have juice, pop, and beer back in the cooler they left at the yurt, but for now water would do.

After breakfast was done and dishes were cleaned, it was time to break camp, pack everything up, and head out. The temperature was rising a bit and they were all in a good mood and ready for the day. They agreed to follow Jane's uncle's map. No reason why not to. The park is marked and it would be difficult to get lost for too long. So, after Todd and Jack made sure the fire was totally out, they headed north following Jane.

CHAPTER 19

Cuyahoga Peak

"THIS IS THE Carp River," said Jane, shortly after they headed north from their campsite. "It's probably the best spot to leave the trail and head west," she commented, leading them off the path along the river.

"Looks like there's still a trail," said Jack.

"It'll look that way for a while," said Jane, "because a lot of hikers leave the trails to check out these river beds. Some like fishing where there's nobody else around to scare the fish away. Some just like watching the fish. The water here is both crystal clear and shallow enough that you can see the activity easily.

They walked another ten or fifteen minutes when Gail spoke up. "You're right Jane. The path is starting to disappear."

"It's also getting muddy," said Todd, as he was barely able to pull his boot out of some muck as he stepped to close to one of the little streams.

"Let's go this way," said Jane, leading them further north and uphill, away from the area where the river seemed to be turning more and more marshy.

She kept her compass out, just to be sure, but continued to keep the river in sight. It helped verify her direction. She led them about fifty yards north of the river's tributaries.

"Is it my imagination," asked Jack, "or are we going a bit uphill?"

"It's not your imagination," she said, stopping to point out the difference in terrain. "We are indeed going uphill. I wanted us to get away from the river. It's not really a river anymore at this point. This is where the trickling streams gather together to start what becomes the river. That's why it's so swampy. You can see brush and plant growth changing down there as it becomes more and more wetlands. And the contour of the land coming this way, going more and more uphill, is becoming more and more rocky. I want us to get out of the swamp and head uphill," she said.

"Look at that!", said Gail, as she pointed to the area they had just covered. They hadn't been walking long, maybe an hour at the most. And even that was because of the slow going near the marshy area of the Carp River. But when they all took a break, and turned around to take it all in, it was astonishing.

"You can feel the elevation now," said Jane. "We're just above the main tree line now and if you look, the view below is really incredible."

They all looked around. There were the obvious wetlands they had just left, gathering water, trickling together, and turning into the Carp River as it flowed eastward. And then there were the trees beyond, mostly pine, all full and still bright green. And more trees, birch, ash, maple, and even oak, further on, that showed touches of yellow and hints of pink. They all knew it was still a bit early for the fall colors but with the slight chill in the air and the occasional tree in the distance looking just a bit yellow or pink, you could tell fall was on its way.

"Now I know why everyone likes hiking up here so much," said Gail, ogling. "It's like getting a bird's eye view and feasting your eyes on part of God's creation. Anyone walking through this area of the Porcupine Mountains could see how the river below has it's start," she said, pointing in that direction. "You can see that whole marshy area and how the water is collecting together and forming the beginning of the river," she continued pointing and waving her arms to take in all that she saw.

"How cool is that." she said with calm excitement.

Jane smiled, remembering her first hiking experience and a similar magnificent view.

The others were quiet and just looked around. The marshy area was over to the east of the elevated trail. If they looked a bit west they could almost make out Lake of the Clouds in the distance. It was a magnificent jewel shimmering in the sun.

The four friends decided to rest for a few minutes. It was time for a water break anyway and Gail wanted to use the opportunity to take some pictures.

"My kids will love this," Gail exclaimed. "Look there," she pointed. She saw a bald eagle in the distance. It wasn't close enough for a picture but the visual of its majestic flight will last her forever. She did get a nice, close-up of a peregrine falcon, as it flew overhead. She was clicking away and Jack just smiled as he watched her. He knew she'd already taken a hundred pictures.

Looking up toward Cuyahoga Peak they could see that the terrain wasn't going to get much easier. None of them seemed to mind.

"I assume that marshy area was one of the landmarks your uncle talked about," Jack said to Jane. "What's the next marker we should be looking for?"

Jane opened the map she was holding in her hand a bit wider so everyone could see. Gail was too interested in pictures, but Todd and Jack both peeked over her shoulder.

"See this ledge," Jane noted, pointed at a line in the map.

"That's the approximate location of the overhang I had mentioned earlier. The one where my uncle and his friends started to set up their camp. Thing is," she started to say, before jerking her arm back.

"Whoa," she said, hearing the huge BOOM.

They all jumped. Gail ducked, covering her head with her arms. There was no doubt in her mind that was a gunshot, but she had to ask.

"Was that what I think it was?" she asked, taking a quick glance at the others.

Jane was a clearly upset by the gunshot and was about to say something to Todd when Gail asked the question.

"Absolutely," said Todd, securing his rifle a little tighter where he had been carrying it over his shoulder.

"Where'd it come from?" she asked.

"I think it came from the area where we camped last night," said Todd.

"So do I," said Jane.

"We didn't leave any food behind, did we?" asked Jack.

"No!" said Jane. "Todd and I did a once over before we left. Actually, if I'm observant as I think I am when it comes to hiking details, I think you did a once over yourself, didn't you Jack?"

Jack's head turned and he looked straight into Jane's eyes. "Yah! I did," said Jack smiling. "How'd you know? I mean I was just being thorough."

Jane smiled back. "Hey Todd, we like thorough, don't we?"

"Absolutely we do," said Todd, also looking at Jack with a big grin on his face.

"I was trying to clean up everything too", said Gail. "You said 'leave no trace' right? I even packed up my used toilet paper," she said.

They all laughed!

"Gail, we'll make a regular hiker out of you yet," said Jane, still grinning. "To much information, but, good job."

Jack wiped his face with his big hand then put his arms around Gail and gave her a big kiss on the lips.

"Get a room you guys," said Todd.

"Should we do anything," asked Gail, still holding onto Jack.

"Not sure what we could do," said Todd. "Someone could be target practicing, or poaching, neither of which I want to get tangled up in since they're both illegal here. Or, it could be an accidental discharge. Or, maybe someone is facing an angry animal. But we're far enough away, I think we should keep it that way."

"So do I," said Jack.

"Me too," said Jane. "I think we should keep moving."

Todd was leading now as they all headed higher toward the next accessible ridge Jane had spotted. It was a little steeper than the last few hundred yards, but it wasn't too bad. The trail they were now following began to climb along a solid wall of rock that led them to an even higher elevation than the trail they were on. They were now using the sides of the rock to brace themselves as they kept climbing. At one point, they almost did a complete one-eighty turn in the direction they were taking, in order to continue climbing up. This is where Jane's compass proved helpful. It was like climbing through a rocky washout. But it got them about ten or twenty feet higher than where they were five minutes ago.

"Well isn't that interesting," said Todd, coming to a halt.

"What do you think," asked Jane, coming up right behind him.

"It's doable," he said.

"Holy cow!" said Gail, "that's deep!" she said, looking over the edge and then up at Jack.

"You can do this hun," he said seriously, "check it out", he continued, pointing at the log and describing how easy it would be for them to cross. "It's just a small ravine, and this tree is plenty big enough to balance on. Look how the roots on the other side are holding it in place. And check this out," he said, jumping up and down on the near end of the large tree stump." It didn't move.

The ravine scared her some but Gail looked at the tree stump. It was lodged between large rocks on the end Jack had jumped up and down on, and it was held tight by roots on the other end. Both Jane and Todd looked it over. They felt that they could all walk across the fallen tree without difficulty, but Gail wasn't so sure.

"How do we cross that?" asked Gail, a little concerned.

Jane looked at Todd and without a word he took off his backpack, rummaged through it, and brought out a length of climbing rope.

"What's that for?" asked Gail.

"This is why it's always a good idea to come prepared," said Jane.

"I didn't think we would need this but Todd and I brought it anyway," she said, as her and Todd started unraveling the rope.

"Whenever your hiking, it's always safety first. Because we need to cross this ravine, and you especially are an inexperience hiker, we'll be tying ourselves together, so we can cross this ravine safely. Even if you were experienced, safety dictates that we support each other. Todd will tie the rope around himself and cross that log while we hold onto the other side of the rope. Then I'll cross, then you, then Jack will come last. As each of us crosses the others will support us. That way, if someone loses their footing, we'll catch them before they slide down the side of the cliff. It's not terribly high but if you fell you could still get hurt."

Todd checked the security of the log, then he went across first. He was as nimble as a mountain goat and was across the eight-foot expanse in seconds. Jane went next, just as sure footed but not quite as quick. Then it was Gail's turn.

"I can do this," she whispered out loud to herself.

"Yes, you can," said Jack. "Focus on each step and take your time. There's no hurry. Do you want me to take your pack?"

"No-no. I'm good." There was no way she wasn't going to do this, so she did exactly what Jack said. She took her time. She shuffled one foot at a time instead of stepping foot over foot like Todd and Jane did. But it only took her a minute or two longer than them.

"I made it," she said to Jane as soon as she got to the other side.

"Of course you did," Jane said right back, "no problem."

Jack was over the ravine as quickly as Todd and Jane. He helped Todd wrap the rope back up and put it back in his backpack. Then they headed down the trail. In another hundred yards there was another switchback, but this time the trail, although a bit overgrown, was easily manageable.

"Look at that," said Gail. "over there!"

They looked where she was pointing and sure enough, glistening in the morning sun, from what appeared to be behind them, was a waterfall.

"I'm not even sure what waterfall that is," said Jane, "there's quite a few of them here in the porkies. Most of them are on the small side, but they're all pretty to look at."

"That one is really pretty," said Gail, "with the sun shining off of it, especially from this distance."

They waited so Gail could take more pictures.

"It turned out to be a beautiful day, didn't it," said Todd.

"Indeed it did my friend," said Jack.

CHAPTER 20

Reality Check

THEY WERE ALL following single file now, and had walked three more switchbacks. The terrain wasn't bad but they were going uphill with packs on their backs. That made it more tiring than regular hiking. And the distance they were covering was deceiving because of the switchbacks. But they were in no hurry. If anyone fell behind, the others stopped and waited for them to catch up. Jack and Gail were a few paces back now and Jane knew they should take a break soon. Then she looked up, and stopped suddenly.

"What's the matter," said Todd.

"Look," she pointed. Right along the ridge about two more switchbacks above them, Jane had spotted an overhang. It really didn't look like much, just a rocky outcrop sticking out between a couple trees. But she had a gut feeling, and it made her nerves twitch.

"We won't know until we get there," said Todd. "Let's focus on that."

"You're right," she said, "we'll see what we'll see," she said sarcastically, but mainly to herself. It was a euphemism used by her mother, and her uncle. It drove her crazy when they said it, especially now that she was older.

She brought a picture to mind of her uncle back then. He'd always draw her into these adventures when she was younger. He'd lead her along some quest and then at the very end when she asked the old question "what happens from hear", he would always scratch his beard and whisper that very phrase, 'we'll see what we'll see'. What does that mean anyway, she thought? She just shook her head, trying to get the old images out of her head.

Her mind reverted to more recent times. Her uncle was getting older now, still agile, but older. He didn't hike anymore but she always loved talking to him about the hiking he did when he was young. She especially liked his stories about hiking the Grand Canyon and swimming in the Colorado River. But when he talked about hiking in the porkies, his mind drifted off. It wasn't until lately, when he found out that his niece, Jane, his goddaughter, got hooked on hiking the Porcupine Mountains, that he became more talkative. Her getting into hiking seemed to raise the hairs on the back of his neck, and Jane, at first, didn't know why. It was after her and Todd got engaged that her uncle became more and more animated about telling her to be careful hiking, giving her advice, and making them both promise never, ever, to go hiking alone. She always thought he was losing it.

Then after her and Todd got married, she visited her uncle less often, but her visits were more and more pleasant in nature. She would usually go visit her uncle with her mom, but Todd went with them a couple times too, and it seemed her uncle liked Todd. It was during these visits that her uncle started opening up more, about everything. Not as much in front of Todd, but mostly when just the two of them spent time together. It was almost like he was building up the courage to tell her something, but he never did. His memory always seemed to be blocked about certain things. Jane just blamed it on the fact that her uncle was getting older and just losing his memory bit by bit.

She eventually learned most of the story, a little at a time, so she felt she knew most of it, but not everything. She knew a boy, a friend, was lost, never to be found. What exactly happened when her uncle and five other buddies went hiking in the Porcupine Mountains? How did they lose their friend? He gave her bits and pieces of the story over time. But Jane concluded that her uncle didn't know himself what had happened. Just that they literally lost him. He was never found. God knows they looked. The authorities looked. The FBI looked. They just never found him. She knew deep down that her uncle never really got over that loss, and maybe, just maybe, blames himself a little. Who knows what a young person would think under the circumstances. The fact that the mystery was never resolved doesn't help matters any. Part of her wanted to do this for him. It was an old mystery. One involving her uncle. It was all about that very strange day, the day her uncle's friend disappeared without a trace. Once again, she shook her head trying to focus on the here and now.

She took a quick glance over at Todd. She knew he had her back. She knew Todd was doing this for her, just like she was doing it for her uncle. Just to be in the same area that her uncle had been, well over fifty years ago, felt strange to her. And especially since the circumstances surrounding the disappearance of a young hiker was part of the mystery. She took another glance at Todd. He was looking her way, like he knew her thoughts. He just smiled at her.

Even Todd knew. He was quite intuitive and he knew instinctively that this whole trip, although it was a planned hiking adventure between four friends, it also had something to do with her uncle. It wasn't completely about Indian artefacts either, or Viking altars, or hidden caves. He just didn't know all the details, but he was with Jane and willing to give her some rope on this one. He knew for weeks how important this trip was to her. He just wasn't totally sure why. But they were here together and that's all that mattered. Besides, Todd liked Jane's uncle. He was animated and friendly. Just a nice old guy. What he didn't know now, he believed that Jane would eventually tell him, if there was more to tell. And that's all that mattered.

Jane turned back and looked at Jack and Gail down the trail.

"Just a little bit further and we'll be stopping for a break," she yelled back at them.

Jack waved his arm in approval.

CHAPTER 21

Destination Reached

WHEN JACK AND Gail reached the clearing, Jane and Todd already had their packs off and leaned up against the face of the cliff just below what looked like an outcropping of solid stone.

"I didn't think you were ever going to take a break," said Jack, smiling.

"Has it been that long since the last break," Jane said lightheartedly. "I didn't notice."

He just smiled at her. "I'm going to the little boys' room," he said back at her as he walked away.

Jane's heart skipped a beat, remembering part of her uncle's story. But Jack was back in no time at all so she calmed herself.

"How about lunch," said Gail. "I'm starved."

Jane looked at the watch on her wrist. She wasn't sure if they would have cell phone service in the mountains, so she brought her watch just in case.

"It's almost one o'clock," she said. "No wonder my stomach is growling. Sure, let's have lunch. We can have peanut butter and jelly, or, peanut butter and jelly."

"Very funny," said Todd. "got any potato chips?"

"As a matter of fact," said Gail, "we brought Pringles," and she whipped out two cans from her backpack.

They didn't need a fire for lunch so they sat in a circle on the ground. It was a bit rocky so they all sat on their sleeping bags. The girls brought out the food. Jane carried the bread. She had packed it in a sturdy plastic container to keep it from getting squished. It made her pack bulky but they were only going to be out on the trail for a couple days so it was no big deal. Plus, she knew Todd would appreciate something more than health food bars. Gail carried the peanut butter and jelly.

Gail carried a small table cloth to put the food on. She spread it out and Jane put the bread container on it so it wouldn't blow away. They hadn't run into too many bug problems so they weren't concerned about the open bread container. Gail also pulled out the plastic jars of peanut butter and jelly and put them on the makeshift table, and Jack placed the Pringles on the table cloth, after eating a handful of course.

"I also have these for dessert," said Jane, pulling out a bag of miniature Hershey candies and tossing them on the table cloth. "They might be a bit soft but I bet they're still good."

"Whoa! I'll have a pre-lunch test taste," said Todd, grabbing the bag, tearing it open, and taking out several little bars. It made the rest of them laugh simply because at that moment Mr. Calm and collected was acting like a little kid.

It was a relaxing lunch. There was a mild breeze which was what partly kept the tiny flying bugs away from their lunch. The sun was high and bright. And the sky only had a few slowly moving clouds, nothing threatening. And best of all, the temperature had climbed a bit. It was around sixty-five, maybe a couple degrees higher, so their sweat shirts were perfect to keep them comfortable, but not overheated.

Jane was facing the flat mountain wall, just looking at it.

"So, what do you think?" asked Todd.

"Well," Jane began, as they all listened.

"We're kind of at our destination, sort of," she said.

"This is where my uncle and his buddies camped out the night one of them disappeared."

"Right here?" asked Gail, "in this very spot?"

"Yes," said Jane, "right here."

"The way my uncle explained it, or the way my mom and I interpreted it, whichever way you want to take it," said Jane, "one of the guys went off to go to the bathroom. I think that way." She pointed to the west.

"But I'm not exactly sure," she continued.

"Once we're all done with lunch, I'd like to look around the area. Take our time and maybe really look closely at all the crevices or outcroppings in the cliff wall we're staring at, just anything unusual. But I'd like us to kind of stick together. I never had any experience in, as you guys put it, hocus pocus crap. I've read up on mystical events, especially those that have occurred in and around the state of Michigan, and truthfully, I don't really believe in it. I feel everything has an explanation. It may not be logical or one you may feel is reality, but everything can be explained if, and I don't use that word lightly, IF, you have all the facts."

"Did you ever read the book 'Mystical Michigan'?" she asked.

"I've heard of it," said Todd.

"I never heard of it," said Jack. "Me either," added Gail.

"Well, it's just a small book. But it gives you a little detail of some things people have known about in and about Michigan, and a brief explanation of how that event, or events, could have occurred. It's interesting to think about. Anyway, the fact that things can be explained was my whole point. And I'm trying to say that there must be a reason for the events that occurred the evening my uncle's buddy disappeared.

And, I still wonder why none of the hikers he was with, in all the years since the disappearance happened, has ever mentioned the cave my uncle says they found. Why they didn't tell anyone about the cave is beyond me. Maybe they thought they'd get in trouble. Maybe they thought some ghost was involved. Who knows. And I'm not saying that we'll find anything. But to me I thought it would be exciting to look around. The porkies are a beautiful place to hike, so if we get nothing else out of this adventure, we can at least have fun hiking. I truly believe Michigan has the best scenery a hiker could ask for."

"Plus, I got lots of good pictures," said Gail, enthusiastically. "I'm ready, let's do this," she said. "I can't wait to tell my kids about this entire adventure."

CHAPTER 22

Secret Revealed

"O.K. THEN," SAID Jane. "I've been thinking about this a lot. We don't want anyone going off on their own. This might seem weird but that means even to go to the bathroom."

"You're kidding, right?" said Jack.

"No, not really, Jane replied. This area doesn't have trails. It's not marked in any way. We don't know if there are soft spots in the sand that someone could get stuck in. I know that my uncle's friend disappeared over fifty years ago, and nothing has happened since, but I don't want any of us to be the next statistic either. Plus, that gunshot does bother me. I was even going to ask everyone if they wanted to spend another night camping, but, especially because of that gunshot, I think we need to head back to the yurt before dark."

"She has a point," said Todd. "Let's be over cautious. Besides, we still have tomorrow to do more looking, or just more hiking, if we want to."

"Well," said Jack, "I don't like the 'don't go to the bathroom alone thing," he continued mockingly as he rolled his eyes. "But the gunshot bothered me as well so, even though I don't like being babysat, I understand your concern and agree."

"There's one more thing I need to tell you guys," said Jane. "I've actually told Todd a little but I haven't had time to go into any details even with him."

"Like what," said Jack.

"Well remember the last-minute meeting I was called to yesterday right after school?" she noted to everyone.

"That's why you were running late," said Gail.

"Correct," Jane said, continuing, "that meeting was called by the archeologist association to warn all amateur archeologists of some dangerous artefact thieves that may or may not be in Michigan."

"Whoa," said Jack. "Are we in any kind of danger?"

"I would certainly hope not," said Jane, "especially if Todd's friend is around and knows we're here. Remember he told me not to mention archeology. Well I haven't. As far as anyone knows we're up here hiking. Nobody, not even you guys, knew anything about me keeping my eyes open for artefacts."

"I was surprised Todd's friend Arnie mentioned my connection to archeology," said Jane. "I wasn't coming up here to start digging for artefacts. I mean I brought the metal detectors so we could look around if we had time, but I didn't really think we'd find anything. However, I just want to make sure everyone knows, so you don't think my stressing safety, and not being alone, isn't totally groundless."

"But you still think we're all safe up here, you know, hiking and everything, right," asked Gail".

"Absolutely," said Jane.

"Then let's do this," said Jack.

"OK," said Jane, "we can probably leave our packs here if you want. We're coming right back this way anyway. We'll just leave them up against the cliff face there marking this as our starting point. However, I think we do need to take a few things with us, like Todd's rifle, the axe, the rope, and our water canteens. Maybe we can even take the metal detector. What do you guys thing?"

"Sounds good to me," said both Todd and Jack.

"I'd like to take my camera also," said Gail.

"No problem," said Jane.

"Let's start heading west," Jane continued, we'll take our time and just look at all the rock formations on the cliff face. Anything that needs to be investigated, we'll do just that. I don't think it will take long. I mean how far would a guy have gone to take a leak, right?" The guys just shrugged their shoulders.

"If, for whatever reason, we decide to head off in another direction," said Todd, "we'll just have to come back and get them."

"If you see anything unusual, or even think you see something unusual, just say so. Pretty simple really."

So, that's what the four friends did. It was kind of exciting really. They all walked along the edge of the cliff face. Jane, especially was pumped up. She had the metal detector out and was watching the readings. She told everyone she didn't expect to find anything but really, she was hoping they'd find something. But, as they walked further and further, her excitement dissipated. They had walked for a little over two-hundred yards, and nothing. Well, not really nothing since they found a rodent hole of some kind, three birds' nests, or something that resembles birds' nests, a couple areas with small piles of rocks that could have been from long ago rock slides, and a large pile of rocks from what also looked like an old rock slide. She used the metal detector near all the rock slides but didn't get any conclusive reading.

"Are you sure this is the right area," asked Todd.

"That's part of the problem," Jane answered. "I'm really not sure."

"Let's walk the same distance down toward the east. If we don't find anything, well, I don't know. Maybe this map is garbage and there's really nothing to find. At least I can say I gave it a try."

So, they turned and headed the other way. Jane still led the way, with Todd following close by. Jack started after them, then noticed Gail just looking up the side of the cliff. Jack thought she was just day dreaming and didn't make anything of it.

"Are you coming?" he asked her, breaking her trance.

"Oh, yes, of course," she said.

"You O.K.," he asked when he noticed she was awfully quiet. "Is something wrong?"

"No-no, I'm fine she said," smiling at him, "I was just noticing the color differences in the rock. You know, it's that old art major' in me. I just notice color changes is all. I see it in nature a lot. That's why the 'Northern Lights' were so cool," she said, as they started walking after Jane and Todd.

They followed Jane and Todd in the other direction. The four of them passed by the spot where they had lunch and headed east, inspecting the cliff face in much the same way as they did on the west side. They went a hundred yards in that direction as well, but found nothing.

"This just upsets me," said Jane frustratingly.

"I know I said I didn't think we would find anything, but I guess I really thought we would maybe find a sign of that crevice my uncle always talked about, or something, anything. I guess I kind of thought that that cave really existed. I'm beginning to think that he was just an old man haunted by a past tragedy."

She felt sorry for what he and his buddies went through. She turned and looked at her friends.

"Look, I'm really sorry you guys", she started to say.

Todd saw her disappointment but didn't know what to say.

Gail walked past them a little, staring up at the rock cliff again.

"Gail, what do you see?", Jack asked her.

Jane and Todd both turned and Jane was about to ask, 'what's wrong', when Jack just held his hand up in a sign that meant 'don't say anything yet'. They all saw her staring up the face of the cliff just as Jack did. They were all quiet for a minute before Gail turned and looked at all of them quizzically.

"Don't you guys see it?" she asked.

"There's a pattern?" she said.

"What pattern," said Jack.

"Just like the one I told you I saw on the other side," she said to Jack.

"The pattern in the rocks," she said.

"I remember," said Jack. Are you sure they look the same?"

"Pretty sure," said Gail.

Then both Jack and Gail turned to Jane and Todd.

"O.K. are you two going to tell us what you're talking about?" Jane said a little more excited then she meant it to be. "Did I miss something?"

"Well, I really didn't know what you were looking for," Gail started saying calmly, "so I was just looking at the interesting rock formations. I'm sorry, I didn't see any crevices or entry ways into any small cave, but I did see that," she said pointing on an angle up the face of the cliff. There's that different colored rock every so far. But they're staggered, and the pink looking ones stick out a little further then the grey colored ones. And they all seem to head right up to that overhang right above where we had lunch."

Jane stood there with her mouth open as Gail was babbling on. She looked at Todd, who just shrugged his shoulders. Neither of them had quite caught on what she was trying to say, but Jane didn't want to shrug off whatever this was.

"Please continue," she said politely to Gail.

CHAPTER 23

The Pattern

TODD WALKED OVER to where Gail stood and tried to see the pattern Gail was talking about. He thought he saw a bit of color difference in a few rocks but he wasn't sure. Jack was just scratching his head trying to figure out what Gail was pointing at. He knew he was talking to an Art teacher, so there had to be something to what she was trying to explain to them.

Jane finally spoke up. "I'm not sure if I see anything," said Jane. "Go over the pattern you're talking about with me again," she said to Gail, "but remember, you're an art teacher and see colors different then me, so be patient with me."

Gail smiled and then pointed while Jane watched.

"There," said Gail, "and there, and there!"

The rocks she was pointing at climbed up the wall like a small staircase, a jagged mildly tinted, yet recognizable pattern in an otherwise insignificant cliff face.

"I see what you're talking about," said Jane finally, trying not to be too excited or hopeful. Just tell me this," she continued, "do you think that pattern is significant?"

"Well," she said, thinking out loud. "I wasn't sure at first, when I saw them on the other side, you know."

"Wait, wait, wait! I missed that. What did you just say," asked Jane, a bit excitedly, her heart most assuredly skipping a beat!

Gail looked at Jane. "Well, I thought I saw the same pattern on the other side," she said, "but we turned around kind of quickly. I was just trying to explain to Jack what I think I saw, when we started walking in this direction. Then, we passed our packs and I started focusing again, and when I started seeing the same pattern, well you know, I had to say something."

Nobody said anything, so she continued. "And now, looking from this side, I can kind of see the pattern a bit better. They kind of look the same, but I'd like to see the pattern on the other side again though,"

Jane looked at Jack. "Art teacher", he just said, shrugging his shoulders.

Jane smiled. "OK then, we'll have to take a closer look at the other side again," she said. "But for now, since we're on this end, go into a little more detail of what you see."

"Well, most of the rock here is kind of dark, maybe deep gray. As a matter of fact, most of the cliff walls we've been passing are all like that."

"That's called 'basalt'," said Jane, "and it's a fine volcanic rock found in this area of the park, so that's kind of normal."

"Well, then, there's this pinkish rock. What I see is pretty much a pattern, starting low, like right there," she said, pointing to a small pink rock close to the bottom of the rock face. "And then it gradually goes up on kind of an angle, all the way up to that overhang over there."

She pointed to the overhang just above where they ate lunch.

"You know," she said, "the overhang above where we left our packs."

She continued, "the pattern looks like small pockets of that 'pinkish' rock I mentioned. You can really see the difference in color you know, if you look closely. It's kind of like someone put them there for decoration."

Jane was surprised by Gail's comment, 'like someone put them there for decoration'. It just sounded strange. She took a closer look at some of the 'pinkish' rock Gail was talking about. She found some that was closer to eye level.

"This looks like 'Rhyolite' rock," she said to Gail.

"It's the oldest rock in the porkies, but it's usually not found up here. I'm no expert of course, but if it is Rhyolite, it's usually found way south of here. Why here? Why in this pattern," she said out loud, but mostly questions to herself.

"And what about the pattern you mentioned," Jane asked her, popping out of her minor trance.

"Well, come over here," Gail said, "and look up the mountain face on an angle."

Jane did as Gail said. She stood at the spot where Gail had indicated that the pattern began, and she looked up the face of the cliff, on an angle toward the overhang a hundred yards away. And, the puzzle finally came together. She saw the pattern!

Jane was astonished. "I don't get it," she said. "I mean I can see the pattern now that Gail's talking about. And, now that we know it's on both sides, this one and the one on the west side, and both seem to be leading to that overhang, then what does it all mean?"

"It means there's something about that overhang that nobody is aware of," said Todd.

"Like what," she said.

"I don't know," said Todd, "but let's think about this a bit. You were looking for something unusual, right? Well, here it is! Question now is, what's it mean? What's on that overhang? And what about those pockets of pink rock? Are they climbable? Are they steps, stable steps? Or, are they just markers leading to the overhang?"

That overhang appears to be about fifty feet up, right? Starting out a hundred yards to get to a fifty-foot ledge seems strange to me, don't you think? Lots of questions, lots of questions. So, let's answer the most obvious. What's so interesting about that overhang? How about we find out?"

"How do we do that?" asked Jack.

"We climb it," said Todd. "Haven't you ever climbed a cliff face before?"

"Not exactly!" said Jack, hesitantly.

"Well, I have," he said, with a big grin on his face.

"You're just full of surprises," said Jane, smiling. "So, what are you thinking."

"Well, we should at least see if these pockets of pink rock, or whatever you call them, will hold someone's weight. Or, even if they do, are there places to put your hands as you climb? Jack, let's you and I check it out."

"Sure," said Jack. "What do you want me to do?"

"How about I do the climbing."

"Todd!" Jane stepped forward, "you don't have a rope, or safety equipment, or anything."

"I don't plan on going that far," said Todd. "I'm just testing the waters, sort of. I'll see if I can place my foot on the pink rock and then see if I can find a place to hold onto with my hands. Jack here, can be my spotter. If I fall, I'll only be a couple feet up in the air, but if I fall, all he has to do is kind of guide me to the ground so I don't fall weird and break something."

"I can do that," said Jack.

"See," said Todd to Jane, "no big deal."

"Let's just take one more look," said Todd. "I want to know if I should climb from this end or from the west side where we first started looking."

CHAPTER 24

Test Climb

THEY WENT BACK to the campsite area where they left they're packs. They were all looking now, trying to get a good view of the rock face. They stepped back about twenty steps so they could get a better perspective of the rock face and how the rhyolite, as Jane called the pink looking rocks, lined up.

"I can see it even better now," said Gail. "Look," she pointed with both hands, "you can see it now from both sides. Those 'pinkish' stones, what did you call them," she turned and asked Jane."

"Rhyolite," Jane quietly responded, looking where Gail was pointing.

"Yeah, rhyolite," Gail continued. "The rhyolite stones seem to form a triangle with the cliff overhang at the top of the triangle, the apex,"

As they all concentrated it became clear. They could see it from both sides. They were all wondering if the angles were similar, if the formation was symmetrical. It certainly looked like it.

"I'll be damned," said Todd. "I actually think I see the pattern. Amazing!"

"I can't believe you spotted that," said Jack. "It's not that obvious."

"There's no question," said Jane. "There's something here. I don't exactly know what, but something. I don't want my imagination to take off on me, but I can see it. You guys see it too, don't you," she asked. "It means something, right?" she asked.

"I think it does," said Todd.

"Me too," said Gail.

"Are you sure you want to test the rock?" she said, looking at Todd.

"I'm quite sure," he replied. "I'm actually excited to give it a try. I think we need to check out a few of these pink rock protrusions. Let's see if there stepping stones, like it appears, or just decoration. The ones on the west end seem closer," he continued, "let's start on that end."

They headed to the west side of the cliff face. Todd looked at the west angle. He truly didn't think it would be a problem. Just a small test and he would know immediately whether the rocks held his weight or not.

"This looks like a good starting place," he said. "At this low level, the pockets of pink rock appear to be about two feet apart. It's a bit longer stride between the rock protrusions then I would like, but it's low enough to the ground so it's no big deal."

As he looked higher and began to study the formation, he noticed that these pink rock pockets were spread out anywhere from six inches to two feet apart. At least the ones he saw were spread out that far. He could only see so far down the cliff face because it had kind of an angle to it. But he knew the pink rock went all the way to the cliff overhang, and that the spacing was about the same, because they had all spent time looking at it and comparing the two sides.

With Jack at his back Todd placed his left foot onto the pink stone and reached above his head to find a place to grip the rock with his hand, or at least his fingers. That didn't seem to be a problem either. Then he put all his weight on the pink rock under his foot, and it seemed to hold. So, he reached with his right foot to the next pink rock, which was only about eight inches away. It held fine as well. So, he moved his hand along as well, finding a good finger hold. Then he reached for the next pink rock. It broke off as he started to put his weight on it, and he almost fell.

"Shit," he mumbled to himself, wondering if climbing even this far without a rope was very smart.

"Todd!" Jane yelped nervously. There was nothing she could do but watch, but it made her anxious.

"I'm fine," Todd told her.

The next pink rock held fine, so he reached with his right hand for a handgrip. No problem. Then he moved his left foot onto the rock with his right foot, so both feet were on the same rock, and it held. So far, so good. They were west of the overhang so Todd was working left to right. He worked the same way, one foot on the rock then both feet, then reach for the next rock and hand grip, and so on. Soon, he was four feet off the ground, then six feet off the ground, then eight feet off the ground, almost to a height that could make it dangerous should you fall. The others were shuffling along below him, but were keeping quiet so he could concentrate. Jack especially was watching his every move.

It didn't seem like it was taking long, but it was slow moving and nerve wracking to watch. And the spacing between the pockets of pink rock weren't too bad, but he was now twelve or fifteen feet high, and he felt like he was really close. But distance can be deceiving. He knew the distance and figured he was probably only one-fourth of the way to the overhang.

Todd really wanted to continue climbing, but he knew he was getting to high for Jack to catch him should he fall. Plus, he didn't want to hurt Jack, or either of the girls. He knew that if he started to fall Jane would jump right in and try to help Jack catch him. And besides that, he knew he was reaching the point at which the lack of a safety harness was making him nervous. As an experienced climber, he knew it was time to go back and get the proper equipment. He did bring his climbing gear but never thought he'd us it.

He yelled down to the others. I'm coming down. He heard them shuffling but didn't pay much attention. He was concentrating on what he was doing, and sometimes going down can be more dangerous than going up a cliff face. He went slowly and carefully but when he reached a point at which he was about three feet off the ground, he waved Jack back and jumped that last little distance to the ground.

"Is something wrong," asked Jane, almost immediately.

"No, not at all," he said, a little winded. "But once you start getting up that high than it's time to be safety conscious. I think we need to stick to our plan. It's definitely some sort of walkway up to the overhang. At least that's what it feels like to me," he said. I think Gail's eye was pretty spot on," he said. "But I can't quite see the overhang, or what it's made of, or if anything is on it," he continued. "But, I do know that I spent some time climbing. You watched me climb so you know it took a while. I know it has to be at least three o'clock."

"It's actually three-thirty," said Gail.

"Wow! Time flies when you're having fun," said Jack.

"Yes, it does," said Todd, looking straight into Jane's eyes. She knew the right decision. She really, really, wanted to continue, and Todd knew that, but was letting her make the decision herself. As much as Jane wanted to see what was up there, and as curious and anxious she was to find out, she knew it could be dangerous for Todd. So, in the end, her logic, and her love for him, won out. At least without too much hesitation. After all, they still had tomorrow.

"You're right of course," she said. Todd knew it was a struggle for her not to at least ask if he could go a little further, but he was proud that she was being smart about the whole thing. This was just a hiking trip. They both had to keep reminding themselves of that.

"OK," she said. "This is good. We know the next step. We have the rest of the afternoon to hike back to the yurt. We can even take our time. We can clean up a bit, maybe even catch some more fish and have a decent evening meal, and even sleep in some real beds."

"Did you bring your climbing gear," she asked Todd. She thought he did but she had to ask.

"Yup, sure did," he said.

"Cool. We'll hike back up here tomorrow and do some climbing."

"Any questions?"

"No, I'm good with that," said Jack.

"I'm good with that too," said Gail.

"OK, let's get our packs and head out then."

"And hey Gail," Jane said, looking at their most inexperienced hiker, "good eyes".

"Thanks," said Gail, with a big smile on her face.

CHAPTER 25

Scary Hike Back to the Yurt

"LET'S PACK UP then," said Jane.

"We can get a good night sleep tonight, have a decent breakfast, and head out in the morning. That gives us all day to get here, check out the ledge and maybe look further for that cave my uncle talked about, if there is a cave," she said. "Then we can head for home by early afternoon."

"The climbing gear I brought is used," said Todd, "so we'll need to fit it appropriately before we start climbing. It's no big deal," he continued, we just need to do this safely."

"Do we have time to catch fish for tonight's dinner?" asked Gail. "That was fun."

"We can probably catch fish in the small creek behind the yurt," said Jack. I saw some trout in there yesterday."

"Trout sounds good to me," said Todd, with a big grin on his face.

Jane smiled too at Gail's request, but she didn't say anything. They all just grabbed their packs and headed down the slope. They were casually walking down the same trail they came up, making plans for tomorrow, Jane leading the way, when they heard another gunshot.

BOOM!

Gail cringed.

The noise jolted everyone.

"What the hell," said Todd.

"Once I can accept," he said, "but twice, I don't like."

They all felt the care free enjoyment of the afternoon melt away. Gunshots were not normal in the park. They all stopped, looking and listening. Todd pulled his rifle off his shoulder and walked up past Jane, and took the lead. Jane had no problem with that. The foursome stood still, listening for a few more seconds. For what, they didn't know. Anything.

"What the hell is going on," said Jane.

"I don't know," responded Todd. "I can accept one gunshot, for several reasons, but two, now that demands our attention."

"Did it come from the same area as the first one," she asked.

"Hard to say," said Todd. "We're kind of in a different position, but I'd guess it was in that general direction. It didn't sound quite as loud to me," he said, "but I suggest we get back to the trails. At least if it's serious they'll have rangers out patrolling. If we stay off trail and find trouble, that probably wouldn't be good."

They all agreed and started heading down the switchbacks, with Todd in the lead. They were hiking with a boost of adrenaline, not to mention that now they were going downhill, so they made pretty good time. Even when they got to the ravine where they had to cross the log, it went quickly. They roped off for safety and followed the same arrangement as before, with Todd first, then Jane, then Gail, then Jack. They put the rope back in Todd's pack as quickly as possible and headed down to the Carp River. Todd took them down the slope on an angle to avoid as much of the marshy area as possible. From there they could head back to the trail quickly and back to the campsite they stayed at the night before. They thought someone there may know something.

But when they reached the small campground, they found it deserted. There was no sign of campers, or hikers, or even park rangers.

"I don't like this," said Jack.

"Neither do I," said Todd, "but maybe because it's late in the season, there just isn't anyone out hiking."

"Yah! Right," said Jane, "on a Saturday afternoon, on a beautiful day."

"You guys are scaring me," said Gail, "let's just get back to the yurt."

"I agree," said Jack.

Todd took the lead again. He headed them back down Government Peak Trail and turned onto Lost Lake Trail toward the yurt they had rented. It wasn't a hard hike and it wasn't long. It was just a bit nerve wracking to think someone is out there shooting a gun and they don't know why.

When the yurt came into sight, they were all relieved. But as they got closer Jane spotted something tacked to the door jam.

"What is it," asked Gail.

"It's a note from the rangers," she said. "asking us to report to the ranger station as soon as we return to the yurt."

"I wonder why," said Jack.

"There's only one way to find out," said Todd.

"We don't really need to carry these packs," said Jane. "Let's dump them here and head to the ranger station. I'm not sure how long they'll be open and we want to catch somebody so we can see what's going on."

"Well I'm a bit hungry," said Jack. "Maybe we can go get something to eat, since we're in the van anyway."

"You mean head to town?" asked Gail.

"Sure, why not," he said.

But they were extremely surprised to see that, not only was the ranger station open, the place was swarming with hikers, rangers, and, the local police. There didn't seem to be any panic, just people milling around.

"What the heck," muttered Todd, as he pulled the van into a parking spot.

They all got out of the van and headed toward the ranger station. Todd was in the lead this time, with the girls following, and Jack bringing up the rear. They headed directly to the main desk. Todd waited politely as another couple was talking to the ranger on duty. Jane noticed that it was the same guy that checked them in Friday morning. She grabbed Todd's arm and stood with him at the desk so the ranger could see they were together.

"Well, hello folks," he said. "Glad to see you again. Maybe not under these circumstances, but, glad you're checking in."

"Well, we've been out on the trail," said Todd, "and we got back to the yurt we rented and found a note telling us to check in here at the ranger station. So, what's going on anyway?"

"A little country drama is all," said the ranger. "Some yahoo was out camping and swears he saw bigfoot. Fired off his rifle and scared several hikers in the area. Then he panicked thinking he was in trouble. We had to call in the local police to help us corner the guy."

"We heard two rifle shots up near the Union Spring Camping area," Todd told the ranger. "Is that where this guy says he saw bigfoot?"

"Yes, it was," said the ranger. "A couple other hikers said they heard two shots as well, with maybe a couple hours between the two. It took a while to find the guy but they have him cornered now somewhere east of Union Spring. They think he's harmless, just a bit scared, so they're trying to talk him into giving himself up. We should be hearing soon. We're kind of asking that the hikers and campers hang out here until we catch the guy."

"How do you get to all the hikers," asked Todd.

"Well, that's not always so easy," he said. "We send out a couple rangers on foot, and a couple more out on ATV's, to touch base with whoever they run into on the trail. Then another ranger leaves notes at all the rented cabins and yurts. The campsites already have rangers on site so they just pass the word for campers to stay on site until the alert is over. We know we won't run into everyone out there on the trails, but we like to find as many as we can, mostly to give folks a heads up to be aware of the possible danger. We're hoping this issue gets resolved within a couple hours. In the mean-time," he said, "there's dinner out back for everyone who checks in. Nothing big," he said. Just hotdogs and hamburgers, but hey, it's free. Compliments of the rangers for this afternoon's trouble."

"Thanks," said Todd. "I guess we'll hang out then."

Todd and Jane went back to the corner where Gail and Jack were waiting. They explained to Gail and Jack all the things the ranger had said.

"Wow!" said Gail. "Bigfoot? People have good imaginations, don't they?"

"Hey, maybe it's true," said Jack. "The existence of Bigfoot hasn't been proven right or wrong, not really."

"It's not so much that," said Gail.

"Then what," said Jack, questionably.

"All the drama," she said. "It's like everywhere. The reasons for the drama may be different, but drama none-the-less. Even in such a naturally beautiful place as the Porcupine Mountains."

Jane just smiled. She was beginning to like Gail a whole lot.

"Let's head out back," said Todd. "The ranger said there's free food."

"I can handle free food," said Jack. "I'm starving."

CHAPTER 26

Bigfoot – Free Lunch

THEY HEADED OUT back behind the ranger station and was a bit surprised by the size of the area and the number of campers and hikers that were there.

"I guess we found all the hikers," said Jane, giving a side glance at Todd.

"There's the grill," said Jack, heading right for it.

The others followed. And soon they each had a burger, or two in Jack's case, a bag of chips, and a water, they found a place to sit and eat their meal. There were hikers all over just chatting about what's going on. The foursome heard lots of comments about bigfoot, jokes mostly.

"This isn't bad at all," said Gail. "It isn't fish but it tastes good."

"You can catch tomorrow's lunch," Todd told her, "no problem."

"What do you think about this whole Bigfoot thing," Jack asked Jane.

"Well," Jane began, "you know there have been hundreds of folklore stories of Bigfoot all over the world. Legends of 'Sasquatch' have been passed down in stories of Indian mythology in this country for years. 'Sasquatch', as many call him, means wild man. He's been talked about throughout all of North America, including Michigan, both the upper and lower peninsula's, for years. The U.P. has its very own 'Bigfoot/Sasquatch Research Organization' dedicated to finding proof that Bigfoot exists," she said, "and living in the Upper Peninsula. They even have a 'bigfoot' convention. I think it was held this past August and I guess quite a few people showed up. I've heard of this person or that person being the 'bigfoot expert' and having this proof and that proof, but never heard of any proof that this creature is real."

She continued, "the Yooper's, people who live in the U.P., are pretty tight-lipped about bigfoot. They don't always share because they think they'll be made fun of. There's some guy who runs the research organization and he tries to run it with a motto that includes 'no ridicule' or something like that. He tries to get people to share what they saw, or think they saw. They say the Seney National Wildlife Reserve is a hotspot for Bigfoot sightings. We passed Seney on our way here. It's off M-28 on your way to Munising. I don't really remember hearing anything about bigfoot sightings in the porkies. You could do internet searches all day long and find hundreds of documents about bigfoot, but science says, until we have a body, there's no proof."

"That sounds kind of morbid," said Gail.

"Yah, it kind of does," said Jane. "But think about it. People are saying that there's this creature out there, about eight feet tall or so, harry all over like an ape, but walking like a man, born to be wild, and avoids contact with man."

"I'd like to avoid contact with man sometimes," said Todd, under his breath.

Jane ignored him and continued. "No professionally acceptable proof of such a creature has ever been seen, nor has any such creature ever been caught. It's another one of those Michigan Mystery things I'm always talking about. Is it true? Or, is it fiction? Folklore, or fact? Who can say?"

"I need another water," said Jack. "Anyone want anything?"

"I'll take a water," said Todd.

"Can you grab me one too," said Jane.

"Sure. Gail, what about you?"

"How about I go with you," said Gail. "I think I want a hotdog. I'm still hungry."

"Sure, come on," said Jack.

The two of them headed back toward the food tent. Gail was chattering about maybe she'll get another bag of chips too because she was still feeling hungry. Right about then the outside loudspeaker crackled and a ranger came on announcing that the danger has passed and that the hiker responsible for firing his rifle was now in custody. The reaction from the hikers was calm. A few yelps were heard but most of them were talking about bigfoot and what would be the possibility of bigfoot being in the porkies. Hikers almost instantly started picking up their packs and heading out. After all, there was still a couple good hiking hours left in the day.

Gail and Jack came back from the food tent and sat back down. Gail had another plate of food. She brought two hotdogs and offered the second one to Jane, which Jane decided to take without question. "Thanks," she said. Jack handed Todd his water, which was cold and looked refreshing.

"Todd," asked Jack, "do you really have enough gear for us to do some climbing tomorrow?"

"Yeah, I think so," Todd replied. "I mean we're only climbing, what, fifty feet? So, I'm sure I have enough rope. It just depends on whether I'm just going to climb up to the overhang, check it out, and come back down. Or, if there's really something cool everyone wants to see."

"If we're all climbing," he continued, "I was thinking of running some anchor points from the ground to the overhang, attaching the rope, and then having everyone climb from there. I have plenty of carabiners also. I also brought four harnesses, so we should be good there. Like I said, they're used, so we just need to fit them properly. I wasn't sure we would be climbing so even though I brought everything, we'll have to talk about what kind of experience, if any, everyone has. Either way, we'll have to take it slow. In either case, I'll set up a rope so we can rappel down. That'll make the descent much easier. After all, it's only fifty feet so, we'll be down before anyone can get scared."

"Why don't we go around to the top of the ridge and climb down, instead of climbing up," asked Gail.

"Well, if you take a good look up that cliff, you'll notice that it's got to be over three hundred feet high. That would make the climb from the top, both up and down more complicated. I much rather deal with fifty feet."

"Me too," said Jack.

"Have you climbed?" Todd asked Gail.

"No, not really," she said.

"What does 'not really' mean?" Todd asked.

"Well, I've never climbed mountains, or even cliffs, like these. But I've climbed trees when I was younger and at least I know I'm not afraid of heights."

"That's a start," said Todd.

"Have you ever gone zip-lining," he asked.

"Oh yeah, I've done that lots of times," she said, "and I've done high ropes too."

"Well, there you go. At least you know how a harness works. And we'll talk about safety later tonight, after I've had time to check my equipment. Why don't we get out of here and head back to the yurt. Everyone done eating?"

Everyone was done so they cleaned up their area and headed out to the van.

CHAPTER 27

Back on the Trail

I T DIDN'T TAKE long to get back to the yurt. It was still daylight so they had time to clean up and organize things for the evening. They had been out on the trail almost two days, and the yurt had no running water, so when Jane suggested they all pack a small bag and go over to the Union Bay Campground for a shower, nobody argued. They all packed their shower bags, grabbed a towel and headed out to the van for the short ride to the campground. They were lucky because being early September, although there were a lot of hikers, the campground wasn't full. That meant, the bathhouse wasn't full either. They didn't know what to expect but all four of them were able to take their time and enjoy a nice hot shower.

"I feel great!" said Gail. "What a difference a shower makes."

"That's for sure," agreed Jane. I think I washed two pounds of dirt and grime down the drain." The girls headed outside where the guys were already waiting.

"Hey, since it's still daylight, why don't we take a walk down to Lake Superior and check it out." Suggested Todd. "Just for a while. There's the staircase over there," he pointed.

They all agreed, and headed toward the stairs he was pointing at. They took the stairs down to the lake and headed to a smooth outcropping of shale down by the shoreline. As they got closer to the water the wind seemed to pick up dramatically and was more intense than any of them would have expected. Yet it was tolerable for a short time so they sat near the shore line and watched the intense color changes in the clouds. It was amazing. The pinks and purples seemed to be intertwined as the sun traveled across the sky. It was just beautiful and they were all mesmerized, putting a nice calm to the end of the day. They just sat on the rocks quietly absorbing natures show of color.

About fifteen minutes went by before anyone said anything.

"You know, I realize we've only been here a day and a half," said Jane, "but I feel like I've been here a week already, and I'm enjoying it a lot. I'm really glad we were all able to make this trip together you guys," she said. "Maybe we could make it a yearly event."

"I'd like that," said Gail. "I'm having a wonderful time! I have always loved nature and all the colors, not just in the clouds, but in the wildflowers, and even the butterflies that pass us by. I've seen at least five distinct color of butterfly," she said. "And the northern lights, oh my gosh, they're so magnificent," she said.

"I guess that means a leisurely walk through nature, or a pretty sunset really does bring out the art appreciation in you doesn't it," said Jane.

"Yes, I guess it does," said Gail. "It's just that I see colors so vividly and I am always awed by even the slight changes of hue," she said enthusiastically. You could tell in her voice that her artistic roots were planted deep.

"All right you guys, I hate to break this up but if we don't get back you're all going to fall sleep," said Todd. "We need to give ourselves time to prepare for tomorrow, and I need to get some gear together."

"Remind me not to bring you on a romantic dinner date," Jack told Todd.

They both laughed as they all got up and headed back up the stairs to their van.

CHAPTER 28

Decision to Climb

CLEAN AND REFRESHED they headed back to the yurt. They parked in their regular spot down the path from the yurt.

"Jack, you want to help me bring this gear in?" asked Todd.

"Sure," said Jack. "Just point out what you want me to carry."

"Can you grab that blue duffle bag over there," he said pointing to a ragged looking blue heavy nylon duffel bag. "I need to go through everything to make sure we have what we need for tomorrow."

"Not a problem," said Jack, grabbing the blue bag.

"We should also go through our packs and get them ready for tomorrow," said Jane as she and Gail got out of the van. "I think we should get as much ready as we can tonight. It'll help avoid wasting time in the morning getting things together. We should probably take the smaller packs anyway since we won't be spending the night out on the trail."

They all headed into the yurt ready to plan for tomorrow.

"Before we get into exactly what we're packing," said Todd, "I'd like to go over some plans for tomorrow's climb. That way we're packing only what we need."

"Sounds good," said Jane. "Plus, I'd like to review the route we're taking as well."

They all emptied the bigger backpacks they had used the previous two days, cleaning out garbage and organizing what was left. They already had clean clothes on but the girls changed into more comfortable shoes. They all grabbed something to drink and sat down. The guys each had a beer and the girls opted for the Arnold Palmer Tea. Todd did a quick review of his climbing gear and was ready to talk over some details with the others.

"I spread out all my climbing gear so I can show you how things work," Todd began. "The ropes, and we have a couple, the harnesses, and the carabiners are the most important. I brought helmets as well. They're simple, and they're used, but they'll work for what we need them for. And, of course, my anchors. We're talking only fifty feet high, but we're still going to take the traversing route across the cliff, on the pinkish stones Gail spotted. It's longer but it'll be easier. And since none of us really has expert climbing experience, even me, I think that's the best way. A direct route would be straight up the cliff face, but the angle of the cliff face itself would make it a more difficult climb. We're not in any hurry so why not take our time. Besides, from what I've seen, going over those pinkish steps actually provides both foot and hand holds making it less stressful for all of us."

"So, you don't think it's a difficult climb for me," asked Gail.

"No, I don't," said Todd. "You already know about harnesses from zip-lining. And if you've done any high rope courses, they all give you experience to get up and around obstacles. They're a little different but they both provide safety, which is the important thing. And, even though we're only going up about fifty feet, which can freak some people out, we already know you're not afraid of heights. So, with the climbing gear on, it's just another new experience for you. The biggest challenge for everyone will be the finger holds. I suggest everyone try to put most of your weight on your feet, toes, as you're climbing, and use your knees and legs for strength. It'll put less stress on your hands, fingers."

"Jack, what about you? Any climbing experience?" asked Todd.

"I've done a lot of climbing on pretend rock walls," Jack responded. "And I've done high rope courses too. I've never done any real climbing but I understand the whole finger, toe hold thing. I've always had a harness and a guide rope on, so I have a feel for the gear like Gail, but, like Gail this will be a new experience for me as well," he said.

"And Jane," Todd said, looking over at his wife, "you've been pretty quiet. I know you've had a little climbing experience so this small adventure shouldn't be difficult for you, so, what's on your mind."

"Well," she began. "I know I have a pretty good imagination, and I know some of the things going through my mind might seem somewhat far-fetched, but I just want to put my thoughts out there. Please don't laugh."

"Nobody's going to be laughing," said Todd, "well, maybe a little," he smiled. "We all like your tall tales. I mean, we didn't run into bigfoot, but we ran into one of his followers," he said, trying to make her laugh. And she did. The others laughed as well.

"You dork," Jane said.

"I saw you roll those deep brown eyes at me," said Todd. "Come on, we're all friends here. Tell us what you're thinking."

Jane took a deep breath, but continued.

"Well, look," she said. "The whole reason I picked the Porcupine Mountains as our destination was because of my uncle. There's something haunting about the stories he's been telling me over the years. He just goes to this far off place when he talks about those times he hiked up here with his friends. I can't quite put my finger on it. But I knew I was supposed to make this trip. Do you guys ever get that feeling?" she asked the others. "Like you just know you're supposed take one direction instead of another. Or, make one decision over another, when either decision seems fine. Or, even when something goes terribly wrong, but deep down you just know everything will turn out OK. I guess it's a kind of internal guide. I don't know. Maybe it's my belief in a higher being. Sorry, I do believe in God," she said, looking at the others. "I think he's always watching over me, sort of giving my life direction. That's just me."

"We all know about your faith in God", said Gail. "And don't be sorry! We believe in God too," she said. "That's part of what I like about you."

That little tiny comment from Gail washed away any of Jane's concerns about telling the others her feelings. So, she continued. "Anyway, I just feel we're supposed to do this. And I really feel we're going to find something. That's the part that seems unreal. My head tells me probably won't find anything. My heart tells me we're here for a reason. I mean, here we are about to climb up to this small overhang on some obscure cliff, that some old man remembers as a young boy, fifty years ago. There's probably nothing up there but sand and rock and weeds. But my gut tells me otherwise. And God doesn't lead people to treasures of gold and silver, so why do I feel so strongly about this."

She glanced around at the serious looks on everyone's faces, and paused.

"Maybe up here God could lead us to some copper," she chuckled.

Todd laughed, and asked more seriously. "What do you feel is on that cliff, Jane."

"You know," she continued, "I'm not sure. I've had strong feeling about this kind of thing before, and there's been nothing. Maybe that's what'll happen here. We'll get up to the overhang and see nothing but a beautiful view of the porkie's."

"But we'll all have the new experience of a good climb," said Jack, with a smile.

"Then I'll have to bring my camera," said Gail.

"You guys are all way to positive," said Jane.

"It's the high altitude," said Gail. "It makes people goofy."

They all laughed again.

"All right, all right, children," said Todd. "Let's get ready for tomorrow."

Todd spent the next hour fitting everyone to their harnesses and showing them how his carabiners work. He then gave them a short demonstration on how to hook and unhook the carabiner, or 'biners' as experienced climbers called them, on and off the anchors he'll be placing.

Finally, everyone packed. They used smaller day packs as they didn't intend on sleeping overnight anywhere but at the yurt. Plus, the smaller packs would allow easier hiking on the trails. The only heavier thing Todd intended on taking was his rifle. And they would eat breakfast at the yurt, but Jane made sure she packed for lunch. They decided they would take the fishing gear. That way they could catch some fish for dinner on the way back from their little expedition. Jane reviewed the route they would take, pretty much the same as before, only no stopping to spend the night at the Union Spring campground. And with the packing all set, they all settled in for the night.

CHAPTER 29

Hiking to the Peak

J ANE WOKE UP startled. She had a terrible dream. It was about Jenny. She had known Jenny for a while now but never really socialized with her. She seemed like an OK person but there was always something about Jenny's demeaner that kept Jane from getting to close. Call it intuition, call it instinct, call it whatever you want, there was something about Jenny that kept Jane at a distance. She tried to remember how Jenny had acted at the last archeology meeting, when things were so chaotic, but she just wasn't paying attention and just couldn't remember. But these dreams – she had had three of them in the last month. And they weren't nice. Jane decided to try to shake it off. She would see how Jenny acted at the January archeology meeting. Jane didn't want to dwell on it anymore. She looked around realizing she was the first to wake-up. She didn't want to disturb the others so she got dressed and headed toward the door.

She quietly stepped out of the yurt and into the chilly morning. Her eyes were drawn to the stunning rays of the morning sun walking their way over the distant trees and toward the forest in front of her. She listened to the early morning critters, smiled, stretched, and yawned. It was an amazingly beautiful morning. She decided, since everyone else was still sleeping, that she would start a fire in the 'fire-circle' and cook breakfast outside. Since the sun was just starting to rise and it was still a little chilly, she quietly crept back inside the yurt, snatched a sweatshirt and added it to what she was already wearing. She also grabbed dry socks to put on with her hiking boots. She thought about getting out the metal detector and checking out the area around the yurt, but decided to stick to just making breakfast.

She was an avid hiker and camper so starting a small fire was not difficult for her. She gathered twigs and dry pine needles in the area to get the fire started. Then she added a couple small logs for a bigger more sustainable fire. She visited the little girls room while the fire was going, then washed her hands and gathered ingredients for breakfast. They brought a dozen eggs and some bacon with them when they first came up to the park, so, she decided she would cook the bacon first then use the bacon grease to cook the eggs. She planned on cooking all of them so she would just make scrambled eggs for everyone.

The fire was beginning to set perfectly for cooking so she put the wire grate across the fire pit, placed the coffee pot on the side and started cooking bacon in their skillet. She always used a cast iron skillet for cooking in the out of doors. In her opinion, this type of skillet handles campfires the best. The coffee was hot and she had just poured herself a cup when Todd came outside.

"Coffee smells good," he said. "Actually, so does the bacon."

"Grab yourself a cup and I'll pour you some of the hot stuff," she told him, pointing to the cups.

"Ahhhh. Now that's good!" he sighed. Thanks."

"You're welcome," she said to him.

They sat together on a small log near the fire-circle. They both sipped hot coffee as she occasionally flipped the bacon.

"Today's our last full day," he said, "can you believe it?"

"Not really," she replied. "It just seems like the time flew by."

"I know you've been thinking a lot about your uncle," he continued, "but I hope the fact that we haven't found anything from what he's told you, from his stories I mean, I hope it hasn't spoiled the trip for you."

"Oh no, of course not," she said, turning to him. "I love it up here. It's so peaceful. Of course, it would have been kind of neat to find something, anything. But I love hiking. And I love being with you. That's what counts. And I knew we didn't have a lot of time. We didn't even get a chance to use the metal detectors. But that's O.K.," she said.

"And I've really enjoyed Jack and Gail," Jane continued, I like her a lot. And, she's good for him you know."

"Yes, I certainly agree with you there. He seems to have settled down around her. I hope he grabs on and doesn't let go."

Jane laughed, "yeah, you know, I think she'd like that."

They were quiet for a couple minutes and then Todd spoke up.

"Jane, what if we find something up on that cliff? I mean what if there's clues to some ancient people, or Indian artefacts from the last century, or even a cave with some kind of pictograph language on the walls, or something like that? What would you do?"

"Good question," she said. "I think we'd have to contact the right authorities. I mean this is a state park, so anything we might find legally belongs to the state. But it would be nice if I could be involved in any research. Or, anything like that, including any kind of excavation. I guess I'd have to take a sabbatical from work. I would hope the school system would approve something like that. I don't know. I almost think that's like finding bigfoot's lair, if you know what I mean."

Todd laughed. "Is that your way of saying you don't want to count your chickens?"

"Yah," she said. "You got it."

He laughed and gave her a big hug.

"Todd," she said.

He looked at her, just because of the way she said his name.

"Yes," he said gently.

"I just have this strange feeling. Maybe it sounds weird, but it's a jittery kind of feeling, like I'm missing something. I don't know whether it's because I've been rushing around for the last few weeks, or I'm just anxious because I want to find something for my uncle," she said. "I think I should try to ignore the feeling and don't let it bother me, but I can't seem to ignore it. It's just nagging at me."

"Look," he said. "I would never tell you to disregard your feelings. Always be aware. But in this case, we've got each other's back, right?" She shook her head yes.

"Plus, I trust Jacks ability to be aware of his surroundings. Let's trust each other's instincts and let things play out. If you see something that bothers you, say so, otherwise let's just enjoy our time here in the porkies. Sound OK?"

"Yeah, I think it does," she said. "Thanks."

She stirred the bacon more. It seemed to be done so she transferred the bacon over to some paper towels she had waiting. She wiped some of the grease out of the pan, then poured the scrambled eggs she had prepared into the pan. She asked Todd to go wake Jack and Gail while she put slices of bread on the side of the grill to toast. Breakfast was almost ready.

Todd just got to the door when both Jack and Gail came out of the yurt.

"I don't know about you guys but I can't possibly sleep anymore with that wonderful smell wafting through the air," blurted Jack. "My stomach is yelling at me to get my ass out of bed and check it out."

"I guess me too," said Gail, laughing. "The coffee really smells good."

"Help yourself," said Jane. "The paper cups are right over there."

"The bacon is ready, the eggs are almost ready, and the toast will be done shortly. There's plenty of coffee," she continued. "If someone could pull out the plates and plastic forks, we'll be good to go."

"I'll do that," said Gail. And she had paper plates, plastic forks, and paper towels ready by the time Jane brought the hot, egg filled skillet, to the picnic table. The bacon was already on the table under some paper towels. Jane collected the toast and they all sat down to breakfast.

The food was gone in no time. Jane was concerned that all the eggs wouldn't be eaten, but apparently, they all had good appetites this morning because not only did the eggs all disappear, but every piece of bacon and every piece of toast was devoured as well. They had to make one more pot of coffee, but that was no big deal.

"Since you cooked," said Gail to Jane and Todd, "we'll clean up."

"What!" said Jack. "Oh, yah, right. We'll clean up," he said rolling his eyes.

Todd looked at Jane who had a big grin on her face.

"Yup, she's good for him," Jane whispered to Todd as they headed back into the yurt to pack for the day. Todd held the door for Jane, as he watched Jack start helping Gail clean up the picnic table. He just smiled and followed Jane inside the yurt.

CHAPTER 30

Back at Cuyahoga Peak

THERE WAS A small stream behind the yurt where Gail and Jack cleaned the cookware. Once the dishes were done, they headed back to the yurt.

"I'll dispose of all the garbage," she told Jack, "if you make sure the fire is totally out.

"I can certainly do that," he said.

Once those chores were done Jack and Gail went back into the yurt to organize their backpacks for the days hike.

All of them had packed a few things last night, but Jane wanted to review what they had. It would be a one-day trip back up to the overhang near Cuyahoga Peak and back again. At least that was the plan. Todd had already reviewed the climbing that would be involved and made sure he had all the climbing equipment he felt they would need.

"OK," said Jane. "Last check. We all have the climbing harnesses Todd gave us. Todd and Jack are carrying the rest of the climbing gear, ropes and such. Todd also has his rifle with ammo. Jack has the fishing gear. Gail has the food for lunch and maybe a snack, and her camera of course. I'm carrying extra water, flashlights. Today I think I'll leave the metal detector at the yurt. We really don't need it. We don't need sleeping or overnight gear either, but in case we're out late make sure you bring a sweater and/or jacket. And make sure you have plenty of water. Am I forgetting anything?" she asked.

Everyone shook their heads.

"Alright then," said Jane, with a bit of excitement. "Let's head out. I'll lead the way."

And she did. They left the yurt and headed up the way they did before, heading north toward 'Lost Lake Trail'. They'd all been up this trail earlier so there would be few surprises, if any. They would follow Lost Lake Trail up past Government Peak Trail toward Union Spring. This time they would pass the backcountry campsite just north of Union Spring. They didn't have heavy backpacks so they could move quickly. Even with taking short breaks, mostly to let Gail take some pictures, they made good time. And they wouldn't be spending the night this time anywhere on the trail. Even so, it would still be at least a couple hours before they got to their destination.

They didn't stop often but when they did Gail always took the opportunity to take plenty of pictures. The rare sites of small wildlife captivated her.

"I know we've only been here a few days," she said to no one in particular, "but I feel like I already know these trails. And I have lots of pictures of the trails, and the Mountains in the distance."

"It is breathtaking, isn't it?" Jane said, looking around.

Although they were on a mission to reach Cuyahoga Peak, they took in, and enjoyed, the beauty of their surroundings. The clarity of the light blue sky was amazing, and the chill in the air made the day feel crispy.

"I know now," said Gail, "that if we're quiet enough, we can hear all the sounds of nature around us. "You learn fast," said Jane. "That's the trick you know; trying to be quiet. So many people hike and camp and walk the out of doors, but they don't hear anything. They don't know how to listen. If it's not the sound of their own boots then it's the constant chatter going on in their heads. That constant sound of their own hectic lives can be deafening."

"Just listen to it all," said Gail, with a big smile on her face.

They could hear the wind blowing through the trees. They could even hear it change directions by the rustling of the leaves. They also heard small crickets chirping and frogs ribbiting, some close by, some in the distance.

By listening they learned that squirrels are little chatterboxes. And they heard a menagerie of bird song all around them, some cooing, some screeching and screaming. Some were close by while others were far away. They even heard the noise of the many brooks and streams way before they even passed them. The term 'babbling brook' takes on a whole new meaning when you hear it in the deep woods, and especially when you hear it and see it at the same time. They also heard the shuffle of small animals scurrying away as the foursome approached. They enjoyed all these unique sounds coming from all around them. They found that sometimes even the click of Gail's camera echoed like a deafening intrusion in the symphony nature was giving them. It was a wonderfully peaceful hike.

"Here's where we turn off," said Jane, leading everyone off the main trail.

"This time lets head up slope earlier then last time and avoid having to walk through that swampy area," said Todd.

"No problem," said Jane, leading them accordingly. "I'll still keep us parallel to the Carp River, just higher up."

"There's more weeds this way," said Gail.

"Better than getting wet shoes," said Jack.

"That's true," said Gail.

Before long they started to recognize the trail they had taken yesterday.

When they came across the ravine they needed to cross, it was no problem. They still used a rope for safety but Gail knew exactly what to do and had a bit more confidence to do it. She still shuffled along and took a little more time than the others, but it was no big deal this time, and they were over the ravine and back on the trail in no time. It wasn't long before they came into the clearing under the overhang. It was close enough to lunch that they all decided to sit down, have a little lunch, and get themselves ready for their climb.

CHAPTER 31

Todd's Plan

THE TIME FINALLY came that Jane was waiting for. She really wanted to know what was on that cliff, the overhang, whatever. She was tense and knew it, even her hands were sweating. She was trying to settle herself down a little. It wasn't like her to be so wired up. Todd noticed it too. When Gail and Jack wondered over to a scenic area Todd walked over to Jane.

"What's up?" he said.

"I don't know," she responded. "I still feel jittery, like something's wrong. But I know nothing's wrong. You and I have both climbed before. So, I'm not nervous about that. It's just a weird feeling."

"I know what it is," said Todd.

Jane looked at him but didn't say anything.

"Look," he said, "you're really close to your uncle. Right?"

"Well, yes," she responded slowly.

"This whole trip," Todd said, as he waved his arm in a circle, "it's really about finding something for him, isn't it?"

She didn't want to admit it but Todd was right.

He watched her absorb what he just said.

"I know you really want something for him, but you need to accept the fact that you may not find what you're looking for. If anything, you can tell him about the so-called bigfoot siting they had."

She laughed at his attempt at making the conversation light.

"You're right," she finally said. "I had myself so pumped about finding that stupid crevice, or whatever him and his buddies found, or say they found, that I'm not being realistic. I guess admitting that out loud, even just to myself, is at least facing reality."

"Just think of it this way," Todd continued, "you can tell him that you followed his map. Maybe you could even draw another map of your own and put in more details. Use the park trail map you've been using since we got here. He'd like that. Maybe it'll even spark more memories for him. Tell him about this climb we're doing. He'll like that too. Plus, with all the pictures Gail's taking, you'll have those to share with him as well."

Jane put her arms around Todd and held tight. He hugged her back. Todd, of course was right. She began to feel the tension in herself dissolve.

"Thank you," she whispered in his ear.

Gail and Jack came back from taking pictures over the valley. They were smiling and holding hands. "It's beautiful up here," said Gail to Jane and Todd. "We could see for miles, and I got some great pictures."

"You're going to have to share some of those you know," said Jane, with a smile.

"Oh", I will," said Gail. "Plus, I'll have lots to show my first graders."

"You guys ready for a climb," asked Todd.

"Yup," said Jack. "We're ready to go."

"OK then," continued Todd. "First things first. Everyone get their harnesses on. I'll collect my stash of anchors bolts and rope. Jack, if you don't mind, I'd like you to feed me the rope as I climb. I have a few carabiners for myself, but as I place the anchors bolts, you feed the rope to me and I'll feed the rope through the anchors bolts. I'm going to make a type of guide rope, or clothesline for everyone to follow as we go up, and I'll try to put the anchor bolts close together so there will be minimal reaching. We really didn't plan this so let's just take our time and be safe. Everyone wears their helmet. Please remember that we have no climbing gloves, and no specialized climbing shoes. At least our hiking boots will give us some grip, and remember, we all work together as a team. That means if we're going to do this we're doing it slowly all the way. There is a lot about climbing that would be impossible to teach everyone today. That includes climbing terminology, how to make certain types of knots, and what to call certain moves. So, what I'm going to do is make everything as safety oriented as possible. Everyone agree?"

Jane, Jack, and Gail were all listening carefully. They knew Todd was serious and had their utmost safety in mind. And they all shook their heads yes.

Todd continued, "everyone will get two quickdraws. They're two carabiners attached together by a length of thick pre-sewn webbing material. You will all also get an ATC, or belay device. They will all be attached to your harness like such. I'll explain in a minute what we'll use it for. I'm going to show Jack how to be a belayer. That way when we're ready to come down off the overhang, we can come straight down. That's the easy-way".

Jane and Gail just looked at each other. Neither said anything.

Todd attached two quickdraws to each of their harnesses and demonstrated how they open and close. He also attached the ATC and explained how they will be used when everyone is ready to descend. He walked through the belayer's duties with Jack a couple times to make sure he was comfortable.

"OK," Todd said, "I know this climb, straight up, is only fifty feet. It's double that, or maybe even more, if we traverse, or go across the cliff diagonally, as we're going to do. That doesn't seem far, but it would still hurt if anyone fell from that distance. My plan is for nobody to fall. Sound good."

"Absolutely! "said Jane. "I'm hoping this will be an easy trip," she continued. "I would really like to show my uncle that we did a good search of the area he was in as a young hiker. Maybe, as Todd suggested to me, I can draw out a new map for him to compare his with. Maybe I'll even include some of Gail's pictures, which is why I asked you to share a few if you didn't mind," she said to Gail.

"No problem," said Gail. "Like I said, consider it done."

CHAPTER 32

Todd's Climb

TODD STARTED HIS hand grips up the slope at about six feet high. That way he could place the first couple anchor bolts at about eye level. He hooked himself up to the anchor bolts as he climbed and he also had Jack attach the belay rope to add more safety. He placed the anchor bolts just two feet apart, and sometimes only eighteen inches, so the shift from anchor to anchor wouldn't be difficult for his friends. It seemed a little overkill to him but he knew none of them were experienced climbers. He was just learning the whole mountain climbing sport himself and felt he knew enough to add a little safety to their climb. But, although he had climbs under his belt, he didn't consider himself an experienced climber either. He was extremely happy that the cliff shelf they were heading to was only fifty feet high.

Jack followed Todd along as he traversed the cliff wall. He was holding tight to the belay rope knowing that Todd had told him that he should never let go of the lower rope. He was giving Todd more rope as he needed it but was trying to make sure he kept the slack out of the belay line.

The girls were watching in awe as Todd went further and further up the cliff. It was kind of exciting to watch. Jane had gone with Todd to some of the indoor climbing walls when he first started to practice climbing. But as he got better and better and some of his friends offered to take him to some of the easier cliffs and peaks in the area, she declined the invitation. She was beginning to think that she should have gone with them. Maybe next time she thought to herself. Maybe next time.

Gail was snapping pictures as Todd moved higher and higher. She had pictures of Todd, and pictures of Jack holding the belay rope, and pictures of Jane. At one-time Jane took Gail's camera and took some pictures of Jack and Gail together in their climbing gear. If anything, they would have a good collection of snapshots of hiking in the 'porkies', and climbing part of the Cuyahoga Peak cliff face.

It didn't take long for Todd to complete the climb, even being careful, going slow, and placing anchor bolts along the way. His plan, once he reached the top, was to place at least four anchor bolts at the top, so that each of them had a safety latch to secure themselves. That way, as the four of them were all up on the shelf together they could safely hook in and prevent any accidental falls. He was securing the fourth anchor when he saw it.

"Holy 'shit'," he said to himself. "Jane's going to have a canary."

In front of him, but mostly hidden from view by brush, was a small opening in the cliff. He knew it wouldn't be visible from above. It was low to the ground, and maybe, just maybe, big enough for a normal size person to crawl into. If he pulled away some of the brush and moved some of the sand, he hoped it would be big enough for the four of them to squeeze through. It depended on what's on the inside and he couldn't tell without looking if an animal is or isn't camping out in there. Anything was possible. There is no way he could look now. If he disappeared from Jane's view, she'd have a conniption. He'll have to tell everyone about it when he went back down, and they'll all investigate it together.

"What are you doing up there," yelled Jane.

"Just placing extra anchors," he yelled back.

There's no sense in delaying he thought. She's going to want to check this out, without a doubt. He really wanted to look inside himself, but who knows what's in there. His thoughts went immediately to all the jitters Jane's been having. Maybe he shouldn't have blown them off so easily. Some people just have a sixth sense about things. Maybe there's a reason Jane's been having these weird feelings after all.

He looked around. The actual cliff overhang was bigger than he thought it would be. The brush growing in the area hid a lot. He estimated it to be about eight feet long and four feet wide. Much bigger then what it looked like from below. That's plenty big enough for four people to stand, or even sit on. He went to the edge of the cliff and waved down. He was directly above the campsite area.

"Hey Jack, you ready for your first test?"

"I think so," Jack yelled back.

"You better be more than thinking you're ready," Jane squealed at him.

"I got this girl, relax," he said back to her.

"Belayer ready," Jack yelled.

"Starting to belay," Todd yelled back.

It was perfect. Todd belayed down while Jack released the rope little at a time to allow for a gradual descent. They were in sync and Todd was on the ground in just a couple minutes.

Todd hit the ground softly and turned to Jack. "Good job my friend. Maybe you'd like to try rock climbing with me and my buddies back home."

"I think I'd like that," he said.

Jack felt great. He thought just maybe this rock climbing might be something he could get into.

Then Todd turned to Jane. "We need to talk!" he said.

Jane's blood pressure just went up a notch. "What'd you find," she said.

CHAPTER 33

The Cave Discovered

"LET'S SIT FOR a minute," said Todd. They all sat. Then he took a big swig of water before he began.

"There's something up there," he said. "I'm not sure what exactly because I didn't want to investigate by myself. But I can tell you this much," he continued. "There's a small opening to what looks like a cave up there."

"Oh my gosh, oh my gosh, oh my gosh!" Jane jumped to her feet! She was mumbling to herself with such speed and exhilaration that she could hardly contain her thrill at such news. Her mind was spinning with possibilities. She suddenly felt restless, which is exactly what Todd knew would happen. He let her be for just a second then got up, went over to her and grabbed her shoulders.

"Take a breath, will ya," he said to her, grabbing her shoulders to stop her from pacing.

"Look at me," he told her.

She looked right at him. "I know," she said. "I know. You don't even have to tell me. It's obvious I'm excited. And, I definitely am, no doubt. But, I also know this could be nothing, but then it could be something. I also know we're talking fifty feet in the air and we need to play it safe."

Todd was pleased with her response. Sometimes her mind went fifty miles an hour and because this was so high off the ground he wanted to talk things through before deciding on the approach they would take.

Let's make a plan," she said. "You know me. I'm better if I can make a plan."

"OK, let's sit," he said, as he started to explain again what he saw.

He looked directly at Jane, "I found what looks like a small opening to a cave at the back of the overhang. I didn't see it at first because it's covered over with weeds."

"No shit," said Jack.

"Wow!" said Gail.

"Yah, I know," he said to everyone. "It was a bit of a surprise to me too. But let's all take a breather and, like Jane said, make some plans. Can I assume everyone wants to investigate?" he said. "I know Jane and I do but let's hear it."

"Hell yah!" said Jack.

Gail was quiet.

"Gail?" asked Todd. "What do you think?"

"It's kind of creepy weird," said Gail, "but yah, I'm kind of interested. What do we need to do? And if I go in and don't like it, can I come back out?"

"Absolutely," said Todd and Jack at the same time.

"You don't need to even go up there if you don't want to," said Jack.

"Oh, I want to go up there," she said. "I just don't know about going in the cave. Can I make up my mind when I get there?"

"Sure. No problem," said Jack.

"Nobody has to do anything they don't want to do", said Todd.

"Let's go over everything and then everyone can decide for themselves what they want, or don't want to do," he continued.

Todd let everyone have a second then explained.

"First, the overhang is bigger than it looks from down here. It only sticks out four feet, but it's about eight feet long, maybe longer.

That means there's plenty of room on the shelf for all of us. Plus, I secured four anchor bolts so that we all have a safety anchor to latch onto. I didn't do any investigation when I was up there. The opening, like I said, is kind of covered over by weeds and such. However, I believe any weeds or bushes in the way can easily be pulled out. We may also need to pull some sand away from the opening, to make it big enough for all of us to get through.

For this trip, if she wants, I think I'll let Jane decide who goes in the cave first."

He looked at Jane. "What do you think?" he said.

Jane just smiled. She had calmed down now.

"You know me way to well," she said. "You know I want to go in first."

"Any objections," he said, looking at Jack and Gail. They were both smiling.

"We both know what this means to Jane," said Jack. "We have no objections at all."

"Well, that was easy enough," said Todd. "I just have some conditions first."

"Conditions!" said Jane, gazing at him. "Like what?" she asked questionably.

"First, any sign of danger, you retreat," he said looking at her.

"Second, you wear a safety rope the whole time you're in there."

"Third, you take a flashlight and the first several feet, before your whole body is in the cave, you describe to us what you see."

"Fourth, and I repeat, any sign of danger, you retreat."

"Those are all good conditions," she said. "I have no problem with any of them. I'm not out to put myself, or anyone I'm with, in any kind of danger. Todd, you know I like adventure, but I hope you also know I try to be realistic. Besides," she said, "we just got married and I'm not done with you yet."

She got up and hugged him.

"OK, you two," said Jack. "Let's do this. How do you want to proceed Todd?"

"Since all of us are going up there, we'll have to do without a belay rope. Everyone will hook together, and we'll each individually hook to the anchor bolts I placed. Do as we talked about and find a foot hold and a hand hold every step of the way. Go slow and careful. There's no hurry. If someone falls, we may have to lower them down and start over. Everyone's safety is primary to anything else, including that cave. Everyone agree?" he asked.

They all agreed.

"Just like we did when we crossed the ravine," said Todd. "I'll go first, then Jane, then Gail, and Jack you'll follow everyone."

They all agreed and their ascent began.

CHAPTER 34

Jane's Cave Adventure

THEY FOLLOWED EACH other closely. Todd took his time, waiting for Jane to catch up before getting to far ahead. Gail was better at this than going across the ravine so she was keeping up just fine. Finding an area for foot and hand holds wasn't as difficult as she had imagined. And Jack had no problem bringing up the rear. Their pace wasn't fast but it wasn't slow either, and before they knew it Todd was at the overhang with Jane right behind him. They both clipped into the safety anchors Todd had placed as Gail and Jack both arrived at the top of the climb as well. They also clipped into their safety anchors fairly quickly.

Gail turned around and saw the view from fifty feet higher than she did before.

"Oh, my, goodness," she said. "How beautiful is that!"

They all turned and looked at the view of the lush forest of the Porcupine Mountains. Gail took pictures in all directions, including down. They all carried their small backpacks up with them so there was nothing below but the small clearing they were in and the trees surrounding it. They all sat for a moment, took in the view, and drank a little water.

It wasn't long before Jane turned to the area near the back of the small overhang they were all standing on. That's where Todd had mentioned he spotted the cave. It wasn't hard to examine. Her and Todd pulled a few weeds away so they could see the opening more clearly. Being on the cliff together was like everyone being in someone's kitchen while they were cooking, busy and crowded. Except for the cliff of course. That's why Jack and Gail just watched as Todd and Jane pulled brush away exposing the cave opening. Todd was right, it wasn't big. But it was definitely big enough for a person to crawl through. They used their hands to shovel some of the sand away from the opening as well, making it just a bit bigger. Then Jane looked at Todd. She was ready to go.

"OK," said Todd. "I'm going to attach you to the belay rope we have and clip you to me. If anything happens just pull on the rope. Do you have your flashlight?" he asked her, as he put the appropriate knots in the rope. She took her backpack off. She pulled out a small headlamp she was carrying in her backpack and put it on. That would give her light and leave her hands free. Her plan was to leave her backpack on the overhang. She didn't see any reason to bring it in the cave with her.

"Anything else you think I'll need?"

"Not that I can think of," said Todd. "Remember, you're only going in to look around. And watch for bats or other small animals. Don't go to deep into the cave either. Verify that there's room for all of us and we'll be right behind you."

"Understood," said Jane.

Todd double checked her harness and ropes and Jane was ready to enter the cave. She had to get down on her hands and knees to go forward. With digging away the sand the cave entrance was now over a foot in height. It was wider though so not too difficult to get into.

She noticed it as soon as she entered the cave. The entry went down gradually. She went in about three feet and down about six inches before the cave actually opened up, and wow, did it open up. Todd still had sight of her feet and asked her what she was seeing.

"You won't believe this until you see it," she said. "The cave opens up about three feet inside. I mean it really opens up! The first three feet are like out there, sandy, but it angles down slightly as you enter. Further on in it looks rocky, just like any other cave. Let me go a little further and I'll see how far I have to go before I can stand. Todd let go of her feet and let her crawl further inside.

"Don't go too far," he said.

"Can't go too far," she said, "I'm attached." He laughed at her cute joke.

The other three companions listened to her describing the inside of the cave.

"The cave opens up about three, maybe four feet in," she said.

"The walls don't appear to be anything special. They look like cave walls but they do have a mixture of both the grey basalt rock and the pink rhyolite rock. I can tell there's also something else mixed in with it, maybe some copper. It's hard to tell. Maybe we can check it out later with the metal detector. Seeing rhyolite this far north seems weird to me," she said, "but at least it's all dry here at the entrance."

She was quiet for a minute while she looked around, then she began speaking again. "I can hear water trickling from somewhere. The left wall is a couple feet from the opening and it's dry as well. But the whole things kind of goes around to the right. The ceiling appears to be maybe eight feet high in most places. I don't see anything special, but about ten feet in it goes around a big boulder, and then it appears to take a left and seems to go down a bit. After that it's hard to see. I'm standing now and the ground seems firm. It's not slippery or anything. I don't even see any bats, yet. I can't see past the big boulder so I'd like to check out what's around the bend from there. What do you think?"

"OK," said Todd, but just around the corner. Don't go further, OK?"

"Sure thing," she said.

"Do you have enough rope for her to go further," asked Jack.

"I have about a hundred feet," said Todd.

As they were talking the rope went taught! Todd tried to pull in slack but there was none. Something happened!

"Holy shit," said Todd.

"Pull!" he told Jack.

They both pulled on the rope.

"Jane!" Todd yelled.

"Jane! Answer me!"

"Dammit Jane, answer me."

They couldn't hear her. She wasn't responding, and they couldn't pull the rope any further. It was taught.

He could barely here an audible noise coming from inside the cave. But the rope wasn't moving. They weren't losing any more length, but they couldn't seem to pull it back either.

"I'm going in there," said Todd. He switched the belay line to Jack. "You two keep a good grip on this rope and don't let it slide. I have another smaller rope in my pack. If it's just the rope stuck and I can loosen it, I'll pull once on the rope for you to start pulling in the slack." He was talking and pulling at the extra rope as he talked. He didn't hesitate but dove into the cave after his young wife.

"Jane," he called again. No answer.

Todd got out his small headlamp and put it on. He also pulled out a flashlight and took a good look around. Unlike Jane, he left his backpack on when he came into the cave. It had climbing gear in it in case he needed something. He noticed that it was pretty dry inside, just like Jane had said. Then he spotted where the rope Jack and Gail were holding onto, had gone. Around the huge rock Jane mentioned. She said she was going around a corner so he knew Jane was on the other end of that rope, but he couldn't see the other end. He took a step closer but heard the faint trickle of water that Jane described. He didn't know what happened to Jane but he didn't want to fall into the same predicament so he attached a couple anchor bolts to the inside walls of the cave and hooked himself up using the extra rope. Once he felt his ropes were secure, he continued forward.

"Jane," he called again. As he got around the huge rock he noticed the ground was damp. He took another step forward and almost slipped. As he moved further he felt the ground take a noticeable dip. Then he saw her. She was tight up against the left wall of the cave, holding onto what appeared to be a huge tree root.

"Hey Jane," he yelled.

She looked up when she heard her name.

"You OK?" he asked.

She shook her head yes and motioned for him to come down to her. The going was slow but he hugged the wall she was on as he went, noticing the trickle of water increased as he went further down into the cave, making the noise increase as well. He noticed the number of tree roots also increased, so he used them to hold onto along with his rope. When he reached her, he thought she would be terribly frightened but that's not what her facial expression indicated.

"I'm caught on this branch," she said. "I tried calling but the noise made by the water is kind of loud down here so I didn't know if you even heard me. Anyway, I'm OK, but, you need to see this. Then we'll get out of here. Look down over there."

She pointed to the right and aimed her flashlight so Todd could see what she was pointing at.

CHAPTER 35

Todd Goes in After Jane
– Mystery Revealed

THE SLOPE TOOK a steep dip as it progressed forward. He looked around as best he could with the small headlamp he had put on his helmet. He could tell there was some kind of bottom to the cave, at least he thought it was a bottom. But it was still too hard to tell. The water seemed to come from both sides and it was gurgling and rushing from both sides. Yet, it wasn't getting deeper, so it had to be going somewhere. He didn't know for sure. But what caught his eye was what was on the far wall where she was pointing.

"Is that what I think it is?" he asked her.

"I think so," she said. "But it's wedged pretty tight into that corner, and there's a lot of tree roots all around it. Whoever it was had to have slipped exploring this cave and has been there for a very long time. If they were alone, that would explain why they're still here," she said.

It was a skeleton! No doubt!

"Are you thinking what I think you're thinking?" he asked her.

"Well, it's a possibility, don't you agree?"

"I think it's a very good possibility," he said. "I would love to try to belay down there and check around. I can't see much detail so there's no telling if whoever it was has ID on them or not. However, he continued, you're already stuck and I don't think we should take the chance of both of us getting stuck."

"I'm sorry about that," she said. "I didn't realize the floor was so slippery."

"That's why we hooked you up," he said. "Safety first, remember."

He saw how her rope got tangled in the tree roots as she slid down the cave floor.

"OK," he said. I'm going to go above you and untangle your ropes. I may have to cut away some of the tree roots. Then I'll send Jack a signal to pull you up. You ready?"

"Yes. I'm ready," she said.

He pulled himself up a little above her until he found the problem. He had to take out his knife and cut away a couple of dangling finger size tree roots that had wrapped around her rope. Once he did that, and freed the rope, then Jane was free to maneuver.

Jack felt the tug on his end of the rope and slowly started pulling out any slack he felt. He knew it was a little unorthodox the way he was doing it but none of them were experts so he did his best to belay whoever was on the other end. Between him pulling and Todd helping Jane up the slippery slope of the cave, they managed to get to the dry area of the cave and better footing. And from there they were back at the cave entrance within minutes. Jane exited the cave first, then Todd. Gail grabbed Jane into a big bear hug. "I'm so glad you're safe," she said. "Are you OK? Oh man, you're soaked."

"Thanks," said Jane, out of breath and only a little tired. "I'm glad I'm safe too. It was dry at first but then I went around this huge boulder a few paces into the cave, and took one step to many. It was like taking a left-hand turn and it was wet and slick, and I slid about twenty feet before I could catch myself. I actually think the rope in this doohickey thing Todd gave us locked, which was probably what stopped me from falling further."

Gail knew immediately by the way Jane was acting that something was up. Jane was not scared. She was exhilarated.

"OK, what's going on," she said. "You don't look like you almost slid into oblivion in a cave. You look excited. You saw something didn't you?" Gail said.

"You're very observant," said Jane. "Yes," she continued, hardly able to contain herself. "You guys are not going to believe what we found," Jane said. She looked at Todd.

"Go ahead," said Todd. "Tell them."

"There's a skeleton in there!" Jane told them, with a bit too much excitement.

"EEW," said Gail. "That's nasty."

"Was it human," asked Jack.

"Definitely!" said Todd. "I wanted so bad to go check it out, but under the circumstances, with Jane's rope tangled, and the steep downward wet slope of that area of the cave, I thought it better we come back out for now, maybe discuss it a little."

Todd was excited now. The more he thought about the fact that this could be the missing boy from Jane's grandfathers story, the more he wanted to go back.

"Remember the story Jane told us about the missing boy?" he said.

"You don't think that could be him!" Jack said, surprised.

"It's the right area," said Todd. "Plus, we couldn't even hear Jane when we knew she was in there. And she said she yelled for us. I bet any shouting for help he did, was never heard. Plus, it's a skeleton. It, he, could easily have been in there for fifty years or more. I'd love to check it out."

"You're kidding, right? It's too dangerous," said Jane. "We couldn't even see for sure if there WAS a cave bottom. And what happens if what we saw is not the bottom? What then? What if the water gets higher and has a current, and you get dragged under? Don't you think this is the time we call the authorities?"

Todd took a good long look at Jane.

"Is that what you want?" he said, looking at her. "Really?"

"Oh man, honestly," she said, "No! That's not what I want. You know me, the adventure queen! I would love to find a clue to that persons' identity. I would love to go back to my uncle and be able to tell him we found his friend, if indeed our assumption is correct. But, I don't want you, or Jack, or Gail, any of us, to get hurt, or worse," she said quietly. Remember, I told you when we started this trip, that there would be no danger. Things have sort of changed. I mean I didn't expect this to happen, really. I have to admit, it was scary sliding down that wet slope. I mean before the rope caught and I was able to grab those roots. It was damn scary!"

"What you just said," Todd told her, "about the danger that's involved, is very true. There is danger involved. I'll be the first to admit that. And the first step of getting through the danger is understanding that it exists. This is not something any of us should take lightly. But think about this. There's four of us. All we want to do is see if this guy had ID on him. That's all. If something happens, someone goes for help. All those nervous twitches you've been having could have led us right to this. But it's your call. This is your trip, really. I mean it, really. We'll do whatever you say. What do you think?"

CHAPTER 36

The Skeleton's Identity

TODD WAS WAITING for Jane's response. She loved the out-of-doors. That's no question. He also knew that sometimes she overthinks things, so he needed to give her a minute to work through this in her head. Jane looked at both Jack and Gail.

"What are you guys thinking?" she asked.

"I'm all in," said Jack, just a little too quickly.

"It's a guy thing," Gail said, mostly to Jane. "But," she said hesitating, "I think we should do this one thing. You went in there not knowing about the slick downgrade. But now we know, and we're prepared. This is what you want to do. You're more concerned for all of us than getting what you want. That's exactly why I want to do it. You're thinking of others, not yourself. I kind of like that."

Jane gave Gail a friendly hug. "OK, let's do this," she said. "But safely!"

"OK", said Todd, taking that as his que. "The immediate interior of the cave is dry and easy to walk on, plus there's plenty of room for the four of us, so I think we can all go inside without ropes. Once we're inside I'll set anchor hooks like I did out here. I already set a few so we just need a few more. The plan is just to go down and see if this person we spotted has any kind of ID or anything. It was hard to see any detail from where Jane and I were located. The remains were down about fifteen or twenty feet, and on the other side of the slope. Plus, there's water running downhill which makes it really slippery. And we don't know where it goes. I believe we still have enough rope to do what we need to do without taking our guide rope down that we used to get up here. But we need lights so our headlamps and any extra flashlight will come in handy. And Gail, I don't know how your camera does inside a dark cave, but if you can take some pictures, I think we should try."

"I can certainly do that," said Gail. "I already took pictures of the cave entrance, and the guide rope you put up to get us up here as well. I just thought it was like keeping a photo journal that we could look back on later."

"Good job," said Jane.

"Just one more question," said Todd. "Jane, do you remember if your uncle said anything particular about this missing kid. I mean was he carrying anything that could be identified?"

"You know", she said, "I do remember him talking about how they all would wear those bandanna's. He said they all wore red so if anyone got lost they could spot it. That was kind of their thing, you know, wave the red bandanna if you need help. Doesn't help if you're stuck in a cave though, does it?"

It was a rhetorical question that nobody answered.

"All right," said Todd, "let's head inside. Once inside and everyone gets their bearings, we'll decide where to place the anchor bolts. Jack, you can be on the belay rope if you don't mind. You've done it a couple times already so that helps. We'll do a true belay this time, with you and I working together as a team. Then I'm going to set up a second rope on the opposite wall," he said, pointing to where the wall on the far side of the cave would be. "I'm hoping you and Gail can hook up there and shine some light on where I'm going," he said to Jane. "And Gail can take some pictures," he said directly to Gail.

"We can do that, right Gail?"

"Absolutely," she responded.

They all headed inside the cave.

Once inside they could look around and get their bearings. The cave, once pitch dark, lit up with the bright glow of their lanterns. It was bigger than they originally thought, made of the dry grey basalt rock and the pink rhyolite rock they saw outside. It somehow seemed to shimmer in the light. They saw the other color Jane mentioned as well. It looked like copper but they really weren't sure. Some parts of the walls were jagged yet there was no sign of any speleothems, like stalactites or other such protrusions on the rock surface. There was no sign of bats either, or any other small cave dwellers. Further in, as they looked toward the boulder Jane had stepped around earlier, the cave seemed to shimmer and the dampness became apparent. That's when they also became aware of, and heard, the running water.

Gail was awed by the size of the cave, not that it was that huge, only about the size of a small cottage, but that it expanded out of such a small opening. Todd set his anchor bolts and he and Jack discussed the belay process. They checked their gear once more to be sure everything looked good. Jack found a nice dry area on the cave floor where he could get a good foot hold for support. He was also secured by rope to a couple of Todd's anchor bolts on the cave wall. Then Todd began his descent. He went slowly on purpose to prevent any sliding, and he used the tree roots as well. The water started trickling around his boots but it was never deep enough to go over his ankles. Even as he got closer to his destination, the water never got deep. Todd was very aware that the water got really noisy as he got further down the slope. It was echoing but it was also gushing from or to somewhere, but it never got deep. It wasn't long before he reached the remains. Jane and Gail were safely hooked into a couple of Todd's anchor bolts, and they had their headlamps as well as an extra flashlight Jane had brought, focused on Todd. And Gail was taking lots of pictures.

When Todd reached the skeleton, he felt a wave of sympathy for this poor fellow. He looked at the hands still wrapped tightly around the surrounding tree roots. He noticed the smaller bone in the left leg had a crack in it. He was thinking that was the fibula bone. Whoever this was broke his leg, but there was no way Todd could tell if it happened in a fall or if it happened after death. What he did notice was the dirty bandanna still around the neck. He gently untied it and put it in his pocket. Then he searched what was left of the clothes worn by this poor fellow. His leather boots were in bad shape but still on his feet, and his belt held up most of his pants, or what was left of his pants. Todd found a wallet in the back pocket and took that as well. The shirt was torn to shreds as were his lower pant legs. It appeared that this poor fellow probably died of starvation, or if he had any cuts, he could have died of infection or fever. It was sad really. He was so close but still so far away from help. Todd couldn't help but wonder how this poor guy even got into this predicament.

"We'll get you out of here," Todd whispered. Then he tugged on his rope signaling to Jack to start pulling him up.

The way up took a little longer because he was climbing up slippery rocks, plus the water coming down had a current and the splashing water was soaking him. He reached his hand up to grab a rock he saw embedded in the wall. But when he grabbed the rock and tried to pull himself up his hand pulled the rock right out of the wall.

"What the heck," he said out loud. Parts of the wall were wet and muddy and as Todd grabbed at it sometimes mud would come away in his hand. Perplexed by that, he aimed his headlamp in that direction. He had to make sure he got a better grip so he could pull himself up. That's the last thing he needed was to fall back down the wet cave floor. He just wanted to get out of there and back to solid ground. But he also wondered why the wall was so saturated. That's when he noticed the trickling water. It was a small amount, but it was coming down the wall. He figured some of it must be rain water soaking in from above, but it hadn't rained in a few days. He knew because he and Jane had kept an eye on the weather for the past two weeks. It was a strange phenomenon that he couldn't readily explain. He knew it rained maybe ten days ago. But, he'd have to know more details about the peak and the type of earth it's made of to really make a good guess. Is that the cause of this much saturation, or not? He decided to see if he could dig into the wall. Maybe this is a fake wall. Or maybe there's more caves in this place. The mud wasn't as soft as he dug deeper. He had dug about eight inches in when he almost decided to quit. The dirt was soft, but it wasn't wet anymore. But the last handful he took broke through to the other side of the wall.

"You OK down there," yelled Jack.

"Yah, I'm good," Todd yelled back. I think I found something. Just give me a minute.

"O.K., just let me know when to pull you up," yelled Jack.

"And be careful," added Jane.

Then he saw it. "What the hell!" he started to say, as his voice trailed off. Then he looked again. "Oh, my god!" he said, totally out loud this time. "Is that really possible," he said to himself, temporarily stunned. Then his eyes started darting in every direction. He couldn't see much because the hole wasn't that big, plus it was about a ten-inch wall he was looking through. He didn't want to move. He wanted to see more. It was simply amazing that the second cave was even there!

He pulled himself closer to the hole he had made. He thought it would allow him to focus his light all around, but he couldn't see much so he turned his headlamp off. He focused on a spot in the distance where he couldn't believe his eyes. It was a light, no, a small campfire. And it appeared as if there was a man holding a stick. No, it was a rifle. He took another minute to look and with his light off he could see a little better. He didn't know if the person down there was friendly or not so he decided it was time to leave. He took another minute to absorb what he was seeing, but also wondering what Jane's going to say when he tells her about this.

"She'll go ballistic," he said to himself. He didn't want to drag his feet anymore so he signaled Jack and continued his ascent as efficiently and safely as possible. He took one more peak around and then pulled back and headed for safety. Once he made it to the top, and to his friends, he gathered his companions to a dry safe corner of the cave, where they all sat.

"OK", said Jane, overflowing with anxious energy. "Did you find anything? Why were you down there so long?"

Todd looked at her and smiled. "Check this out," he said, pulling out a filthy 'red' bandanna. Jane almost started crying. She was that emotional. After all, this was her uncle's story she heard about for years but never knew whether it was fact or fiction.

"Oh, my god," she said, taking the bandanna in her hands as if it were a precious souvenir. "It's him, isn't it? It's my uncle's friend, DB?"

"Well, let's see," said Todd, pulling out a dirty, wet, wallet.

Jane's eyes lit up like lanterns as Todd started to open the wallet. He did it carefully knowing that it could fall apart in his hands because it was so old. But inside, in plain view, was an identification card from 'Michigan Technological University' with the name 'Charles B. Denton'.

"That's him!" said Jane, with such absolute belief that the others knew it to be true. "That's him! Oh my gosh! Can you believe it! Holy shit! That's him."

"Now what?" she asked. "What do we do? Do we call in the rangers? We need to get him out of there. We need to see if he has, or had, relatives.

"What," she said, looking at Gail.

"There's a picture in there, look. I don't think you should try to move it because of how old and damaged it is, and, right now it's covered with that see thru plastic in the wallet so it's protected. But, it looks like three kids. If this Charles is the older one, that means he has siblings."

"We need to do something, that's for sure," said Jane. "Oh my gosh, I can't even imagine what my uncle will think. Wow! How do I tell him? What do I say?"

Todd let her absorb the incredible discovery before he continued. She was already excited that they had solved the disappearance of her uncle's friend. But he had more to tell all of them.

CHAPTER 37

The Second Cave

"OK," SAID TODD, after all the excitement settled down. There's more."

"What do you mean 'there's more'?" said Jane, staring at Todd. "That's plenty to identify him," she continued. "Plus, if he does have siblings they can do DNA analysis and that kind of thing." She was totally focused on the fact that they found her uncle's friend, or at least she believed they did. Todd let her ramble on and on, waiting for her to settle down. She realized he wasn't saying anything and turned to look at him.

The look Todd gave her made her realize this wasn't about Charles B. Denton. Her and Todd have learned to read each other quite well. This was a totally different look. This was one of those 'I've got a secret' looks. She recognized it and could barely wait for him to explain.

"What?" she finally said to him. "Spit it out," she said.

Jack and Gail looked at Jane, then looked at Todd, who was obviously holding something back.

"I need to tell you another detail about what I found when I went down that slope," he said.

"OK," said Jane, somewhat puzzled.

"As I was coming back up I was holding on to my rope, but I was also holding onto either small roots, or available hand grips within the cave wall itself, anything I could use for support. Sorry Jack, but I let you do most of the belay work. I was concentrating on not sliding back down."

Jack waved him off. "No problem," he said.

Todd continued, "I grabbed onto for what I thought was a small rock in the cave wall, you know, a place to grab and haul myself up a little further. Well, it came right out of the wall. So, I looked for something to grab but all I got was mud. When I looked at the wall I noticed water trickling down. Not a lot, but enough to make it muddy. So, just for the heck of it I dug at the wall, just to see how far in the mud went. It got dryer of course by about three or four inches in, but the soil was soft so I kept digging. About eight inches in it was still dry and I was about to quit digging. I just grabbed one more handful of dirt when it happened."

"When what happened," asked Jane.

"A small opening appeared in the wall," said Todd. "What does that mean", said Jane. "What do you mean by 'a small opening'?"

She could feel the adrenaline start to surge through her veins.

"Exactly what I said," Todd told her. "It was a small opening. It was only about as wide as my fist so it was like looking through a six-inch round by ten-inch deep hole."

I had been focusing my light on it to see what I was doing so I saw it when the last bit of dirt fell away to create the opening. I pulled myself closer and was amazed at what I saw! I mean really amazed. At first, I just saw the cave, you know, just another cave. But then I turned my head lamp off to see if the other cave had any light going through it. Don't forget, I was looking through an eight-inch tiny tunnel that I had dug in the wall, so I didn't see a lot. But, I saw a little creek. I mean I think it was a creek of some kind. The water from this cave must trickle into that cave and form that creek. It probably exits somewhere from there. Then I realized."

"Realized what," Jane said.

"Jane," he said, looking directly at her, "think about this. It's another cave. And who knows what may be in there. I could see something was there, I didn't know what, but something. I thought I saw markings on one of the walls. It was dark so I couldn't really tell. But I'd love to check it out. You know, like a dig," he said with excitement.

"I couldn't see enough to make anything out because it was too far away. I had to be careful! I mean really careful," he enunciated. Jane looked puzzled. Jack and Gail didn't know what he was talking about.

"Jane, I know in my gut just how incredible this is going to be," he said, grabbing her by the shoulders. "This is an amazing find. But there's a problem," he said looking at her with intensity. Then he looked at the others. "We all need to be careful," he said.

"What do you mean?" asked Jane.

"You're scaring me a little," said Gail.

"I didn't just see a cave," he continued, looking seriously now.

"I saw a man with a rifle."

Jane tilted her head, looked at him like he was talking crazy. Gail sucked in too much air and almost choked herself.

"Holy shit!" said Jack.

"I want to see it," she said. "How can we get in there?"

"Jane," said Todd, "this is where that whole thing about making the right decision comes in. You know, the one about safety, and being careful, and not letting any of us get hurt. Now is when we need the experts. Now, it's time for us to make some calls."

Jane hesitated. She was so excited she felt like a kid that wants what she wants, right now. She really didn't want to wait, not even one more second. But, Todd was right. This could get dangerous. Who was the guy with the rifle! What was he doing in there? Why the rifle? There is no way for the four of them to know the answers to those questions. Todd was her voice of reason. He was the one that made her stop and think things through. She knew that. So, she took a deep breath, and she exhaled slowly.

"You're right," she said, and then she was quiet, but only for a second.

"Oh my gosh," she said. "Look, I know you're right, he's right," she said to Jack and Gail, that's not a problem. But I can't believe all this. I was hoping to just do a little hiking and maybe see the place where my uncle had hiked as a young man. Never in my wildest dreams did I think this would be the outcome. I mean I dreamed it but never really thought that cave existed. I was thinking of the angle this cave here takes. Think about it. It slants to the left. I think that's the direction the original cave was in, you know, the one the boys spent so much time in before their friend disappeared. What if there's more than one opening? You're right she said again to Todd. I need to make some calls to a friend I have at Michigan Tech. She belongs to their archeological society.

You guys," she continued, "thank you so very, very much for going with me, and being trusting through all my wild stories. I know you must have all thought that I was crazy. Except Todd of course," she said, "he already knows I'm crazy."

Todd looked at her with a smile. "No, I don't," he said.

"You know," said Jack, "I hate to break this up, but I don't see light outside the cave anymore, at least not much of it. I think it's getting late, and we need to get out of this cave, and off the overhang, or we'll be sleeping here tonight. Plus, we know nothing about the guy with the rifle."

"Is it really that late," asked Gail.

"Yes!" said Jack, "I bet if we went out on the overhang outside the cave, we could watch the sun go down."

"I'm not so sure we want to do that," said Jane. "It'll get cold tonight, even if we stay in the cave. Plus, we have no provisions. How's everyone's water holding out?" she asked.

"I'm out," said Jack.

"I'm almost out," said Gail.

"I have some left," said Todd, "But not much."

"I only have a little myself," said Jane. "And, we still have a couple hours walk back to the yurt. I don't want to do that in the mid-morning sun tomorrow, without water. I know we could get some by any of the many streams here in the woods, but I don't think we're to the point where we really need to depend on 'mountain spring water' to drink. It's probably OK, but, I don't know about you guys, but I don't want to deal with diarrhea all day tomorrow."

"Me either," said Gail.

"OK," said Todd, "let's get out of here. I really don't want to lose all my gear so I'd like to pull my anchors both in here and out on the slope outside."

"I'll help you," said Jack. Just show me how to pull them."

Todd walked Jack through the process of pulling his anchor bolts. Todd had a device to help pull the anchor bolts so the process went by fast. Jane and Gail left the cave first and started repacking their equipment. Jane had left her backpack and the metal detector outside the cave and wanted to make sure she retrieved it. She really wanted to use the metal detector on those cave walls, to see if the colored rock she saw was copper or not, but they simply didn't have time.

Todd had his gun on the inside of the cave and made sure he retrieved it as he and Jack left the cave. Gail especially felt safer going down the way they came up, so instead of doing a quick belay straight down the face of the cliff, they all walked back down using the safety rope Todd had secured for them to come up on. This time Todd waited at the top for all of them to reach the bottom. Then he descended after them, pulling his anchor bolts as he descended. To keep himself safe he left one anchor bolt at the overhang and tied himself to it with the extra rope he had, giving the end to Jack. If Todd fell as he was pulling his anchor bolts, Jack could catch him and lower him down the cliff safely. But, in the end, there was no problem. Todd retrieved all of his equipment except a couple anchor bolts. Everyone stored their harnesses in their small backpack then they left the clearing and headed back to the yurt.

CHAPTER 38

Evening Scare – Last Minute Decision

THE SUN WASN'T down yet but it was getting there. Jane wanted them to move quickly. She figured that if they got back to the trail before the sun was completely down, the chance of getting lost would be minimal. Being on the trail at night, in the dark, would still be slow going, but they would at least be on a path that can be followed easily.

They all felt the chill, but Todd and Jane felt it the most because they were soaked from going down the water flooded slope in the cave.

"If you guys don't mind," said Jane, "I would really like to make a trip to the campground showers again tonight. I'm getting a chill and a hot shower would sure help."

"I'd like one of those myself," said Todd.

They made it down the slope of Cuyahoga Peak, crossing the ravine without a problem, and were back on the main trail as the sun was setting below the horizon. Jane was concentrating on the trail and just keeping warm. Gail was right behind her and beginning to get a little antsy. She was hearing different sounds at night than she heard during the day. And they weren't all pretty sounds. Jack was behind Gail and Todd brought up the rear. He had his rifle out. He heard things in the brush he didn't like either. They passed the Union Spring Campground where they had spent the night what seemed like forever ago. Jane had thoughts of asking for hot coffee if someone was camping, but it was empty. Nobody was camping. They moved on down the path to Government Peak Trail and were almost to Lost Lake Trail when they all heard it. It was a growl! It was loud and it didn't feel, or sound, like it was very far away.

"Keep going," murmured Todd as quietly as possible.

They all tried moving faster. They were quiet because they were tired. A tinge of fear was starting to crawl at their nerves. Todd and Jane were traveling in wet clothes and only their fast-paced walk kept them from shivering.

They all felt it. Something was following them, something big. They all knew it but nobody wanted to say it out loud. Lost Creek ran along the path they were on and suddenly they heard a load splash, then a scream. It was an animal scream and it was full of terror, and the growling snapping sound was not that of a twig someone just stepped on.

They kept moving. The growling sound became distant but it was still too close for comfort. Jane caught a glimpse of their yurt not far away, and picked up speed.

"Look you guys, she said as they entered the yurt, "we've had a long day. I'm tired and cold. Would it be too much to ask to head into town and spend the night in a nice warm hotel?"

"I'm for that," said Gail. I'm not cold like Jane, but I just didn't like whatever it was out there. It sounded like one animal attacked, and probably ate the other, or at the very least killed it, or whatever. If there's something not nice in the area, this canvas hut isn't going to keep it out."

"I really don't think we have anything to worry about," said Todd, "but I'm cold too, and a nice warm hotel room would be great. Let's grab what we need for the evening and we'll come back and pick up the rest of our things in the morning. Everyone OK with that?"

"Sounds good to me," said Jack.

They didn't waste time. Each of them grabbed a small bag of clothes, toiletries, and whatever else they felt they needed for an evening stay in a hotel, then they left. They decided not to stop at the campground. They decided to just check into the nearest hotel, each take a shower, then after a break from that quick nerve wracking hike, they could plan for dinner.

They stopped at a place called 'Lake Superior Resort'. It was on M-64 halfway to Ontonagon. It was a small place and it fit their needs perfectly. They ended up taking a room together that had two huge king size beds. There was something about tonight, that nobody mentioned. They didn't know what to say, even though they all felt it. Tonight, they just liked the idea of being together.

CHAPTER 39

Watched by the Bad Guys

"DID THEY SEE you?" Carl asked. "Of course not," said the prowler.

"But they found the upper cave. Don't know how they did that. There's no sign pointing to it and you can't really see it from below. But I saw them go in. They were in there quite a while. But then they came out and left. They didn't appear to be carrying anything so I didn't interfere. Once they left the cave they hiked out. It was getting dark so they were keeping up a pretty good pace. Tomorrow is the end of the weekend so they'll probably head on home."

Carl didn't like the man but he used him when he had to. There was a lot going on and he didn't want his plan to unravel because of the likes of her. Carl didn't like Jane. She was too smart for her own good. Someone making him nervous was not a good sign. Plus, she was too close to the professor. And now, the professor was wavering, starting to get a conscience. He might talk to someone. Jane could be that someone.

"Shit," he said out loud.

He was usually pretty calm, but this bothered him. These kids were just to close.

He needed a contingency plan. He picked up his phone and dialed the number. The voice on the other end answered immediately.

"Jenny. This is Carl. I need you to do something for me."

Hiding his stash up here was a great idea but for the final step to be successful he couldn't have any want-a-be archeologist in the way. He knew Jane from down state. She was one of Professor Simmons students. She was part of the old man's archeology group too. So far, their paths hadn't crossed, and he was hoping to keep it that way. Right now, he had other things to do. He had to keep an eye on the rangers, that meant keeping up a good front.

"Alright," he told the prowler. "Just keep an eye on their yurt. If anything appears strange, let me know."

"Will do," said the prowler. Their conversation ended so the prowler headed out the back door.

CHAPTER 40

A Safe Hotel Room and a Hot Dinner

J ANE TOOK THE first shower, then Todd. Mostly because they were both soaked and they were both feeling a chill coming on. Jane came out of the shower wrapped in a huge hotel robe. She looked cozy and felt delighted to be clean and dry again. The chill she felt earlier was gone. Todd was not far behind. He came out of the shower wearing blue jeans, and a towel wrapped around his neck. Gail and Jack both took quick showers and came out in street clothes.

"Remember dinner, "said Gail. "I'm hungry."

"Oh yeah, right," said Jane. "That shower just felt so good, and I couldn't resist this big comfy robe. I'll get dressed and be ready in a quick second."

Todd was pulling on a jacket over his t-shirt. "I am extremely hungry," he commented. I think this is a steak night."

Jane was ready in just a couple minutes, and they headed out the door, straight to the on-site restaurant. It was late and they were lucky to get in and seated since it was close to closing time. They ordered immediately and as it ended up, they all had steak. It came with a salad, baked potato, and green beans. All of them ordered beer. They needed it to settle their nerves. Jane spoke up first.

"So," she started. "What the hell was that thing back on the trail? I almost felt like it was following us."

"I think it was following us," said Todd. "I also thing we were lucky another smaller animal crossed its path. I was right there with you Gail," he said looking at her, "when you said you didn't like the sound of that animal. I didn't like it either. It sounded mean, not like the normal predator/prey sort of, I'm looking for food thing. Maybe it was hurt. Animals can get mean if they're hurt. But it did sound mean, like it wanted to kill something sort of sound. And I don't think my little rifle would have stopped it. It sounded big, maybe a big bear. I'm not sure, just big."

"I think you're right Todd," added Jack. "Maybe it was hurt. I've done a lot of hunting growing up and that sound was definitely an angry something. I was already questioning us staying at the yurt when Jane suggested we come into town. That took no persuasion for me to agree to that at all. As a matter of fact, I think we should report it to the Rangers in the morning."

"Probably a good idea", said Todd. "If I remember properly, there was no siting's of bear in this part of the park, so, where'd that thing come from? We definitely need to report it to the Rangers in the morning."

They talked and ate and drank their beer. The bear, or whatever kind of animal was out there, took their mind temporarily off their discovery in the cave just below Cuyahoga Peak. But eventually the conversation reverted back to C.B. Denton.

"It's an interesting coincidence, don't you think," stated Jack, "that this bear, or whatever thing, started following us, after we made the discovery we did. Not that I believe in hocus pocus type stuff, but maybe some spirit thing is watching over that cave. Maybe it's what tore up your uncle and friends' campsite way back when. Maybe C.B. climbed the side of that cliff to get away from something, and maybe he found the small cave by accident, climbing in there because something scared him on the outside. I was just wondering, maybe."

"I'm not a hocus pocus sort of gal either," said Jane. "Besides, it's been fifty years or more since the incident with my uncle and his friends. And from what I've read about bears, they only live to maybe twenty. Some have been known to live up to thirty, and the longest life span ever recorded was a black bear somewhere in a National Forest in Minnesota, a female I think, lived to be forty. So, if anything, it's not the same bear. I could however believe that a bear protecting her cubs could get mean, or maybe a bear protecting his food source, but black bears especially, which are those usually found here in the U.P. are not usually aggressive. That animal we heard, was quite aggressive. It was growling like it was angry. We all heard it."

"But," said Gail. "Do you think that's what happened to C.B.? Do you think he climbed the cliff wall to get away from something?"

"I suppose anything is possible," said Jane. "But how would he have climbed that cliff wall?

"Same way we did, without the ropes of course," said Jack. "Remember, if he was scared he could have tried anything," Jack added.

"The fact that we found him where we did would indicate that he got up there somehow," said Todd, "and there had to be a reason. But what was the reason? What happened to put him in that cave? His friends were supposedly in a cave down below, so why would he have climbed the cliff? Why didn't he run to the cave?"

"That's the thing", said Jack, "why didn't he just go to the cave his friends were at?"

"Maybe he tried", said Todd. "Maybe he couldn't find it. I'm thinking one of the rock slides we saw when we first arrived is probably hiding the entrance. We really don't know how big the entrance was. Maybe it was small like the one we went into."

He turned to Jane. "Do we know anything about it Jane," he asked? Did your uncle describe the entrance or say how big it was?"

"No, he never really did", said Jane. "He was just caught up in losing their friend. He never even really explained why the cave they found was never revealed. That part I really don't understand.

If there were people all around looking for this kid, you would certainly think one of them would have come across that cave. And, could the entrance now be covered by one of the rock slides we saw? Who knows when the rock slides may have occurred. My uncle didn't say anything about them either. But I do know one thing", Jane continued, "I think we need to stop off at the ranger station first thing in the morning. We have a lot to tell them. Plus, tomorrow is Labor Day, remember, and we should be heading home. I don't know how things work up here, or how long it would take them to get a crew up there to extract him, but I'd like to be here when they bring C.B. out of that cave. I haven't figured that part out yet", she said, looking at Todd. "I don't know how I could manage another trip up here, or we could manage," she continued, still looking at Todd.

"I would think they would do it before winter sets in, but who knows. And school starts back up Tuesday."

"First things first," said Todd. "It's getting late. Let's get back to the hotel room and get some sleep. It's been a long, and a very unusual day at that. Plus, I don't know how you guys feel but I'm tired. We'll head over to the ranger station first thing in the morning. I also want them to investigate that guy with the rifle. I suppose it could be legitimate, but I doubt it. We'll see if anyone's at the ranger station. If nobody's there because they don't open until whatever time, we'll head over to the yurt and pack our things so we're ready to head home. Then we'll go back to the ranger station and wait for someone. We can tell them what we found and see what happens. How's that sound?"

"Sounds good to me," said Gail, starting to yawn.

"Oh, don't start that," said Jack.

They all laughed. They needed sleep and they all knew it, so they paid their bill and headed back to their room.

The Northern Lights were visible again, and brighter it seemed tonight. Probably because they were that much closer to Lake Superior. They watched for a while, mesmerized once again by the beauty of the moving, living portrait. But they were all tired and soon went inside, and to bed.

In the shadows, the prowler enjoyed the northern lights as well.

CHAPTER 41

Federal Marshal's Step In

"YOU HAVE TO help me on this one," Arnie said. "These are friends of mine. And they're in more danger then they realize. Sargent Martinez saw them. They don't know that, but he noticed their light in the upper cave. He was lucky to spot it but the back of the cave was dark. That made the small light easy to see. I'm not even sure how they found that cave. We've been looking for other caves in the area and never spotted that one. They're probably the first to discover the thing. But I know them. If they saw Sargent Martinez with a rifle, they'll be careful, and they'll probably report it to the Rangers first thing in the morning. That could cause a big problem!"

"Are they safe?" his brother asked.

"For now, yes" said Arnie. "I'm not sure why they decided to go to a hotel tonight but at least that way we can keep an eye on them. Post someone you trust there tonight would you please. Just tell him to keep his eyes open for any threat that may cross their path.

"Sure thing," his brother said.

"Also, I want you to be at the Ranger Station first thing in the morning. If they show up, be the mildly curious ranger would you please. And if Carl shows his claws, make sure you call in the cavalry. Remember, Carl is pretty slick, and he's a smooth talker. Don't let him catch you off guard.

"Sure thing big brother".

"How do you want me to handle Jason?", asked his brother.

Arnie thought for a minute. He liked Jason, but the kid was young and always seemed to be in trouble. He just made bad decisions. If Arnie's suspicions are correct and Carl sweet talked the boy into getting involved in this artefact theft ring, well, if that's what happened and Jason made the wrong decision, then he'll be going to jail with the rest of them.

"We have to play this one by the book," Arnie told his little brother. "It's too big. Don't give away your cover. Follow the plan all the way. If you, or our guests, or any other civilian in the porkies, are in danger, protect them. I know Jason was once your friend, but you can't trust him, not now. I'm sorry."

"I know," said his brother, half sulking. "I was just hoping, for once, he'd do the right thing."

"Does he know you're a Marshal?" asked Arnie.

"No!" said Arnie's little brother. "Only you, mom, and dad know."

"Good. Let's keep it that way for now."

Arnie left and headed back to his meeting with the other marshals. Tomorrow was the day. Everything was in place. The buyer was already in town and under surveillance. He knew now that his friends were in danger. He was hoping they were also smart. They could easily get in harm's way depending on what they're up to. Arnie didn't tell them how big this operation was. He couldn't. He knew these thugs were ruthless. He didn't have the heart to tell Jane that her once loved professor had already been a casualty. At least he was able to provide some really crucial information to the Federal Marshals before Carl had him killed. Professor Simmons death will go down as a freak archeological accident. Arnie just hoped Todd's wife Jane didn't meet the same fate. He had to close this case to make sure her future wasn't in danger.

CHAPTER 42

Reporting to the Ranger Station

JANE WAS AN early riser so she was the first to wake in the morning. That was normal. No dreams, so that was good. She took a quick shower and by the time she was done, Todd was awake. While he was taking a shower both Jack and Gail were moving around and ready to get up as well. They both took showers too. There was no question that after being out on the trail off and on for three days that the showers felt good, and invigorated all of them. They were ready to go so they packed what they had and headed out.

Todd had put the hotel room on his credit card so once they were all up and ready, it was easy to stop at the office and check out. They ate a small breakfast at the restaurant, and were on their way back to the park by nine. They headed back to the park fully expecting the Ranger Station to still be closed. However, to their surprise it was not just open, but the parking lot was full and there was a lot of activity. They parked and headed inside somewhat perplexed by the commotion. Jane spotted the older ranger that had checked them in when they first arrived. He was behind the counter but when he saw them he waved them over.

"I am really glad to see you," he said with a surprise that startled them.

"Why is that," said Todd.

"Let me explain," he said, "but in here," he continued, pointing to a small conference room over to the side.

"Ranger Steve, isn't it," said Jane.

"Yes, that's right," he responded back to her. "I was the one that checked you in, remember? We talked a little about volcanics."

"Sure, I remember," Jane responded politely, with a smile. "What's going on here? We noticed all the activity but we didn't think you were even open until ten o'clock," she said, as they entered the small conference room.

They were amazed to see two other rangers talking near a large map of the porkies. They were placing little red tacks in several spots. It seemed too early for there to be anything important going on, but something unusual was happening. The other two rangers turned around as the foursome entered the room. Jane almost had a heart attack! It was the guest ranger that had come to the last couple of her archeology meetings. She wasn't sure if he recognized her. There were lots of people at the meetings and Jane never actually talked to the guy. But Todd felt his hand suddenly being squeezed abnormally tight by Jane, but he wasn't sure why.

"Sir," ranger Steve said to one of the men. "This is the group I mentioned."

"Jane, and, I'm sorry, what were your names, he said to the others?"

They all introduced themselves. Jane saw no indication that he recognized her so she didn't say anything.

"This is my boss, Carl," said Steve. "I'd like him to tell you why I asked you back here to the conference room."

"Glad to meet you," said Carl, looking directly at Jane.

It made her skin crawl and she immediately heard warning bells go off in her head.

"I can see you're perplexed," the head ranger said," so I'll get right to the point. Have a seat."

They all sat, just a little to confused to say anything. Jane wanted to tell Todd who this guy was but she didn't want to say anything out in the open. Something just wasn't right, but she didn't know what.

"You were assigned to the yurt over by Lost Lake, right?" asked Carl as he began talking, temporarily putting them on edge. They didn't even respond when Carl continued.

"Don't worry, you didn't do anything wrong. But, there was an incident," he continued, "and we were a bit worried about you."

They all looked at each other unsure of what to say.

"Can you tell us where you were last night?" he asked politely.

"Sure," said Todd. "We got a little wet on the trail, and the temperature was dropping so we wanted to get back to the yurt for the night. Then we heard what sounded like a bear, with a pretty mean growl. We just didn't like the sound of it, plus because we were wet, we decided a nice warm shower in the local hotel would really be nice, so we spent the night at 'Lake Superior Resort' up on M-64. We actually decided to stop by the Rangers Station here on our way back to the yurt, to report the bear thing."

Carl knew they were at the hotel. He just smiled. At least they didn't lie.

"Well," said Carl. "Staying at a hotel last night may have been the best decision you've ever made."

Now they were really mystified, and a little concerned as well.

"What exactly are you telling us," asked Jane. "What kind of incident?"

"Well, let me just tell you the whole story," Carl said, eyeing each of them like they were little kids, gaging what to say and what not to say. "The rangers got a call from one of our campers about nine last night. It was just past dark. Someone wanted to report a bear. OK, we have bears and it's good to know where they are so we can give advice to the hikers and campers. Then we got another call, and another, and another. The last two said it was a mean bear, growling and snorting. The first came in from the north side of 'Union Bay Campground'. That's a huge campground so, at first, we thought it was looking for food. The second one came from the south side of 'Union Bay

Campground. That's a lot of ground for a bear to be moseying along looking for food. The third one came from campers in a rustic cabin over by the Union Spring Trail. It scared them but they were in a safe building so they just stayed put. The fourth one came from Lost Creek Outpost. A couple had already set up camp there. It's a rustic camping spot and they were the only ones there. They heard the growling from a distance just before they had planned to go to bed. They said they were sitting out watching the northern lights, which was probably a good thing. Then they heard the growling even closer and decided not to chance an encounter with a growling bear, so they got in their car and waited."

The Ranger watched his captive audience eyes turn into saucers, but he continued.

"They saw the bear enter their campsite. It was bleeding and they watched in horror as it trashed their campsite. They didn't take any chances. They left the area and called us immediately. Because the bear was bleeding we instantly dispatched two rangers. They were out searching the area when they found her, at your yurt."

"Holy shit!" said Jack, dumbfounded.

"Oh my God!" said Gail, instantly putting her hands to her mouth, as if to stop a scream from coming out.

Todd and Jane just sat there speechless. They didn't know what to say at first. Then Todd spoke up. "Do you think this bear could have been wounded by that guy shooting at bigfoot the other day, whatever day that was?"

"We think that is definitely a possibility," said the ranger.

"But I'm afraid there's more," he continued. "We did find the bear, like I said, at your yurt. We didn't know where you were," continued the ranger. "We've been out all morning looking for you."

Carl felt his heart race. He knew exactly where they were. He liked when people got scared. He fed on fear and enjoyed the reactions from people. He was enjoying himself. He wanted to get in their faces and tell them about the gory bloody mess that the bear left behind. He wanted to describe every detail, but there were other rangers around, so he controlled himself and only gave the essential parts of his little speech.

"It was obvious you hadn't left yet," he said," at least we didn't think you left. There was too much left behind. We were hoping you were still out on the trail, camping somewhere safe or something, but there were backpacks all over so we just weren't sure."

"What do you mean there were backpacks all over," asked Todd.

"We were concerned about you," said Carl, looking directly at Todd, "because the yurt you were staying in was trashed. The bear was still trashing the place when the rangers got there. They heard it from a distance and approached it slowly. We didn't know if anyone was in the yurt or not, so we couldn't just start shooting. Obviously, we're glad you weren't there."

"So am I", said Jane.

The yurt you were staying in, like I said, is trashed," he repeated bluntly.

"Holy Mary, mother of God!" said Gail.

"What about the bear," asked Todd.

"We had to put her down," said the ranger. "She was removed shortly after that."

"We would like a couple of rangers to escort you back to the yurt so you can gather your things, or whatever is salvageable. Your cooler was trashed and any food you had left is gone. It didn't look like much, candy bars, trail mix, beef jerky. Fishing equipment looked trashed. You'll have to go through and make a list of everything. We'd like a list for our report if you don't mind. You know the Park can't reimburse you for anything, sorry about that. When you camp in this type of environment you take your chances with the wildlife. Sorry!" he said again.

Ranger Carl was about to get up. He thought he appeared as straight forward and honest as possible and he wanted these young people to be on their way. Maybe they would head home after all, and out of his way. But something bothered him. He looked back at Jane. She knows something he thought. He was about to give orders to one of the rangers but turned back to the four hikers.

"I'll be assigning a ranger to escort you back to your yurt," he said. "Could you just wait here," he asked.

"Sure," said Todd.

Todd was going to interrupt him, and tell him about C.B. Denton, but Jane grabbed his hand. When he looked over at her, she mildly shook her head no.

The rangers left the room.

"Somethings wrong," said Jane to her friends, "I feel it she told Todd. This is big and I'm getting that panicky feeling."

"I understand," said Todd. He knew. This was Jane's thing. The blessing, and the curse, she always told him about. He looked deep into her panicked eyes.

"Let me make a quick call", he said.

Todd dialed Arnie's number.

Todd stood in a corner talking quietly. Jane and the others didn't hear much of what he said. Just an 'O.K.' here and an 'I understand' there.

He whispered carefully to Jane and their friends. Arnie said go ahead and tell him about C.B. but don't say anything about the cave. Arnie said he'll have our back and not to worry. But that comment had the opposite effect and now, they were all worried. None of them really knew what was going on.

A few minutes later Ranger Carl came back into the room, along with Ranger Steve, and two other younger looking rangers. Jane told him they had something to tell him.

"Something to tell me," he responded curiously, his eyes going wide, almost worried.

Todd thought he spotted fear in the man's eyes, but the look went quickly away.

"Well, whosever in charge," Jane said.

"Oh, well that would be me," said Ranger Carl.

CHAPTER 43

Secrets Revealed - The Lost Boy

J ANE DIDN'T KNOW quite how to start, so she just jumped in by asking a question.

"Have you ever heard the story of the hiker from Michigan Tech that disappeared about fifty years ago?" she began, "hiking with five friends." Jane heard a gasp behind her and turned around to see the shocked look on Ranger Steve's face.

Carl had only been in the Porcupine Mountains for about a year but managed to get himself the lead ranger position in that brief time. It was his cover. He made quick study of all the rangers under him, and he knew the story about the missing boy.

Now he was the ranger in charge. He looked over at them. "I'm fairly new here," he said to the four hikers, getting up out of his chair. "But Steve here, Steve, come on over and sit down," he told the elderly ranger. "Steve has been here a long time."

"Jane," Carl nodded, "Todd, Jack and Gail," Carl looked to each one in turn. "I would like you to meet Ranger Steven Jacobs," he said as his hand gently padded Steve on the shoulder.

"Steve was one of the six boys that went out on that fateful hike fifty years ago, fifty-one actually, right Steve." Steve just nodded. "Steve was born in 1944. He's now seventy-three years old. And yes, we know about the lost Michigan Tech boy of the Porcupine Mountains. On occasion, we discuss it in meetings and are always watching for information that may give additional clues for us to follow. Steve here has repeated the story a hundred times to new rangers as they come on board. Now, why do you ask?"

Jane's voice shook and she wasn't sure if she could talk at all. She was barely comprehending what she was hearing. This gentleman, this man that checked them in when they first arrived, this man who talked to her about the mountain with such pleasure, this man was a friend of her uncle's.

"Go ahead Jane," said Todd. "Spit it out."

She looked at Steve and touched his hand gently from across the table. She could feel it shaking. "My uncle," she started slowly, looking at Steve, is David Porter."

Steve's reaction was immediate as he squeezed her hand.

"I'm up here, in the porkies," she continued, "because of all the stories he's told me over the years. He never forgot C.B. and he talked about how confusing that whole experience was. I could tell over the years that that was the one time in his life that he wished he could live over. To try to do something differently. So somehow, his friend would never have gotten lost."

Jane's voice quivered as she talked about her uncle. Steve felt the emotion and looked up at her. They both had tears in their eyes.

Todd noticed how intensely Carl was listening. He suddenly saw a look of anger go across Carl's face, but Carl hid it well. He suspected that Carl didn't like what Jane was saying, but he didn't know why. That, he thought to himself, might be a problem.

"We lost contact over the years," he told Jane, his eyes watering. "I always liked Dave. He was just a nice guy. The hiking was mostly his plan. We all had a great time, you know, hiking and such. It, he, taught us how to appreciate nature. I was a year younger then him but he always treated me as a friend, not an underclassman, a friend. I liked him."

Jane looked at Todd. He knew this next part would be difficult but she continued.

"Steve," she said, looking him in the eyes, "we found C.B."

She didn't say anymore. She waited for the information to sink in. Todd saw the immediate look of controlled anger on Carl's face. It was weird. Why would Carl be angry. Was he reading the guy right?

It took a minute to register on Steve's face, but it finally did. Steve let go of Jane's hand. He stood up. He didn't believe her.

"You couldn't have possibly found him," he told her. He wasn't mad, but he was on the verge. "I've been looking for years," he continued. "I've never found even one clue."

Jane could tell that he was visibly upset. She looked at Todd who then took a wrapped item out of his pocket and placed it on the table, opening it carefully. There for all to see was a dirty red bandanna, and a wallet. Steve sat back down with a thud.

"Holy shit," said Carl. "Where'd you get that?" he asked them, a little too aggressively. But before they could answer Steve dug into his pocket and pulled out a clean, neatly folded bandanna, and placed it on the table. It was an exact match to the one Todd had placed there.

Jane tried keeping her emotions under control as she began to talk. She wanted to tell Steve more.

"My uncle gave me a map. It wasn't real detailed but we followed it up to a small clearing near Cuyahoga Peak. There's an overhang above the clearing. We didn't think anything of it at first. Then Gail here noticed a particularly strange change in the rock formation leading up to the overhang. She's an Art teacher," Jane said shrugging her shoulders. "She said there was a color difference," Jane said, and we were all curious, so, we ended up climbing up to that overhang. Once we were there, we found a cave. He's in that cave Steve," Jane said.

Todd was watching Carl as Jane talked.

He saw Carl looking at Jane with deep seated anger. Carl had slid back behind everyone else there. His fists were clenched and he didn't seem surprised at what Jane was saying. He was angry. Todd also saw the quick scowl cross Carl's face, and the man was beginning to sweat. Something about this guy bothered him. Jack saw it too. The two of them looked at each other. They knew something about Ranger Carl was wrong.

Jane and Gail were just focused on Steve. "His remains are in there," she said. "We need to get them out. We need to rescue him. We need his family to know what happened." She was talking fast now explaining a little more detail about getting into the cave, and how slippery it was, and how noisy it was and how, even if he yelled for help, nobody would have heard him. And how they decided to look for identification. And how badly she wanted it to be C.B, for her uncle.

They were all listening to Jane go on and on. Several more rangers hearing her voice get louder and louder walked over to the door, listening, wondering what all the commotion was about. They were all astounded by the story. Could it be true. Could this fifty-year mystery of the porkies be solved? They all wanted it to be true. They all wanted to believe. They all knew Ranger Steve. They gathered around Steve. They had all heard his story. They liked Ranger Steve but some of the younger ones weren't sure if they believed the old mans' story, until now, when they heard it with their own ears. After all, here they were, listening to this unknown hiker say they found the old mans' friend, the fifty-year-old missing hiker. There was proof, his bandanna and his wallet, sitting there, on the table.

Carl didn't wonder any more. He knew this girl and he also wanted her gone. He wasn't sure how to get it done but it needed to be done. She was going to ruin everything. She still didn't let on that she knew him, but he couldn't take the chance. He'll have to do something about that.

Carl calmed himself. Then he stepped up and turned to Jane. "Young lady," he said. "Would you and your friends like to guide us to this cave you found?"

"Absolutely," said Jane. She looked at the others. "you guys OK with that?" she said. They all shook their heads affirmatively. Todd and Jack looked at each other. They were highly concerned.

Carl barked a couple orders to a couple other rangers to have the rescue team called. Then he looked at Steve and asked, "do you want to call her, or do you want me to?"

That came out kind of cold thought Jane, but maybe I'm being too sensitive she thought. She turned and looked at Todd. She saw something in his eyes. She knew that look and she became even more concerned.

"I'll call her," said Steve, excusing himself from the room.

"Do you mind me asking what that was all about?" asked Jane. "Who is he calling?"

Carl smiled a small anxious smile. "C.B. has some living relatives," said Carl. "He has two younger siblings, and," he paused a minute, "his mother is still alive."

"What?" said Jack. "Are you kidding?"

"Not at all," said Carl. They all live over in 'Silver City'. His mother is ninety-five. She's frail, but she's a spunky old gal. Northern Michigan born and bred from what I hear," he said with what seemed to be a heartless tone to his voice.

CHAPTER 44

Bear Attack at the Yurt

J ANE LOOKED AT Todd and smiled, then looked back at Ranger Carl.

"Thanks Ranger Carl," she said, smiling at him

Ranger Carl smiled back at her, "you're welcome," he said, then just left the room.

He was steaming. He was sure now. He knew Jane was a member of the archeology chapter and she must know something. She's just too damned smug. She must be a better friend to that stupid professor than he thought. Poor professor he thought to himself. Won't she be surprised to find out that an accident had taken her dear professor just this weekend. Carl wasn't about to let this amateur get in his way. He wasn't sure how much she knew, but he wasn't going to take the chance. She was a loose end and he wasn't willing to chance her screwing things up.

The four friends waited for the head rangers' response. They needed to prepare for the recovery of C.B. Denton, but none of them were moving very fast. They watched as Ranger Carl signaled to two younger rangers.

"I'll see what we can do about the recovery of D.B.," he told them. "Wait here for a moment, please," he said walking out of the office.

The four friends weren't sure what to make of it. They thought Carl was giving his Rangers instructions on taking them to the yurt and then up to Cuyahoga Peak to watch the recovery. Todd was a bit uneasy. Just something bugging him. They didn't get to talk to Ranger Steve again. Jane wanted to quietly ask about the second cave. But Steve was kind of whisked right out of the office. That seemed strange to Jane.

Within minutes two young rangers came into the room.

"We have been assigned to you," the blond said. "My name is Jason. My partner here is Ron. We'll escort you to the yurt so you can go through and find anything worth saving. Sorry," he said again. "Then when the recovery team arrives and we're notified we'll ride up as far as we can toward Cuyahoga Peak. We can ride part of the way on ATV's but I'm sure you know we'll have to hike part way to get there."

"Yes, we know," said Todd. "Thankyou. We'll need to make a couple of calls before we leave. We were all supposed to be back to work tomorrow. Now, I'm not so sure if we'll make it back on time so we need to let some people know."

"Not a problem," said the young Ranger.

"If your cell phones don't work in here," said Ranger Jason, "we have a land line you can use."

"Thanks," said Todd. "We'll be ready to go shortly."

Then Ranger Jason left them to their calls.

"So, what does everyone think?" asked Jane.

"I would at least like to see this kid recovered," said Jack. "I'm calling the sub line, and have them get me a replacement teacher for tomorrow."

"Me too," said Gail. "I'm going to call my principal and let him know what's going on, just a little info. I'll fill him in on the rest when I get back. Then I'll call the sub line."

"We'll both be calling for substitutes as well," said Todd. "But I think Jane needs to make a call to her uncle as well."

"That's for sure," said Jane. "I'm not sure if he'll believe me, but I'm calling him first. I should probably call my mom as well, since she knows this story as well as I do. But, one more thing you guys," Jane said quietly and hesitantly. "Be careful what you say to anyone. Somethings going on that I just don't like, and we don't want to put anyone in danger."

"I agree," said Todd. "Just give the principal the basic excuse, we're running late and can't get back until Wednesday! No details! They don't really care anyway."

While Jane was on the call with her uncle, Todd made one more call to his friend Arnie. Things weren't feeling very comfortable he told Arnie, and Todd wasn't too proud to say how nervous this whole thing was making him and his friends. Arnie lived in the U.P. and Todd trusted his friend implicitly. He knew Arnie had some connections and he just had to trust his friend.

Now that he met him, Todd didn't like this Ranger Carl any more then Jane did. He just had a bad feeling about him. He couldn't explain it, but he felt he needed to call Arnie. Now, he's glad he did. The information Todd acquired from his friend was quite valuable.

Jane hung up after talking to her uncle.

"How did it go?" asked Todd.

"Apparently, he knew that Steve worked as a Forest Ranger up here", said Jane. "He told me the same thing Steve did, that they just got out of touch over the years. He said to give Steve his regards. He said I can fill him in on all the details when I get home, and that he was glad I was staying for C.B.'s recovery. It was weird though," she said. "He sounded funny."

"He's probably emotional about you finding C.B. Jane, and trying to hide it from his niece," said Todd.

"I suppose," she said.

Just then Ranger Jason ducked his head back in and asked if they were ready to go out to the yurt.

CHAPTER 45

Bad Guys Discovered

THEY ARRIVED AT the yurt shortly after they left the ranger station. Rangers Jason and Ron drove individual four-wheelers and led the way to the yurt. They all parked in the area reserved for cars and hiked the short distance up to the yurt. Nothing could have prepared them for what they saw. The cooking area was a mess. The picnic table was torn apart and looked like kindling. The whole area looked like someone just kicked and smashed things like they were angry at the world. Everything was just torn apart. They were almost speechless as they just looked at the mess.

"Holy shit," said Jack.

"This gives me the shivers," said Gail, "we could have been in there."

Parts of the canvas yurt were flapping in the wind and the door was smashed in. There were things all over the place. They finally walked up to the yurt to see if anything could be salvageable.

The backpacks were thrown around but only Jane's was ripped. The straps had been torn off and there were three tears down the back, like claws had ripped into it. She picked it up twirling it around with two fingers.

"Oh man!" she said. "I was thinking of buying a new backpack but I thought I'd use this one as a back-up."

"Not anymore," said Todd.

"No offense," he said, "but I'd rather lose your old backpack than all my climbing gear." He found the bag with his climbing gear. It had been tossed in the corner but it was intact. The cooler, which was a good solid 60-quart Coleman cooler on wheels, had the sides basically crushed in and there were pop and beer cans all over the place, some smashed and some still intact.

"Is this still usable?" asked Jane, picking up one of the metal detectors. It was bent at the handle.

"Yes," said Todd. It's still good. Just a bent handle.

The other metal detector was fine.

"Oh man!" said Jack. "Look at this fishing gear," he said with frustration.

The two rods they brought were bent and fish line was all over the place and in tangles. They were inexpensive rods but that didn't mean he didn't like how they worked. "I guess these can be trashed," he said.

His fishing box was upside down but intact, so that was good. Some of the clothes they left out were in shreds but nothing anyone felt was terribly important. Gail's camping blanket was intact but her pillow was ripped apart.

"This was my favorite pillow," she said, picking up the left overs.

Todd had brought his gun with him so it was still in the van, and fine. Same with Gail's camera. She had it with her so it was fine as well. The axe that belonged to Jack had a busted handle, but handles are easily replaced. Any food, such as trail mix, candy bars, health bars, and even individually wrapped oatmeal packets were torn apart and all over the place. Most of the food was gone. They just saw wrappers. The five-gallon water jugs were smashed and water was all over the place. The peanut butter jar was smashed on the floor and had a claw print in the peanut butter. The jelly jar was found under an overturned bed, cracked but not smashed. One set of bunkbeds was overturned. The other was moved around but still upright. And the table was smashed.

Basically, they didn't lose too much. But the yurt took a lot of damage. It may even need to be replaced.

The four friends picked up what they could salvage and hauled it back to the van. Anything that was destroyed was replaceable. Out of instinct Gail clicked off a couple dozen pictures.

"I'm glad we made the decision to head into town last night," said Gail. "This is terrible. It gives me the shivers thinking what could have happened. I think my guardian angel was working overtime last night."

"I'll agree with you there," said Jane. "All of our guardian angels were working overtime last night," she said. "I've been camping in a lot of places and I've never, ever, seen anything like this before."

"This was an unusual circumstance," said Ranger Ron. "We're talking about a wounded bear, shot by a crazy hiker. At least we think that's how she was wounded. Thank goodness we don't encounter that problem too often."

Just then Ranger Jason walked up. "We're ready to head up to Cuyahoga Peak," he said. "Are you guys all set?"

"Yeah", I think we're done here," said Todd. "We just need to put what's left of our gear in the van," he said to the rangers. And I need to grab my rifle," he added.

"Oh, you won't need that," Ranger Jason told him, as they all walked down the trail to the parking area. You can leave it in your van for now. "Ron and I are both armed, in case we run into any problems."

"Oh, OK," responded Todd, with trepidation.

The four friends headed toward their van to stash what they recovered from the yurt. The two rangers headed toward the ATV's. Todd was sure he heard a few harsh words being said between the two rangers but he was too far away to hear any details. Right now, it appeared as if Ranger Jason was in charge.

He took a quick glance at Jack, nodding his head so Jack would follow him around the side of the van. The two friends had a quick discussion before heading over to where the girls stood waiting with the rangers. The only thing the two girls took with them, were their water bottles. They really didn't need anything else. They were with rangers who were carrying guns, so they were safe. So, they thought.

Todd and Jack weren't so sure. They each secured a knife in their boot.

"Is the recovery team already on their way," asked Jane.

"Yes," said Jason. "I just got the message. As we get closer we'll probably see the helicopter bring in their gear. We'll take the four-wheelers," he said. "They're both equipped with passenger seats in the rear. Two of you can ride with me and two can ride with Ron. We'll have to leave the ATV's once we go off trail. But the rest of the way shouldn't take long."

They reached the area where the four friends had left the trail the last couple of times they had hiked this way.

"We passed the place we should go off trail," said Jane. Her and Todd were riding with Ranger Jason.

"I know a quicker way," said Jason.

Jane was about to argue but Todd poked her, to get her attention. She peeked over at him. He had that look on his face. Something was wrong. She was beginning to be leery of these two young rangers, especially Jason. He was driving the ATV just a little faster than she thought necessary for the terrain, so she was holding on tight to the roll bars. Todd slid his arm around Jane's waist and whispered in her ear, "trust me", he said, "take your hands off the roll bar and put your arm around my waist and hold onto me. Stay with me and jump when I say; now."

The ATV veered around a sharp bend and Todd felt it start to go over. He whispered "NOW!" just as Ranger Jason jumped off. Todd had braced his feet and jumped off in the other direction, carrying Jane with him. They rolled down a small hill but came to a stop in a shrub covered ravine. They heard the ATV crash end over end down a steep slope, dust flying everywhere. The quiet eeriness of the forest animals was deafening. They didn't see Jason.

"Shhh", whispered Todd in her ear. They didn't make a sound but they heard another crash and a scream, Gail's scream.

"Shhh", Todd said. "Jack is aware", was all he dared say.

Then they heard the two rangers.

"Mine went over the cliff," said Jason. Carl said make it look like an accident so it looks like an accident. What about yours?" he asked Ron.

"There done for," answered Ron. "You heard the scream, right?"

Todd and Jane heard inaudible mumbling, then angry words, then fist hitting flesh. The struggle went on for a few minutes before the silence came. They didn't dare move until finally Ranger Ron yelled out, "Todd Bowman, "you got a friend named 'Arnie?'. He's my brother dude. Come on out."

Jane saw Todd smile, then he helped her to her feet.

"Come on," he said. She was confused and a little shaken but no broken bones. She followed him out of the brush.

They walked about twenty paces up the slope before they saw Ron. He had Jason handcuffed and on his knees.

"You were pretty smart calling my brother," said Ron. "Are you two OK?" he asked. "We're good," said Todd.

"What's going on," asked Jane.

"We've had these guys under surveillance for months," said Ron, "but could never catch them in the act. They've been stealing artefacts from National Parks all over the country. This guy here was stupid enough to join up with Carl and his brothers. They were all working under assumed names. There's one other brother involved and we suspect two other guys but a couple friends of mine should have them in custody by now. This is a huge bust you guys. Whether you realized it or not, you helped! Thanks."

Jane was still in shock when Ron looked at her and said, "Your friends are hiding back there about fifty yards. Don't worry, they're OK. I had the girl scream for me to make it real. She did a good job, didn't she?" he said smiling.

Jane went to find them, slapping Todd as she turned saying, "you could have warned me."

"There wasn't time, hun. It all happened to quick".

Jane found Jack and Gail walking toward them. "You knew about this too," she yelled at Jack.

"Not all of it," said Jack innocently.

"I certainly didn't know Ron was one of the good guys. He stopped us back a way and told us he was more than a Ranger, he was a Federal Marshal and that he was Arnie's brother. Can you believe that? He said we needed to just trust him. Then he told Gail here to scream like she was really hurt. How'd she do?"

"Scared the shit out of me is how she did!"

Gail smiled. "Sorry," she said, hugging Jane.

They walked back to where Todd and Federal Marshal Ron Sorenson were still talking. Ron looked at all of them and explained just a little. "I'm sorry for what I just put you through," he said, "but I was undercover and couldn't break silence or someone would have been killed. They are already recovering the remains of C. B. Denton, thanks to you. By now they will also be placing Ranger Carl under arrest, and from what I hear we will be recovering a great treasure near where the remains have been located. I'll have to fill you in on everything. Then you can tell me about how you discovered that little cave. We still need to walk up to the recovery area but we took some time arresting this idiot so the remains will probably already be gone. You will, however, be able to meet C.B.'s family. Ranger Steve has been working under cover with us. He's a great guy and will be happy to see that all of you are OK. We need to head out this way," he pointed northwest. Everybody ready?"

"We're ready," they all said in unison. "OK," said Ranger Ron. "Let's go."

Todd and Jack had no problem hauling 'ex-Ranger Jason' to his feet and shuffling him up the path to the recovery area.

CHAPTER 46

D.B. Denton Recovered

T HE HELICOPTER WITH the remains of C.B. Denton was lifting off as they approached the clearing. That's when Ranger Steve Cook saw them coming.

He eagerly walked over to them.

"I want to thank you," he said to all of them, then he walked over to Jane.

"May I hug you?" he asked, looking at her with a big smile on his face.

"Yes," Jane said, with a slight bit of dampness in her eyes.

And with that, the gentle elderly man wrapped his arms around Jane and hugged her. Then he whispered, "please give half of this to Dave for me, would you?"

"I certainly will," she said, her eyes starting to water more freely.

"Come on over here," he said. "I would like to introduce you to a couple of people."

Jane wiped her eyes as Steve led her, Todd and their friends a short distance up the hill, stopping in front of three individuals standing amidst two rangers and two Federal Marshals. Steve introduced them to the Federal Marshals and then led Jane over to a frail looking elderly woman.

"Jane," he said, "this is Emma Denton, C.B.'s mother.

Jane was astonished at how healthy the elderly woman looked, and amazed at how alert and attentive she was to every remark being made. And these two," he said, pointing to the elderly man and woman standing next to C.B.'s mom, is C.B.'s brother and sister," he said

"Emma", Steve said to the elderly lady, "this is Jane Bowman, who happens to be," he continued, "David Porter's niece."

Jane became slightly emotional when the older woman took a step forward, and grasped Jane's hand holding it tightly, looking directly into Jane's eyes.

"My dear," said the old woman, looking at Jane intently. She held Jane's hand in hers more firmly. "You are an answer to my prayers young lady, you and your friends," her eyes darting to the others, barely able to focus through the emotional tears that clouded them.

"I have accepted my son's death a long time ago," she said, "but my final wish on this earth was to at least go to my grave knowing something of what happened to him. We may not know all the details, but we do know where he ended up, that he didn't run away, or he wasn't kidnapped, or anything like that. And now, I can bury my Charley peacefully."

"Thank you," she said leaning up a bit to give Jane a kiss on the cheek. Jane bent down enough to hug the fragile elderly woman.

Jane and her friends also met C.B.'s brother and sister. Elderly, yes, but obviously younger then Ranger Steve or Jane's Uncle Dave. They also verbalized their gratitude. All of them had only a minute or two to talk before the Denton family's ride arrived and they had to leave. They thanked Jane and her friends one last time before departing.

"Todd," a voice boomed.

Todd turned around to see his friend Arnie. The two grabbed hands then pulled each other together into a manly bear hug. The foursome had met Arnie before, at the restaurant, but somehow, he looked much bigger. For sure he could have squashed Todd in that bear hug if he wanted to.

"I've been trying to get you up here to visit for a long time you bugger," said Arnie in a rather loud voice.

Then he looked to Jane and spoke a bit softer. I heard Todd had a wife! I am glad to finally meet you properly," he said to Jane, bowing to kiss her hand.

"I know this is a hell of a way to introduce a friend to your wife," he laughed. "Perils of the trade I guess."

"Yeah," said Todd, "this wasn't the introduction I was hoping for either."

Jane just smiled at them both. They were acting like school boys.

"But seriously", he said more quietly, his voice becoming very professional. "This was dangerous. There is more going on here than you realize. It was a good thing you made that call Todd," he said directly to his friend. "All of you could have been killed. This group of thieves wouldn't have cared."

"That being said", he continued, "do you know what you four just completed?", he asked them all, looking from face to face at the four friends. They all shrugged their shoulders.

"Just so you know, this ring of thieves had infiltrated several archeology organizations across the Midwest," he noted, looking right at Jane. "Your archeology chapter president was sweet talked into joining them, but later when he tried to back out, I'm sorry to be the one to inform you Jane, but he was murdered."

"Oh my god," said Jane, almost falling over.

Todd was right there to support her.

Then she composed herself. "I knew something was wrong. I could tell. He was a nice man. I really liked him, but it was heart breaking to see his personality change over the last couple months."

"You need to know a couple things," Arnie said, grabbing her hand.

"First, he did not die in vain. He provided us with much needed intel before he was found out. He was attempting to get more when he was killed. He's really a hero to his cause, protecting Michigan's artefacts."

Jane's emotions were already running high, but this, this was wrong! Her tears were replaced with anger at losing a friend to such greedy, uncaring and ruthless thieves. She hated how he was used, but there was nothing she could have done.

"And two", he said, "and this is important," he said, looking into her eyes, "nobody will know the extent of his fall from grace, nor of his heroism, only you. The world will only see that a beloved college professor of archeology died in a terrible accident."

"But why can't people know he died a good guy," said Jane.

"One can't come out without the other Jane," Arnie said. "Keep this to yourself and nobody will know that he did anything wrong in the first place."

Jane nodded. She was overwhelmed. "I liked him," she said. "Knowing he chose the good side in the end helps take away some of the not so nice thoughts I was beginning to have about him. I will miss him."

Arnie let go of Jane's hand and focused on Todd and Jack.

"Carl and his rats also infiltrated the Forest Ranger Service. Ranger Carl, and I use that title on him with distain, is already in custody. And you saw his partner Jason get arrested. There were two other rangers we also captured. There were a few others in other states arrested as well. And a couple dealers of old artefacts that just went out of business."

"What about the man with the rifle that Todd saw, in the cave," asked Gail.

"Well, he actually was one of ours," said Arnie. "He posed as a buyer and was able to join their group. They were using that lower cave to stash their goods before selling them off. From what we have been able to determine, there seems to be quite a few old tunnels winding through Cuyahoga Peak. We've only found a few small entrances but they're barely big enough for anyone to crawl into."

"I'm guessing that CB, your Uncle's, and Steve's friend, somehow came across one of the entrances and somehow got lost in the tunnels. That's where you found him. We can only speculate about how he got there. I don't think we'll ever really know."

"The man you saw with the rifle, and my brother Ron, who you've all met, were also working under cover. As well as Ranger Steve, whom you've also met."

"Wow! It seems they had quite an elaborate enterprise built up here," said Jack.

"Oh, the conspiracy goes pretty far and took advantage of a lot of good people," said Arnie. "And, with the help of good people like you we've put a lot of crooks out of business."

"Glad to help," said Jack, as the two men shook hands.

"It's taken a lot of man hours to get this far, and make these arrests," added Arnie, "but you're right, it was quite an elaborate production."

CHAPTER 47

Rangers Step Up

"WELL LISTEN FOLKS, I've got to run," said Arnie. "Lots of work left to do."

"But, I just have one last request," said Arnie. He waved his brother over to listen. "Ron here heard you tell the story of how you found C.B. and he relayed that to me. Pretty interesting. But, we are still both curious as to how you found the other cave.

Todd smiled and looked at Jane.

"Go ahead, you tell them," he said.

Arnie and his brother listened to their story. They stood across from Jane and Todd as Jane enthusiastically told the story of the second cave, accidently found by Todd. She told them about her accidently sliding down the floor of the cave and getting stuck, and how Todd came to her rescue, with the help of Jack and Gail of course. And most importantly, how Todd went back down to look for ID on the skeleton they found. She mentioned how thin the wall between the upper and lower caves must have been that allowed Todd to dig through it. She mentioned that Todd had spotted the man with the gun, which scared them away and actually helped them decide to go to the rangers.

"I knew that was what happened," Arnie said, looking at his brother "My guy saw your light," he told Todd.

"Well, it was kind of intense up there," he told Arnie, "and overwhelming."

"Oh, I can imagine," his friend said.

Jane continued. She decided to tell them more details of her uncle and things that her uncle had told her concerning the cave found by the boys over fifty years ago. She told them how she desperately wanted to find the cave for her uncle but that just wasn't happening. She told them of Gail's keen eye for color and how they discovered the kind of out of place rhyolite. She talked about how they really didn't know if it could possibly be the same cave the boys were visiting when their friend disappeared fifty years ago, but she suspected it was. She thought she was telling them the short version of the discovery but when she was done talking she knew by their smiles that she had talked quite a while. She took a quick look at her watch to confirm that she had been talking for well over thirty minutes.

"We'll have to talk to Steve about that," said Ron. He saw the look on Jane's face, "gently of course," he said, "gently."

Jane did have one last request of the rangers.

"I was wondering," she said. "I wasn't sure about mentioning the discovery of artefacts in that cave, and obviously you know about them, but could I be invited as a guest on the archeological team that researches that cave? If it's the one from Michigan Tech, I know some people over there. I would love it, plus it would mean a lot to my grandfather".

"Jane, you, Todd, and your friends have done a lot, no question," said Arnie. "And you know I can't make any promises, but I will make my recommendations in your favor, saying whatever I can to the team that does the research. That's the least I can do," he said looking up at both Jane and Todd. "Besides, you would bring in a lot of history from your uncle. I think you would be an asset to them."

Arnie looked at all of them now. "Do you four have any idea how you've settled that man's soul," he said, nodding over toward

Ranger Steve. "Trust me, I'll do my best to keep you involved one way or another. Now if you'll excuse me."

"Todd!" he yelled as he trotted off. "Don't be such a stranger."

Todd just laughed.

"Oh my God!" Jane cried suddenly, tears filling her eyes. "Wait, Arnie, wait!"

They all looked at her. Arnie walked back to where the others were standing.

"Todd!" she said. "Remember what I told you happened at the last meeting?"

"No, what," he started to say, "oh my gosh!" Todd blurted out.

"What is it?" asked Arnie.

He waited for Jane to compose herself. "At my last meeting," Jane started. "Remember you guys," she said to Jack and Gail.

"Yeah," said Gail. "You were late getting started because they called a last-minute meeting of the archeological chapter you belong to."

"Something happened at that meeting," she said. "The professor asked if he could talk to me. He slipped a small envelope in my hand. It was very strange! He told me not to look at it when he handed it to me. He wouldn't let me ask any questions. It was real cryptic, spy like shit," she said, half laughing at it, half crying at the circumstances.

Arnie was perplexed.

"Where is the little envelope now," he asked. "Do you know what was in it?"

"Sorry Arnie," it's at home. "Probably still in my pants pocket. I was in a hurry when we left. I just took a shower, changed my clothes, and we left. But I know this," she said. "There was a key in it," she said. "I felt it."

"Wait here he told the foursome," then he walked away to talk to another marshal.

CHAPTER 48

The Rangers Story and Archeology Thieves

ARNIE CAME BACK about ten minutes later. "Things have changed," he said.

"Look," he continued, "we normally don't go into detail about cases with private citizens. Sorry, but that's what you are, no offense."

"We don't take offense," said Todd and Jack at the same time.

"We are indeed civilians," said Todd.

"OK," said Arnie. "Let me explain. But we need to be in a lot more secluded area. Ron here will take you where we're going. I'll meet you there shortly. I need to contact a few people." With that, Arnie left, and Ron directed them to a couple ATV's.

"I'm not sure if I want to ride on those again," Jane whispered to Todd.

Ron overheard. "Don't worry Jane," he said, with a chuckle. This time Todd will be driving the second ATV. Here are the keys," he said to Todd, handing him the keys to a second ATV. "Just follow me he told him. You two will still be with me he said to Jack and Gail."

They all climbed into the all-terrain vehicles. Ron drove back down the trails past Union Spring and down Long Lake Trail toward their once rented yurt. He didn't stop but headed toward the Ranger Station. Once at the Ranger Station he had all four friends climb into a small private SUV. Todd sat in front with Ron and the others climbed in the back. He drove toward Silver City but passed it about two miles before pulling onto a dirt road. He went about three miles down the road and stopped at what looked like a private home.

"This is my place," said Ron. You can barely see the house from here. Just go over that foot bridge and at the fork turn left. "You'll see the house when you come to it. Make yourselves at home," he said, handing the keys to Todd. "There's food and beer in the frig. Also iced tea if you'd rather have that. I'll need the keys to your van," he told Todd. Do you have them on you?"

"Yeah, sure," said Todd, handing them over.

"I'm going back for your van, then I'll explain what's going on when I get back. It shouldn't be more than a half hour, maybe forty-five minutes, tops. Oh, and don't turn on your cell phones until I tell you, OK?" he said. "That's very important."

They were so distracted by the quick drop off by Ron, that they barely looked up at the house. They were all watching him leave. Jack was the first to turn around.

"Holy shit", said Jack. "Look at that". They all turned toward where Jack was pointing. They only saw the top part of the house, but that was enough. High up on a ridge, not far away, stood a very magnificent looking log cabin.

"If this is country living I want some of it," said Jack.

They walked over the foot bridge and turned the corner. When they all saw the full extent of the log cabin they thought sure they had entered a dream.

They could see as they approached from the road that it had an impressive looking covered porch stretching around three sides.

"Wow!" exclaimed Gail.

Once they all came out of shock at the houses obvious beauty, they walked up closer and up to the porch, slowly taking in every detail. The home was rectangular and smelled of cedar. The roof covered the house and extended over the porch with beams that looked humungous. Pillars were along the full length of the porch and helped frame in the house. Flower pots all along the three sides of the porch added a beautiful country style to the outside. Todd unlocked and opened the door. They all walked in to the open floor plan of a beautifully decorated home. It had huge windows on three sides that gave you a panoramic view of the surrounding forest. The furnishings were not elaborate but looked comfortable. They were all fascinated by the simple grandeur of the place.

"This is simply amazing," said Gail. "I love it."

"What exactly are we doing here?" asked Jack.

"I'm not sure," said Todd, "but I have a feeling there's more to this quandary than even Jane knows.

"I don't know much," said Jane.

"I have never had such a weird week in my whole life," she commented. "But I know this," she said. "This house feels safe. It feels warm, and it feels inviting."

"This is tops for me," said Gail. "I'm just wondering if this is all a dream and when exactly will I wake up."

They all took a few minutes to look around. Gail still had her camera so she took a few pictures. Todd wondered over to a huge map on the west wall. It was a very detailed map of the Porcupine Mountains and it had a laminate of some kind on it that allowed you to write on it.

"Look here," he said to Jane, waving her over to the map he was looking at.

In the corner of the map someone wrote 'Todd & Company', with a symbol next to it. And on the map, that symbol appeared in every place the four of them had traveled throughout the porkies.

"I think they've been watching us," said Jane, "but I think that was a good thing." Jack and Gail wondered over to the map.

All four of them were looking at it wondering, trying to take it all in when Ron and Arnie walked through the door.

CHAPTER 49

Putting the Pieces Together

"WOULD YOU LIKE to know the details?" Arnie asked.

They all turned around when Arnie and his brother walked through the door.

"Come on in the kitchen. We'll grab something to drink and then I can give you a few facts about what's been going on."

They all took a beer. Jane and Gail would usually have iced tea but today called for a cold beer. Ron also set out some snacks. He knew they were hungry. They had to be. It's almost one o'clock. They were probably still stunned by all of today's happenings. He put some cheese and crackers, chunks of salami, and some sliced cucumbers out on the table, along with some of his wife's homemade cookies.

"I brought you here because I know it's safe," said Arnie. "Plus, Ron and his wife, she's at work by the way, have a military style alarm system. A little overkill for Michigan," he said, looking at Ron. Ron just shrugged his shoulders, "but it works."

"Anyway, I have permission from 'my' boss to share some details with you. Mostly because of what Jane told me about Professor Simmons giving her something," he said looking directly at Jane. "We're hoping it's a key," he continued. "I still think all of you could be in danger, especially Jane."

Todd and Jane looked at each other. He reached for her hand to give her support, not knowing what was coming.

"You two," he said, pointing to Jack and Gail, "I believe to be safe, however, I'm not counting on maybe's, so all four of you are now under federal protection."

"Oh my God," said Gail. "I'm just a small-town school teacher. What is happening?"

Jack moved closer to her and put his arm around her for comfort.

"Let me start from the beginning," said Arnie. "The collection of artefacts from earlier cultures has helped us understand the processes of human life, including migration, across the globe. Obviously, our country is not nearly as old as India and Europe, however American Indian artefacts have dated back ten thousand years or more in this country. Jane, you probably know a lot about the archeological history of Michigan and are aware that there are Indian artefacts all across our state, including the upper peninsula."

Jane shook her head yes, fascinated by how much Arnie knew.

"Here in the U.P.", he continued, "many of the artefacts found have been connected to the Chippewa Indians. And because the U.P. is less populated, many places where artefacts are found have been untouched by progress, you know, population growth, cities, etc. so the relics found here are in better shape than some found in lower Michigan. Some of the artefacts found are worth a great deal of money. That's really what this is all about, money! And there can be a lot of money in artefacts," he said. "Sometimes," he continued, "you get a high-level collector who will pay top dollar for certain items."

Arnie stopped to take a sip of beer and since no one seemed to have any questions, he continued.

"Out west there has been a huge crackdown on these artefact thieves, so what do you think that does? The heat put on them pushes the bad guys out of the west and sends them looking around places like Ohio, Illinois, Indiana, and Michigan. Most of these thieves are small time crooks, cockroaches, no big deal, until you get to many. We catch them one at a time. But this group!" he said with emphasis, "this group is very well organized. They have an invisible leader, someone who hires the most notorious, the most disreputable, the most skillful thief. The group we just broke up, led by Carl Handly, was most dangerous, because Carl had a bit of a silver tongue, and he was ruthless. He could convince anyone that the work he did was legitimate, and honorable and right. One person he persuaded to help him was your Professor Simmons," he said, looking at Jane. "Thing is, Carl was not very tolerant either. He has killed before. He doesn't care who gets in his way. He hired a young idiot here in the U.P. to get rid of your four, however, Ron was under cover and in the right place at the right time, so you got lucky."

Gail started trembling as Jack held on to her. "Are we still in danger?" she asked Arnie, her voice shaking. "This stuff you're telling us means something could have happened to us while we were hiking."

"Actually, I don't think Carl suspected you were anything but young hikers out on the trails. He used his Ranger cover to watch everyone who came into the porkies. They used the Porcupine Mountain caves to stash their loot. One of those caves was the one you accidently spotted," he said to Todd.

"You were not on his radar at all, until," he paused, "until you reported C.B Denton's body. Sorry Jane," he said looking at her. "Doing the right thing kind of exposed you. That's when he started suspecting. And when you all met him I think that's when he knew. He thought he recognized Jane but he wasn't sure at first because you," Arnie said pointing to Jane," didn't seem to recognize him."

"I ignored him on purpose," she said.

"Nice try," said Arnie, "but he didn't like that. It made him uncomfortable. He didn't want to take a chance in having you suddenly recognize him and start asking questions. That's when he decided to send his goon Jason after you. I'm just glad Todd called and let me know you were heading up here so I could keep an eye open. I was able to warn Todd when he called from the ranger station just before they took you to your yurt."

"By then I had no time to warn you, "Todd said to Jane. "I didn't know Ron was a good guy. All I knew was that Jason had something up his sleeve. When he started speeding, I just guessed what his plan was."

"And with Ron here, under cover," Arnie said, pointing to Ron, "it made it easier for us to intervene."

"Anyway," let's get to the important stuff," he said.

He turned and looked at Jane.

"I think you have the key to wrap up this case completely," he told her.

"I don't understand. What do I have?" she started to say, "Oh, the key!" she said.

"Yes!" said Arnie. "The key. Professor Simmons gave you that key for a reason. Let's see if we can find out what that reason is. We still don't have the last connection. Who is buying the artefacts, and is there a middleman? Where is the little envelope you mentioned that he gave you?" asked Arnie. "Do you have it on you?"

Jane blushed. "I'm really sorry," she said. "It's still in my jeans pocket, in the clothes hamper, in my bathroom at home. We were in a hurry and I wanted to take a quick shower before leaving so I just took my shower, put on clean clothes, and left. I completely forgot about it."

Arnie looked surprised. Todd smirked. Jack snickered under his breath.

"You have to admit," said Gail, "it's safe in the dirty clothes!"

Jane smiled a bit but her face turned a light shade of pink. She felt a little ridiculous for not putting it in a safe place.

Arnie sat back. You could see the wheels in his mind turning, thinking, finding an idea. Then you knew he had it when he smiled. "When do you report back to work?" he asked them.

Jane looked at her watch. It was already past three in the afternoon. "Wow!" she said with a gasp. "We should have left by noon so we could get home no later than midnight. We're all teachers and are supposed to report back in our classrooms tomorrow morning."

You could tell now that Arnie was going over a plan in his head. He just had to think it through.

CHAPTER 50

The Unusual Trip Home

"YOU FOUR SIT here and have some more snacks," said Arnie. "Ron and I have some business to take care of and we'll be right back. Nobody has used their cell phones yet, right?" he asked.

"No, not at all. Ron asked us not to," said Todd.

"OK, good, keep them off until I tell you it's OK again to use them," he said, "please," he added.

Once again Arnie and Ron left the four friends alone.

"I am so sorry I got everyone into this," said Jane, her eyes watering. "I know my nerves are twitching and I certainly didn't mean this trip to be scary or fearful. Don't get me wrong, I'm glad you're hear," she said, with frustration. "I just feel like I put your lives in danger, and I feel terrible about that."

Gail got up and went over to her. She hugged Jane and then putting her hands on her shoulders, and looking into her eyes, she told her, "Jane, we are all good friends. Friends stick together. That's what they do. They help each other through good times, and bad. And they certainly don't regret helping when help is needed. Besides," she continued, "you wouldn't have found the cave without spotting the pink rock, so whose fault is that?"

A big grin came across Jane's face, even amidst the tears. She hugged Gail with both arms. Todd and Jack joined them. "So, what are we," said Jack, "the four musketeers?"

They all laughed. They knew they would get out of this, somehow. They talked for another hour before Arnie came back.

"OK," he said, as he walked through the door. "This is what we're going to do. First, grab everything you have, we're heading out. I'll go over the details in the car."

They didn't have much. The day had whizzed on by and they were taken here and there and everywhere, so their gear and supplies were all in their van. Then they got out to where they 'thought' the van would be, but it wasn't there. The only thing in the parking area was Arnie's big SUV. They weren't sure what was going on but they trusted Arnie, so they all hopped into his car.

"OK, this might be surprising, but I think it'll work," said Arnie, with almost too much enthusiasm. Right now, we're headed for a small air strip used only by the federal marshals. You're in protective custody so I can do this. You will board the plane. Your vehicle will be loaded as well."

"What! Really!" said Todd.

"Yes, really," said Arnie. "You'll be flown to Camp Grayling. It's a National Guard Base I'm sure you're all aware of, just outside the city," he said looking at Todd, who was in the front seat. "What that does is basically put you about three hours, or so, from home. Then, it's business as usual. You'll go home as if nothing happened, and please don't talk to anyone about the, shall we say, unusual events, of your trip. Talk about hiking. Talk about the wild life. Talk about camping. Just none of the other stuff. Jane," he said, "this will be a bit harder for you, with your uncle and all. I want you to make an excuse about how you can't come over. Tell him you'll make it over on Saturday. Tell him that you have a lot to say about C.B. and Steve and everything. But, tell him the beginning of the school year started and you've got meetings or something and can't make it over until Saturday. I'm sure he won't like it, but he'll have to deal with it. If everything ends the way I'm hoping, maybe I'll go visit him with you."

There was silence in the car for a minute, then the questions came. The biggest one of course from Jane, "are we still in danger?" she asked.

"I'm afraid so," said Arnie. "We suspect a couple other members of your archeology group," he told Jane, "but I'm not at liberty to mention names at this point. Please bear with me. We have them under surveillance and if they come near you we'll know."

He continued," each of you will have a shadow. You may not see them, but they'll be there. You may see yours Jane, it'll be Ron," he said.

Jane just smiled. She liked Ron.

"OK," we're here, he said, as they pulled up to a small shack with a military transport standing ready a short distance away. They all boarded the plane, were strapped in, and the plane was in the air within fifteen minutes.

C H A P T E R   5 1

Midnight Visitors

T
HE TRIP TO Camp Grayling took thirty minutes. They were in their van, with Todd driving, and on I-75 headed home by six o'clock. It was like the long weekend, with all the strange experiences they just had, and the cool plane ride, were all just part of some strange dream. Arnie and a few of his federal marshal buddies were on the plane with them, but all of them departed in a different direction. The four friends knew they were out there. They just didn't see them. Arnie said he would contact Jane and let her know how to pass off the key she had received from Professor Simmons to either him or Ron. "nobody else," he had said. "Nobody!

She understood.

Two hours later they were past Flint, heading down I-69 toward Romeo. Todd was driving.

"We're going to meet and talk about all this on Sunday, our house, six o'clock. OK you guys?" said Jane.

"Sounds good to me," said Gail.

"I agree," said Jack. "I'd like to hear everyone's take on this," he continued, "without other ears around."

"It's a plan than," said Todd.

They pulled into Jack's Aunt Dianna's driveway at around nine-thirty. Jack went in to get the car keys while the other three pulled out Jack and Gail's gear from the van. They thanked Jack's Aunt for watching over the car, said their pleasantries, telling her they had a great time, but begged off from visiting, saying they were tired and needed to head home. They all hugged each other vowing to keep in touch. Both couples headed off in different directions, both to their own homes.

Todd watched the surrounding area as they turned onto their street. He also took a quick look around before pulling into their driveway, and then their garage. Everything seemed normal. They were finally allowed to turn on their cell phones, but still didn't call anyone. Jane had umpteen text messages from various members of their archeology chapter, quite a few from her friend Jenny. She didn't respond to any of them. She was tired and wanted to go to bed. She had one thing to do before collapsing for the evening.

It was late but they had to empty some things out of the car.

"Let's get this done," said Todd. "I know you want to check for that key, but we need to get this stuff in the house before we're too tired."

"Here," he said, handing her the metal detectors. "Put these in the basement and I'll bring in the rest of our things."

Jane gave him a quick kiss and headed into the house. She put the metal detectors in the corner between the basement and the kitchen, then headed straight to the bathroom. She walked directly to the dirty clothes hamper and opened it. All the things that were there when her and Todd left, were still there now. She pulled out the slacks she wore and checked the pockets. The small envelope was still there. She was nervous for some reason and quickly tucked the small envelope into her back pocket, then changed her mind. She had that feeling again. She didn't want to ignore it now so she got some surgical tape out of the bathroom cabinet, cut off a piece, took the little envelope and taped it with surgical tape, under the top drawer in the bathroom cabinet. She decided she wanted to look around the house before she opened the envelope, so she took a minute to go to the bathroom, and then headed toward the kitchen. She wanted to talk to Todd about where he thought she should hide it.

She left the bathroom and went around the corner to the kitchen. She took one step into the kitchen and almost had a heart attack! There standing in the kitchen was her friend Jenny from the archeology club, and a young guy, probably their age, whom Jane had never met. He had a gun poked into Todd's side! Todd's looked panicked.

"Holy shit Jenny! What the hell are you doing here?" Jane yelped.

"Hi there, Jane," Jenny said glaringly, "how you doing these days? Have a nice vacation?" she said sarcastically, walking up to about two inches from Jane's face.

Jane stared at her friend but something was really off, besides the gun in Todd's side that is. Jenny's voice was funny. The voice Jane was hearing didn't sound at all like the Jenny she knew. The whole situation was just wrong and made no sense.

"What are you doing here?" Jane asked again. "And why the heck does he have a gun on Todd?" she asked, pointing to the man holding a gun to Todd's side.

"Why didn't you return my phone calls?" said Jenny, angrily. "I tried calling you, and texting you, and you never answered!"

"Jenny!" said Jane emphatically, "I was on vacation. Our phones were turned off! You don't get reception in most of the U.P. and least of all in the porkies, so there was no need to have them on! Then we were so tired coming home, I never really thought about it. What's wrong with you? Are you crazy?"

When she said that Jenny almost lost it.

"Don't say that," she screamed at Jane, spitting all over as she yelled.

Jane backed off, and even though her blood was boiling, she kept her temper under control. If it weren't for the gun she's have punched Jenny. But as it was she was beginning to panic. Her eyes darted to Todd and back to Jenny.

"What do you want?" she asked Jenny.

"I want what Professor Simmons gave you at our last meeting," she said to Jane coldly, "when he asked to talk to you, remember?"

"What are you talking about," said Jane, "he didn't give me anything. I told you that night he was acting weird, that he told me to be safe on vacation. He's been acting strange for a few months now! You know that! You were at the same meeting I was. You saw him."

Todd was trying to watch his captor's face, trying to read it, to see if he was a cold stone killer, or Jenny's pawn. It was hard to tell, until he spoke.

"Let's get out of here," said Jenny's male companion nervously.

"Not until I get what I want," she snapped at him.

"Do you know what happened to the old man, to your precious professor?" she asked Jane, with a sneer on her face.

Jane's heart went cold but she tried to hide her emotions.

"What do you mean, what happened to him," Jane said, trying to act surprised and concerned.

"Oh, you didn't hear?" Jenny said cynically. "He had himself a little bitty accident. It was terrible really. Some big rocks fell on him, and he died," Jenny said without any emotion or sorrow.

"What!" Jane said, trying to appear surprised, and concerned at the same time. "How could that happen. He was always careful, always!" she whispered. "Where was he? Where did it happen?" Jane said again, with grief in her voice.

"Well, lots of people wanted him to have an accident Janie, but I helped the accident along. It was quite simple," Jenny said, "remove a brace here, and another there. It was fun watching everything fall on top of him," Jenny said laughing. "He never knew what hit him," she said nonchalantly.

Jane had her hand around one of the metal detectors, squeezing it hard. She could feel herself shaking. She was angry and scared at the same time. Her emotions took over and both muscles and nerves seemed to react at the same time as she moved.

"Don't tell them details," Jenny's companion shouted. "Matthews will kill us."

"Oh, don't worry honey. They won't live to tell anyone."

Jenny barely finished her sentence when the metal detector smashed into her forehead knocking her unconscious.

CHAPTER 52

The Final Episode

WITHIN SECONDS RON and the other federal marshals were right there. Jenny's companion was startled by the entrance of the federal marshals which made it easy for Todd to wrestle his gun away.

Ron had slipped in the front door without being noticed. Another marshal came in through the garage, and another had come in the back door and was waiting around the corner. Ron must have given them a signal because they all moved at one time. Ron easily placed Jenny's friend in handcuffs and collected his gun from Todd. The young man was still stunned at the appearance of the marshals and didn't resist at all.

"She's crazy," he said, nodding to Jenny, while they hauled him out the door.

One of the other marshals hauled Jenny to her feet as she regained consciousness, a lump starting to form near her left eye. He had her in handcuffs before she could even blink. Jenny didn't appear to be armed but when they searched her, they found a six-inch knife in one of her boots.

Jane looked at Jenny as the marshal were searching her.

"Why Jenny?" Jane asked. "Why would you harm Professor Simmons?"

"He's an idiot," Jenny spit back. "He didn't care about the money. Well I wasn't about to let him ruin it for me. Do you know how much money is in Indian artefacts? Well, do you?" she shouted at Jane.

Jane couldn't understand the hatred pouring from a girl she thought she knew!

It made her angry. "Not enough to kill for," Jane murmured, slapping Jenny hard across the face.

Jane stepped back a bit, into Todd's arms, as one of the marshals took Jenny away. The two intruders were whisked away by the federal marshals in separate cars. Only Ron remained behind.

Shall we sit?" Ron asked. He sat in a big recliner. "Nice chair" he said to Todd.

"Where were you?" Jane asked, feeling emotionally drained.

"We were here when you got home Jane," said Ron.

"Then why did you wait so long before rescuing us?" she asked, tears streaming down her face.

"They were talking" said Ron. "I have everything on tape. You did good by the way," he told Jane. And I'm glad you didn't try any heroics," he told Todd.

"We have plenty of evidence to convict them of Professor Simmons murder, plus, we know who Matthews is!" he said triumphantly.

"Who is he?" asked Jane.

"First things first", said Ron. "Do you have the little envelope?" he asked Jane.

"Yes! Of course," said Jane.

Jane went into the bathroom and retrieved the hidden envelope. She came back into the front room and handed it to Ron. Ron opened the envelope and found two things. One was a key to what Ron suspected was a safe deposit box. The other was a tiny piece of paper folded carefully, with Jane's name on it. Ron opened the piece of paper, perused it, and handed it to Jane.

"You can read this," he told her, "but I'll need it back."

The words in the note were written very tiny.

"It's from Professor Simmons," she told Todd, and she read the note out loud so Todd could hear.

> *Dear Jane, I want you to know that you were the best archeology student I have ever had. I have always been extremely pleased with your work, your questions, and yes, even your inability to admit that somethings are unexplainable. I have gotten myself in trouble Jane. I regret what I have done, mostly because I have let my students down, especially the ones that deserved more from their professor. Please accept my apology and maybe after all this is over, we can chat. In the meantime I am placing in your care a key. I am now working with the federal marshals to resolve some archeological issues. If something were to happen to me please give this key to federal marshal Donald Lacrosse. Donald has told me that he has a friend named Arnie Sorenson who knows your husband. These two names I trust. Please give this key to one of them. Nobody else Jane, Nobody! I am sorry for this cryptic note. Regards, Professor Simmons*

Jane looked up from the note with tears in her eyes. She didn't know what to say. She handed the note back to Ron. He accepted it graciously.

"Jane," Ron said. "I will tell you this much. Professor Simmons came to us. He told us what he had gotten himself into, and he agreed to help us stop these thieves. He has been compiling a list of names for us. This Matthews character Jenny mentioned we believe is at the top of that list. This key," he said, holding up the key she had given him, "will give us that list, and stop a lot of bad guys."

"It cost him his life," said Jane.

"I know Jane, and I'm very sorry," said Ron, "but, in the end, he did the right thing."

"Will you please let us know what happens?" she asked him.

"We will be in touch Jane," he told her. "I promise. But be assured, you will probably be reading at least some of this on twitter, or facebook, or hearing it on the six o'clock news. Right now, I need to be on my way. Please take care of yourselves. Give Arnie and I a call the next time you're in the U.P.," he said as he walked out the door.

Ron left, and for a second Jane and Todd just sat there, still stunned. Then Todd got up and went around the house closing and locking all the doors. He also made sure all the windows were locked and the shades were drawn. It was almost midnight. They turned off all the lights and went into their bedroom, took their shoes off, and laid down next to each other on the bed. Jane cuddled into Todd's arms.

"Well," he said, "you finally got to use my metal detector."

"Not funny," she said.

They talked only a few seconds, then there was quiet. They were sleeping by the time the digital clock on the night stand clicked over to twelve-fifteen.

CPSIA information can be obtained
at www.ICGtesting.com
Printed in the USA
LVOW11*1535150318
569988LV00007B/64/P